THEO AND SPROUT:

A Journey of Growth

Joseph Gergen

For Tony

Jo3

Everybody wants to be someone; nobody wants to grow—

--Johann Wolfgang Von Goethe

CHAPTER 1 – A SEED

SPROUT. My brother had no idea the impact the nickname he derisively gave me would have. Neither of us knew how unwittingly appropriate it would become. Was it destiny or self-fulfilling prophecy? I don't know. Memories and dreams and possibilities like to mix together. As far as my past is concerned and the makeup of who I am and what shaped me, I can make no distinction between memory and reality and dream. I usually don't try.

While I certainly don't remember all of my childhood, and many aspects are densely foggy, I remember with clarity the day my life changed. I was preparing for school in the basement bathroom—the small, cramped bathroom that seemed more like a large porta-potty with a shower than an actual bathroom. Wet towels covered the floor and almost all available surfaces. Countless toiletries jumbled themselves wherever space allowed them to balance or stack. Most of these did not belong to me. They belonged to my collection of brothers and sisters. I had a toothbrush. I knew that. Usually, I found toothpaste. If I absolutely needed a less common toiletry, I picked through a baffling array of products, many of which I had no understanding, until I found something useful.

The bathroom door could have been used in a magic show, presenting only an illusion of a door. The useless expandable accordion door secured itself with a weak set of magnets. No locking mechanism whatsoever. Talk about a constant childhood fear. Forever filled with anxiety a sibling would barge in on me as I did my business. Brothers would barge in like some bad slapstick comedy knowing, like we all knew, if the door was closed, the bathroom was in use. If the boys heard the shower, they wouldn't hesitate to sneak in and use the toilet. The girls exhibited more restraint. They at least would knock before they told you to hurry up, which would never sped up your business. Of course, just because the door was closed didn't always mean someone was on the toilet. The girls fondly engaged in hours of preening before the mirror. So, privacy—that wasn't a thing growing up.

The day my life changed I don't recall anything out of the ordinary going on, neither in the bathroom nor the world at large. Spring had ushered in milder weather and the near ending of the school year. My freshman year of high school. And have I mentioned I was an average 15-year-old boy? I was short and lean, a sprout. My hair buzzed close to my head. My face was angular, all the fat sapped away from constant running. I didn't spend much time worrying about my body image. It just was.

When puberty enters the scene, the body has a few topics it wants to talk about. You should probably pay attention or ask for guidance. I did not. Deep down I knew I needed guidance, but since my parents and family hadn't provided any in the first 15 years of life, I suspected any request for guidance would have ended in terrible awkwardness. I guess my older brother BJ gave me guidance, if you call tough love and admonishments to be more manly guidance.

Of course, when adulthood and puberty started to barge their way into the picture, I felt I had no recourse. I don't think puberty existed for my parents, except for the girls because you couldn't ignore it. Or maybe they didn't have time to explain it. Too many children and too many other worries. They treated us like the eggs turtles laid on the beach, left to fend for ourselves, on our own once we hatched.

Mom knew about becoming pregnant, her primary concern was for her girls to not become pregnant before marriage, somehow believing zeal, abstinence and ignorance would achieve that. Dad travelled for work, and when not travelling, drank often, which didn't leave much time to teach the boys much of anything. He managed to shave every day and create a dozen kids, so he must have known a few things about life. I never learned what he knew. No wonder I had Peter Pan Syndrome. Growing up in our house wasn't even a thing, a topic. God forbid you talk about that thing called life.

I stepped out of the shower to towel myself off in front of the mirror where I could see my lean body from my head down to my belly button if I stood on my tip toes. I bent over to dry my legs and feet, not bothering with my feet too much since they waded in a pool of water from the leaky shower. I popped back up and looked in the mirror again.

And there they were. The breasts of a young teenage girl looking back at me. Small and perky and undoubtedly, breasts. What the hell? I looked down. They were actually there. I raised my hands to them. Shit! Those are real. I slapped myself in the face and looked back in the mirror. The owner of the breasts stared back. Her face, her breasts, her everything reflecting back. She resembled me but she was not me. Her face was rounder with fuller cheeks, a softer nose and wider eyes. And, of course, the breasts. I know I didn't have breasts. She certainly did.

I felt my face. Looked at my hands. They didn't look any different. Looked at the breasts again. I looked back in the mirror. She looked back and popped her eyes a bit wider, as if to say, "what?"

"Who the hell are you?" I didn't know what else to say.

She smiled and said, "Well, hello to you too. I'm you. Who else would I be?"

"I don't think so," I said. "I'm pretty sure I don't have breasts." I stared at the breasts. I felt paralyzed. I looked back at her face. She smiled. I looked down again at the breasts. What was I going to do with breasts? "This has to be a dream."

"Does it feel like a dream?" She raised her hands to her breasts. "These feel pretty real." She raised her hands to her cheeks. "And these. You are way cuter with these." She tugged at her round cheeks.

"Knock it off. I don't want to be cute. I don't have time for this."

"The moment you saw our breasts this stopped being about having time, now didn't it?" She flashed me an impertinent smile.

"Our breasts? You mean your breasts."

"What's mine is yours," she said touching her breasts softly again.

"Stop doing that. I can't go to school like this. I can't go anywhere like this. This has to be a dream."

"Stops saying that. I'm obviously not a dream. I think we'll be fine. I mean, we seem fine so far."

"We won't be fine! What the hell? Shit, I'm talking to myself."

"Sort of," she said. "You're talking to me, who happens to be you, a cuter version of you."

The bathroom had turned into a fun house with distorted mirrors but instead of a distorted me I saw her, a young teenage girl. Disoriented and light-headed, I placed my hands on the sink to steady myself. I closed my eyes. Wake up. I slapped myself. This isn't real. I opened my eyes again. Looked down. Breasts. I touched them. Shit, those are real. I looked in the mirror again. She was looking at the breasts too.

"They're nice, aren't they?" She gave me a knowing wink.

"How would I know?"

"Oh, you know."

I did know but this wasn't the time to talk about it. How do I escape this dream? The slap didn't work. Cold water. I splashed my face with cold water, brisk, cold water, four or five handfuls. I looked in the mirror. Still there. "Shit!" At a loss to explain this, I wondered whether I was in a waking dream? A hallucination? If I ignored them and her, maybe they would disappear when I woke.

She chuckled. "I'm not a dream. I think you're stuck with me."

Bang, bang. Someone pounded on the wall next to the bathroom door.

"Who the hell are you talking to, Sprout?" BJ yelled. "Get out." He didn't wait for me to respond and before I could grab a towel, he crashed in and pushed me hard into the corner. "I have to piss."

I crumpled naked into the wet towel infested corner. He started to go about his peeing. "Get lost, Sprout, Jesus." He ignored me crumpled in the corner, focused on his peeing. I grabbed a used towel off the floor, leapt out of the bathroom, ran back to my room and closed the door. My bedroom door didn't have a lock either, but I could dress before he came back this way.

I looked down. The breasts hadn't gone anywhere. I needed to hide those until I figured out what to do. I grabbed my underwear and pulled them on quickly. I rummaged through my shirt drawer and looked for a baggy shirt to hide the breasts. I found a patterned button up and pulled it on. The breasts still made themselves known but I could camouflage them a bit, though I had my doubts they wouldn't be noticed. Once I covered them as well as I could, I sat on my bed, composed myself and decided I needed answers.

"What the hell is going on? What's happening? Who are you? Why are you here?"

"Those are tough questions. Good questions." She raised her hand to our face and scratched at our chin. "I'm here because you want me here, you need something from me. So here I am."

"I need a lot of things, but they don't usually show up because I want them to." I could feel my heart pounding. I labored to breathe. "I don't remember wanting this. Why would I want this?" I was talking louder, faster.

"Shh. It's okay. Take a deep breath."

"What?"

"Just do it." I took a deep breath.

"Now take another one." I took three more deep breaths. "Let's be calm." She spread our arms out and wiggled her finger. "Okay. Better?"

"Sort of."

"Okay, so try to think of it as a subconscious need. You might not be aware of it until it shows up."

"This can't be real."

"But it is. Subconscious thoughts often feel unreal. But now you've made me real. Don't know why yet. So here we are."

"Yes, here we are. What am I supposed to do with you? I can't become a girl out of the blue and be okay with that. You understand that, right? You think no one will notice?"

"We'll be fine."

"You seem to be unrealistically confident about being fine. Gawd. Not only am I hallucinating, I'm hallucinating a delusional person. Go away. Just fuck off." I swiped at the air in front of me, some imaginary enemy. I needed to find a way to snap out of it. "Go away."

"Don't go all apoplectic on me, Jesus. I'm not going to hurt you." She patted our face.

"I'm not apoplectic. What does that even mean?"

"I'm your spirit guide, not a dictionary." She laughed.

"And you're sassy. Great. A sassy hallucination who's going to guide me."

"I might be sassy, but I'm not a hallucination. I'm you."

4

"So you keep saying."

I heard my brother coming down the hall. Crap. Don't let him poke his head in here. I looked down to see how well the shirt hid the breasts but they had vanished. What the hell? Was she gone too? I looked around as if expecting to see her. "Hey," I said, but she didn't respond.

I sat down on the bed. What in the hell just happened? My heart continued to beat fast. Was she real? She sure felt real. Why would I dream her up? I put my hands to my flat chest. That was weird.

CHAPTER 2 – GERMINATION

I JUMPED as high as I could and pulled a pinecone off the tree branch. I liked to jump. To jump and touch objects I shouldn't have been able to touch. To soar like a hawk beyond my physical limitations. To compensate for my shortness. Maybe it made me feel tall. Maybe the sense of flying invoked a form of liberation. I definitely wanted liberation. Perpetually jumping, jumping toward a liberation always out of reach.

Not like jumping well was going to help any athletic pursuits. No amount of jumping prowess, which I am sure I didn't actually have, was going to augment my stature and land me on a sports team. I wouldn't have tried anyway. I knew better. I loved physical movement, not competition. I felt tortured having to compete in anything. I would have preferred actual torture. I did manage to grab the pinecone. A small win, I suppose.

I ran with the track team, the long-distance team, a rag tag group of teenage boys out for a semi-disciplined run in the local park. If jumping teased liberation, running teased freedom, or at least independence. We may have started out in a pack, but as we ran along the pack stretched out and you ended up on your own. Or you started to breathe too hard to talk and retreated inside yourself to muster the will to keep going. I liked the combination of social interaction combined with alone time.

Pinecone in hand as I descended from my jump, I looked for one of the boys to throw it at. I didn't want to hit anyone in the head and actually hurt them, even though the pinecone was weightless. I'd throw it at someone's butt or legs. Annoy them. Boys needed to prod at each other, needle each other. Establishing a connection or a pecking order. Become the instigator, the initiator.

I landed into a crouch, a panther ready to strike. I hesitated. I had felt a movement from my chest underneath my t-shirt. I reached my hand to my chest. Breasts. The girl whose breasts had sprouted a few weeks ago had returned. Her firm breasts hadn't moved much, but they had moved, and they were there. Shit. Pinecone in hand, I stayed in my crouch and pretended to tie my shoe. I reached my hand to the breasts again. Yep, no denying them.

"Hi," she said. "Remember me?"

Here she was. Two weeks had passed since the bathroom incident. I had convinced myself she was a dream or a daydream. I had obsessed on the incident, the dream, for a few days, searching for what it meant. The search yielded no fruit. I couldn't fathom what it meant. I finally chocked it up to the irrationality of dreams and let it go. I wasn't expecting her to come back like a recurring nightmare. I certainly had not forgotten her though.

"Shit," I said. "What are you doing here?" I felt her breasts again. They were real.

"You don't have to keep grabbing them, ya know."

"Sorry, it's weird. If this is a dream, they're not real, and I can make them go away."

"Oh, they're real."

I started to reach for them again.

"Knock that off. They're real. They're not going anywhere."

"I need to know how noticeable they are."

"You have a baggy shirt on. And they're not that big. They're not bouncing all over."

Dream or not, I was in the middle of a run and had to accept the existence of the breasts until I escaped from the dream. If someone noticed her, what could I do? Run away? Run where?

"What about your cheeks and lips. Are they here too?"

"I suppose so. I gotta be me." She patted her round cheeks.

"Someone's going to notice those."

"Maybe. Not like everybody's staring at you all the time."

"What the hell should I do? I can't just stay crouched on the ground."

"Just keep going. It'll be fine." She was at least a confident dream.

I wasn't as sure everything would be fine. The situation would get weird if I tried to escape. Everyone would wonder what the hell I was doing. A few boys passed me. They wouldn't bother to look back so they wouldn't notice me that way. I jumped up and snuck in behind Dave and Danny. I threw the pinecone up ahead. Didn't try to hit anything. Draw their attention ahead and away from me.

I ran with my sprouted breasts as if everything was normal. I wasn't dreaming this time. I had been awake all day as far as I could tell. Was I mentally ill? How did one know? What else could explain this? I didn't have time to figure out the psychology of it all. I needed to keep running, pretend like nothing was amiss.

As I ran, I became more aware of my breasts, aware of my softer, rounded cheeks, my softer body, my softer view of the world. My panic left me. I relaxed. I floated. Euphoric with the sense of liberation I wanted jumping to give me. Like flying in dreams. I felt I had jumped myself free. Did freedom come in the shape of a girl?

She looked around the park, up at the budding trees, the blue sky, the smell of the new grass. She wondered at it all. "The park is so beautiful," she said. "So peaceful. Do you hear those birds? Nature is an amazing thing."

I saw the boys in front of me in a haze now, a fog separating us. Alone in my freedom, life was a glorious place. With a pair of breasts and full cheeks, I ran under the trees, their shadows providing a protective. I felt alive. If this was freedom, I knew I wanted more of this.

When you grow up in a large family in a small house, you are never alone, you are never free. As an introvert, I could have just as well been in prison. Never free from prying eyes and perpetual observation, real or imagined. Those heavy shackles kept me from liberation.

"What is this?" I said. I'd lost my fetters, not even concerned she was there. "This isn't normal."

"This isn't your normal. This is my normal, my way of looking at life. This is what your normal could be. Don't you want this to be real? Isn't it wonderful?"

Yes, it was wonderful. I noticed the park as I hadn't noticed it since swinging beneath the trees as a child, flying up into the gigantic green trees and the endless blue sky. The colors, the shades of gray, the smells, the sounds of the birds. A lost world I was too busy to see anymore.

We came out of the park, heading back to the school, back to the locker room, nearer to the showers, nearer to the naked boys, nearer my naked body with her breasts. My liberation crashed to the ground. My freedom fled. I was back in the pack of running boys. What would I do? I needed a plan to escape unnoticed.

My isolation was ruptured when Jimmy came up from behind and grabbed my butt. Adolescent boys liked to goose each other. I suppose they would have rather done it to the girls, but they ran on their own, which was probably good. Jimmy had goosed a girl and would never know it.

"He shouldn't have done that," she said.

"He didn't know you were you."

"Still."

"Quit dawdling, Theo," Jimmy yelled, as he raced away. "Sprint to the door." And he took off. I sprinted after him without a plan.

I trotted to a stop outside the gym doors. Breathing hard. Put my hands on my knees to recover. We watched the other boys race up and stop outside the gym door and start to stretch.

I dropped to the grass to stretch as well. I reached up to my breasts, panicked. Jimmy sat right next to me. How could he not notice?

"You look like you saw a ghost," Jimmy said as he stretched on the ground next to me

"Maybe I did," I said.

"You wandered off into the ether for a while. Looked like you were tripping out like a space cadet."

Oh gawd, what did he notice? Did he notice my full cheeks, my breasts? I had no idea what I looked like.

"Enjoying the spring weather. Everything is waking up, alive." I diverted the conversation as best I could. I touched my cheeks, but I couldn't tell how full they were. I nonchalantly reached up to my chest. The breasts had disappeared. She was gone, sparing me humiliation.

"Okay, nature boy." Jimmy sprang on me and rubbed my face in the grass playfully. "Maybe you need to eat more hay after running." He whinnied like a horse, jumped up and ran into the gymnasium.

I jumped up to my feet. Relieved but concerned. Where did she come from and where had she gone? Who was she? Was she a ghost? Was she haunting me? I couldn't explain her. I couldn't attribute her to a dream any longer either. Whether she was a dream or I was mentally ill didn't matter. I clearly thought she was real. The feeling of liberation she had brought was real too. I didn't know what I should do with that. Liberation, the mythical, forbidden fruit. While I didn't know what to think of her, I knew I wanted more of the that.

CHAPTER 3 – SPROUTING

I STEPPED through the looking glass when I mowed the lawn. I used to like mowing the grass. I know, an odd concept for a teenager. I liked to mow the lawn because I entered a separate world, alone. Alone literally or alone in the loud roar the mower created, a zone of aloneness around me. Too loud for people to loiter around or talk to me. Total bliss. As an introvert in a small house with a large family I took advantage of any alone time I could find.

The grass intoxicated me when I mowed it, the smell like a magic potion. The fresh organic smell filled me with life. I could be anywhere I imagined through this small but powerful connection to nature. An escape from the cramped house that didn't speak of nature at all, except for the smell of babies. And there were always babies. Babies smell like life. Like musk or peat moss telling you nature is near, organic processes are occurring, that life is near. We spend too much time removing or covering up the smell of nature nowadays. We've sterilized our lives.

Liking to mow is crazy, I know. But it wasn't crazy because mowing meant it wasn't winter. And I hated winter. I still hate winter. One winter as a child, like four or five, I refused to go outside if I saw any snow on the ground. My childish logic connected snow and cold, and cold sucked. I refused to go outside. I committed so strongly to not going outside I wouldn't change out of my pajamas. I relented when we visited my relatives for the holidays and put on real clothes, but dad would have to carry me out of the house because I wouldn't walk on the snow. The wonderful irrationality of a child.

Apparently, my parents tolerated my refusal to go outside. But in a big family in a small house in the winter, the basic mental health of everyone required the children to go outside daily. I suspect the siblings wondered why I got a pass, especially when it was ten degrees below zero. I don't know why

I got a pass. Was something wrong with me mentally, emotionally, physically? I guess I could have asked my parents what they thought, but I was too young to contemplate such things.

In hindsight, the pass did me a disservice. Allowed me to rationalize my reaction to my hatred of the cold. Didn't force me to overcome discomfort or develop coping skills. Allowed me to wallow in a prison of hopelessness as I stared out the window at the snow unable to imagine a faraway spring. I know now I can adapt to the cold. I know how to do it. The body acclimates. Your body is pretty smart. But I don't acclimate to the long dark pit I fall into with the first snowfall of every long winter. I know the darkness might last.

Mowing the lawn demanded physical engagement, forcing me to move. I always needed to move. Young energy expressing itself. Putting perpetual motion to good use. Movement replete with satisfaction and completion.

One spring weekend I remember the running of the Belmont Stakes was showing on television. Horse racing. I didn't know much about horse racing then and still don't, but the slow buildup of anticipation to a three-minute race that seemed to last forever captivated me.

Horse racing embodied the ultimate in movement. For the horse, the movement existed for its own sake. For the jockeys and owner, competition drove them. For the gamblers, the thrill of beating the odds brought them to the race. I wasn't a jockey or a gambler. The thrill meant nothing to me. For me and the horses, the movement exhilarated us. Powerful, natural movement.

I watched the three-minute race. Revved up by the pulsing movement, I needed to move. I decided to go mow the lawn. I didn't have to ask. No one else wanted to mow the lawn.

I walked into the yard. The grass stared at me like sheep waiting for the shearing. I had a plan, an inspiration. I pulled the mower out of the garage. I began on the outside of the yard and mowed an oval. I pushed the mower around the yard again and cut another swath to widen the oval. I stopped the mower and observed my oval. My race track. Not exactly Belmont Stakes looking but a little imagination could transform it.

I started to run around the race track. We had a small yard. I could have run around the track hundreds of times. While the oval wasn't large, the track still had straight-aways and curves so I had to slow down and speed up. The smell of the grass, the memory of the horse race, the young hormones. I obliviously ran around and around.

On one of the many laps, she showed up. The girl with the sprouted breasts, the full cheeks and gangly legs. This time I could sense her presence. I didn't have to look or feel. I knew. I could feel anxiety at her presence well up in me, but I didn't bother to debate whether it was a dream. This time she just was. With her came the tingling warmth that had spread over my body in the park. I smiled at the feeling she brought. Would she bring liberation again?

"Hi," she said.

I smiled. "Hi."

We kept running. The running began to feel like flying, soaring. I imagined jumping on the wind, flying up to the treetops, wind in our face. The smell of grass and leaves. Effortlessly moving in circles. I became a horse, an eagle, wild and free. I closed my eyes on the straight-aways and escaped. I leapt into the air like a horse running a steeplechase. Unbounded.

"We're flying," she said. "I can feel the wind in my ears and see the world below. Like an eagle."

"I know." We spread our arms out like an airplane. I swooped this way and that. "This is wonderful." I jumped and spun in a circle. I jumped and spun again but this time stumbled and rolled to the ground. We sprang back up and raced around the track again.

"Where are we now?" she asked. "We must be high up. In the mountains, maybe. I see a stream below."

I'm not sure where we had flown too, but we weren't in my backyard. I didn't care where my imagination had taken me. I felt unimaginably uninhibited gliding through the air. "How do you do this? Are you a genie? Able to transport us anywhere?" I had imagined soaring like a bird before but I had never felt it.

"Ha! Do I seem like one who would grant you wishes? I'm much more than that. Anyway, none of the genie stories end up well. You learn a terrible life lesson and end up with nothing more than what you started with."

"How do you transport us out into the universe?"

"I let go." She wafted her hands through the air. "I let it all go."

"Let what go?"

"Cares, concerns, fears, worries, foolish pride. I soar and leave them on the ground."

"Easy to say."

"Yes, it is."

"Hey, hey, knock that off. You'll ruin the grass. Hey."

I opened my eyes and tumbled down to the backyard grass brought down to earth by Dad yelling at me, worried about the grass. He walked to the mower and yanked it towards the front of the yard. "Can't you finish anything? Jesus!" He started the mower and began to destroy my racetrack.

As soon as I saw Dad, I didn't care about the grass or finishing the mowing. I cared about him noticing the unknown young girl running in circles in his backyard. I didn't respond to him. I didn't even acknowledge him. I left the track as far from him as I could and ran and hid behind the garage.

I squatted down and leaned against the garage. Breathing hard from running. Breathing even harder from the fight or flight response. My heart pumped out of control, terrified Dad might see her. I had gone from a soaring eagle in my inner life to a fleeing rabbit in my outer life. I shook form the adrenalin.

"Exhilarating, wasn't it" she said.

"Yeah, until Dad showed up."

"Yes, he seemed unnecessarily crabby. At least you were mowing the lawn. We didn't have to run and hide. We weren't doing anything wrong."

"Oh yes we were. We were you. How was I going to explain you?"

"I don't need to be explained. Be confident in who we are. In who you are."

"You tell him that. He'd freak out. He yelled about mowing the lawn wrong. What would he do if he saw his son was a girl?"

"Learn to accept it?"

"Yeah, right."

I hugged myself to try to calm down. I could feel her breasts right above my folded arms. This can't keep happening. What does this mean? Is this real? It sure felt real. The presence of her breasts couldn't be denied or ignored. Yet this was bigger than her breasts. This was about her. Even though I felt like I was still me, her personality somehow inhabited me without possessing me. We conversed as if that was perfectly normal. I was still there except for the way I felt.

I had felt free. Euphoric. The same euphoria I had felt in the park. I desired that feeling more than anything. Or was it the liberation that brought euphoria? I wasn't sure. I wanted the liberation my introversion subverted in an extroverted world. Liberation from fear of the world, from fear of soaring. Is this how Peter Pan felt? Who needed other people or drugs to soar? I had her.

But fear. My fear overpowered my desire. Fear of being a monster. Fear of having to explain something I couldn't. I didn't know how to handle the fear. I could only run away.

I heard the mower stop. "Theo," Dad yelled. "Hey, come finish this lawn." He leaned around the corner of the garage and looked at me. "Quit acting like a space alien and come out here. I have to take your mother to the store. I don't have time for this."

Shit. Was I caught? I looked down. Nothing. She had disappeared.

Dad didn't linger but shouted as he walked away, "Finish before we get back."

I slumped down into myself, relieved at escaping exposure. But I felt the liberation fleeing and couldn't stop it. Strange as it was for her to exist, she brought liberation and I wanted that more than anything. But in short, I was afraid. My fear drowned me in despondency.

I tried to recreate the sense of liberation as I returned to mowing the lawn, but it had fled with her. I imagined again soaring through the clouds. The euphoria evaded me, like trying to grasp a butterfly spinning through the air. My aloneness now felt empty without her. Her absence, like her presence, left me confused.

CHAPTER 4 – TENDRILS

UNDER A BRIDGE. The strange place I found solitude. Quietude. Lack of stimulation. Lack of people, the biggest benefit to be honest. Not many people under a bridge. No eyes on you. Alone. Maybe a cave would have been better, or a mountain top, but a bridge is what I had.

The crumbling concrete bridge, short and flat, spanned the small river, the kind of bridge a troll might hang out under to wait for the billy goats to cross. I would never have bound up from under the bridge to gobble up the goats. In fact, I'd rather the goats didn't notice me at all. I would have made a terrible troll.

I needed escape from my large family and our small house: a hive always buzzing with activity. My moody teenage ways amplified my need for solitude and to distance myself from my family, establish independence. I excelled at my teenager duties. My inner voice chanted "Leave me alone" in a Pavlovian mantra whenever the family bustle overwhelmed me. As a small child, I would escape to the utility room and hide between the furnace and the water heater, a comforting womb-like experience, especially in the winter, my own personal social bunker. My family wasn't out to intentionally torture me with their presence, but neither did they seem to notice the effect of perpetual togetherness on me.

I had outgrown my ability hide behind the water heater. I turned to wandering along the river when I needed to escape and didn't have anywhere to go. Down along the river I could disappear below the banks into an empty canyon. No one to see me, no one to observe me, no one to notice me. I wasn't hiding in the canyon to smoke or drink or do drugs or paint graffiti. The only rebellious behavior occurred inside my head.

One summer day I ended up under the bridge late in the afternoon, escaping the family, the sun and the heat. The shade from the bridge, the concrete and the rocks along the banks, along with a light breeze, kept it cool under the bridge. In the summer the river ran slowly, a muddy, stagnant cesspool covered in algae. Most people stayed away except the die-hard anglers. I sat on a big rock throwing smaller rocks meant to stop erosion back into the water. Plop. Plop.

"It smells," she said.

'Hey." I looked down. Breasts. Breasts brushing against my t-shirt. Her personality had arrived too, dripping her presence and attitude into my bloodstream. "Yeah, it smells."

"Actually, it stinks." She plugged our nose. Grimaced.

"Yeah, but we're alone. No one is here."

"For good reason, pew! I relate to why you want to be alone. But why here? Double pew! If we only had an assortment of rotting fish to make it completely terrible." She tugged on the front of my t-shirt, which clung a little tight on her breasts and stuck to our skin from the sweat. "This is uncomfortable. You ever wear anything besides a tight t-shirt?"

"Well, I wasn't expecting you to show up, otherwise I might've put on one of my favorite blouses. What can I do when you show up whenever you want.

"I don't show up when I want. I show up when you want me to."

"You're not me. I didn't ask you to show up."

"Oh, you're me. And I'm you. It's not a "we" thing. It's simply a "you" thing."

"I didn't ask you to show up. I'm positive."

"Well, maybe not consciously. I'm not here by accident though. Some yearning in you wanted me to be here right now, under this stinky bridge. Maybe less of a request than a need. If I pondered it for a bit, I might be able to divine a reason. But at the moment I don't know why. Obviously neither do you, but here I am."

"You act like this is real. I'm too old to have an imaginary friend." I threw the next rock with extra gusto. "You don't make any sense."

"You may not understand this but I'm not imaginary. And not understanding doesn't mean not real. You act like it's real. What more proof do you want? You ran and hid from your dad because you thought I was real. Look, you can feel these. They're pretty real." She cupped her breasts. "These are real whether you want them to be or not. No imagination needed. They're real so I'm just as real."

She made a good point. The physical presence of her breasts made a good argument. I didn't understand. If she wasn't imaginary, what was she? What was I? Schizophrenic, delusional? Did I have an alter ego who had the physical shape of a girl? Here she was. I couldn't argue with her presence.

"I don't understand," I said.

"You don't have to." She waved her at the river and the bridge. "The world is full of shit you'll never fully understand. Don't fight it. Just let me be you. Let you be me. We'll be you together. Don't you enjoy it when I'm here?"

Yes, I loved her confidence, her infectious smile. I swam willingly in her be-yourself-attitude, an attitude I wanted badly but could only muster in complete isolation. I came across so reserved around others I probably seemed comatose most of the time. I wasn't comatose though. I told myself I was a private person. I controlled what came out. I knew the truth though. Fear surrounded me and held my real identity prisoner. I had to break out of prison anytime I wanted to express myself and that was rarely successful. No prison could hold her.

"I do enjoy it when you're here," I said.

"See, and that's okay. Let it out. Let it go. Let me be me. Let you be me. It's okay. It's like practicing to be the you that you want to be. No one is around to see what you do anyway."

"Okay." I did want what she had. She made it sound easy. I knew it wasn't. "Let's practice. Let's be you."

"And you." She jumped to her feet. "First thing. This place stinks. Let's go hang out in the park. Much more pleasant."

We climbed up from under the bridge and jogged towards the park. I tried to let go, let her run free. I didn't know how much we looked like her. We had breasts for sure. Did we exhibit her rounder cheeks and fuller lips? Were my legs softer? I don't know. I assumed so. I didn't check. That would not be letting go.

We ran toward the park through a quiet neighborhood. We saw an older lady working on her flower beds. The lady looked up. We smiled and waved. "Hello," we yelled. The lady smiled back and waved at us. We energetically waved even more. I would never have waved at anyone. I started to feel self-conscious. I wanted to give in and retreat back inside myself.

"Stop that," she said as she sensed my fear. "We're letting go."

"I know. I'm trying."

"Don't try. Just be."

She looked around as we ran. She opened herself up to the world, curious about the universe, about everything. Looking at a flower garden. Looking at a broken fence. Looking at a banged-up car.

"See, we can be alone here," she said as we jogged into the empty park. "I know it's hot out but why wouldn't people come and enjoy the shade and nice grass." We ran off the main path onto the grass and beneath the trees.

"Are we skipping?" I said as we bounded over the grass.

"Yes, isn't it fun? It's like super short bouts of flying. You feel like a bird."

I did feel like a bird. Like a balloon, lofted and buoyant. We jumped up at a tree branch and grabbed a couple leaves.

"Too bad the lilacs have passed. They'd smell nice compared to your stinky river."

"Hard to argue with that." We picked up a fallen branch and waved it above our heads. As the motion of the branch became free and fluid, its energy flowed into me and I could taste the liberation in my blood like a vein of chocolate through a scoop of ice cream. We began to float through the park, a butterfly aimlessly prowling for the right flower. The trees and the grass became soft and fuzzy. My feet touched the ground, but my spirit did not. The freedom released us into the universe.

I drifted along, comfortable with this new sensation. If I didn't understand, I could at least accept. But who was she? "Do you have a name?" I asked. If I was going to acknowledge her, she needed a name.

"I'm you. I'm Theo"

"But you need a name. I can't refer to you as me. I'm not totally mental."

"Alright. Let me think." She steered us into a depression in the park circled by bushes, temporarily isolating us even more from the world. "You can call me Sprout."

"Oh, you're funny."

"I'm serious," she said. She laughed. She knew what she was doing.

"My asshole brother calls me Sprout."

She nodded. "Yep. He's always calling you girly. I'm a girl. I'm what he doesn't understand. It's perfect. It's a good name."

I chafed at the idea. I didn't want any part of my brother associated with her. But I had asked. I didn't feel like I had the right to name her. So Sprout she was. She had a name now. Did naming her take me another step into my delusion? I didn't know. None of it made sense anyway.

We skipped up out of the secluded area into the more open park. My vision cleared and my feet touched the ground again when we saw a young boy walking along a path 50 yards away. I didn't recognize him, but he looked about our age. On my own I would have taken a wide berth and made sure not to make any contact. I had handed the helm to her so instead we skipped up to him. My stomach fluttered at the idea of engaging a stranger. I clammed up in the presence of strangers. My brain shut down as soon as it recognized a social interaction requiring speaking. All thoughts left my head. I would even at times lose my voice altogether. My whole body would shrink up into itself. She did not shrink.

"Hi," she said and looked him right in the eye and even held his gaze, which normally made me anxious, but I stayed calm.

"Hi," he said, a little taken by our abrupt appearance, but returning our gaze firmly.

"Nice day in the park," she said. "Doing a little skipping to take it all in. So pleasant, isn't it?" She waved our wand-like small branch between us and the boy like a fan. She danced in place, hopping from foot to foot.

"Yes, I guess so," he said. He eyed us up a little bit. We must have looked a bit fetching despite our tomboyish looks.

"I sense you aren't a staunch believer in the wonderfulness of the day," she said. "Well then, I shall cast a spell on you and transport you to this marvelous place." She waved the branch above our head, whirled it three times and tapped him on the shoulder. "In the name of Gaia I instill you, what's your name..."

"Scott."

"What are doing out here all alone, Scott?" She forgot about the spell. We had his attention, which was better than any spell.

"What are you doing out here, alone?" Scott threw back the question.

"Oh no, I asked first. Are you a loner, Scott?" She pointed her branch at him.

"I don't think so. Are you?"

"Obviously. Don't you have any original questions?" She bounded in a circle around him.

"Sure. Why are you bouncing around out here with a twig casting spells?" He reached out to try and steal the twig from her. She zipped the twig out of his reach and wagged a finger at him.

"It's what I do."

"Are you a witch?"

"Sometimes."

"And when you're not?"

"I'm just a cute little girl." She laughed and twirled around.

"I suppose you are." Scott looked at us appraisingly.

"You suppose I'm what?"

"A cute little girl."

"Oh, do you think so? Well, I'll cast an extra special spell for you for being so kind." She twirled around twice, stopped with her twig high in the air and looked at Scott. "I instill you, Scott, with the joy of the water sprite so you may enjoy the day." She flourished the twig above his head. "Now you will skip with us to the river, a water sprite all but in form." She grabbed him by the hand. I almost instinctively withdrew my hand, but she pressed on. He let us take his hand. I could feel his warm hand, a little sweaty. He hesitated but didn't pull his hand back as she tugged on it. "It's okay," she said and drew him along as she skipped down the path.

We skipped ahead into the park. She had charmed him. She laughed as we skipped. Scott smiled but didn't say anything. She let go of his hand and twirled around a few times. We skipped to the edge of the park where the river curled around it.

She jumped up and tossed the branch toward the river. "You are now transformed, Scott. You will see joy in the day and the world around you." She began to skip away. She looked back and waved. "Til' we meet again."

"Who are you?" he asked. "What's your name?"

She shook her head slowly and placed her fingers to her lips and whispered a quiet "Shhh." We skipped away and left Scott alone. We stopped skipping once we left the park and started walking home.

"That was fun," she said. "Good practice in letting go, don't you think?"

"Yes," I said and smiled. She made me smile too. "Though he probably thinks you're nuts."

"Maybe. But that's okay. He probably needed a little nuttiness in his life."

"Don't we all."

"Exactly. Perhaps you should try to be nutty even when I'm not here. Be free."

"We'll see. Easy for you. Hard for me." Freedom clearly had a price, but the small, sweet taste of liberation she gave me made the cost seem worth it. How free would I be without her though? Where would I find the confidence she had? I could have asked her, but she was basking in the glory of charming Scott as we walked home. I didn't want to chase that feeling away.

CHAPTER 5 – CULTIVATION

I FINISHED SHOWERING late one morning. Late enough so everyone else had already showered and moved on with their day, leaving the basement empty and affording me a little blissful downtime. I enjoyed those rare occasions when I could let my guard down. Sing a tune poorly, awkwardly dance to a song on the radio. Practice being free, like Sprout had said.

I had never worked at being free before. All my efforts had been focused on temporary escapes. At five years old, I learned how to ride a bicycle. The bicycle gave me a set of wings, momentarily setting me free from my earthly chains. I fled to a thousand different worlds. My bicycle turned into a motorcycle, a car, a train, a plane, a horse. I could go anywhere. One time my bike broke down and I couldn't fix it right away. I desperately needed to ride, so I pulled my oldest brother's old bike from behind the garage. It didn't even have tires. I rode it anyway. I made a god-awful racket as I rumbled down the street. I called it my thunder bike. I needed my wings. I guess Sprout was the teenage version of my bicycle, except she wanted our freedom to be permanent.

Sprout. She's what needed understanding. I had reluctantly accepted my neurosis or whatever this condition was, but I didn't understand it. I could only think I craved liberation so desperately I had manifested her to achieve it. I may have had only a shaky grasp on who she was, but I knew for certain she carried with her the freedom to be me. I could feel it every time she showed up though I had no idea how to tap that potential.

I stood naked in front of the mirror drying myself off. I bent down to find my underwear on the floor and out of the corner of my eye I saw her in the mirror, an alabaster statue of a young woman. I stood back up and looked in the mirror. Full cheeks, fuller lips, rounder nose, doe-like eyes.

"Hey." I looked her calmly in the face, much less panicked than the first time she had shown up in the bathroom. This time I knew no one was in the basement. I didn't need to rush back to my room and cover myself.

"Hi." She smiled.

I looked away from the mirror down at our body. I hadn't seen her naked since the first time she had shown up. In my panic I hadn't noticed anything but the breasts. I had time to observe now, to take her in. I ran my hands down my sides along the edges of our breasts, down to her hips, which seemed fuller than mine, around to her butt, certainly fuller than mine.

I dropped my hands from our butt, looked back in the mirror. "We're a little young to be getting hippy, aren't we?"

She shrugged. "What can I say, I'm womanly."

"I don't remember you being this womanly."

"You've been in such a panic before you haven't taken time to notice."

"I don't know. I think I'd remember this." I ran my hands across our butt again. "Fuller." She shrugged.

I looked down again at her breasts, past those to her belly and down to my private parts, but the private parts weren't there.

"Excuse me, but my penis is gone." I reached down to where it should have been. "Where is it?"

"How would I know?" She gestured at where my penis should have been. "Obviously, it's not here. I don't have much need for a penis. Anyway, don't worry about your penis," she said.

"I'm going to worry about my penis. It's kind of important."

"Relax. It'll come back. You're still you. We're just me right now. Trust me."

"Trust you? You can't just say 'trust me' to someone whose penis has gone missing."

"Yes, I can. And you'll trust me, eventually."

"Maybe." I didn't trust her yet. "This isn't helping the trust factor."

"I need a sundress. It's hot as shit out. Sun dresses are nice and cool."

"Way to change the topic. And I'm not wearing a sun dress." I dismissed her and started to pull on my underwear. "I have to get dressed."

She shrugged. "Maybe you could grow your hair out. I'd look good with long hair." She rubbed my short hair, interrupting my attempt to put on my underwear.

"What happened to the sundress?"

"Oh, we definitely still need one. Blue and white would be best."

"Sure. I'll jump all over that." I finished pulling on my underwear, still aware my penis had fled my body. I looked back in the mirror. She pouted back at me. She had a pout to launch a thousand ships. I looked away as if her siren eyes who would lure me to my death. I searched for the running shorts I had picked out to wear.

"Hey," she said. "Look at me."

"What?"

"Don't ignore me."

"Okay, one sec. Let me finish getting dressed." I pulled on my running shorts. I slid my arms into my t-shirt. I had to navigate the shirt around our breasts. I looked back in the mirror. "These seem bigger than last time. How am I going to hide these?"

"Who cares? Look at me." Her tone of voice startled me. I didn't look, certain Medusa and her snakes planned to turn me to stone.

"What? What's so urgent?" I scanned the bathroom to find my toothbrush.

"Look at me." Louder.

I looked in the mirror. Her stern face but no Medusa.

"Better. Do you have time now?"

"Yes."

"Good. Because you don't have a choice. I'm here. Right now. This is you. We are you. When I'm here you need to pay attention. You need to think about me. You have to ask yourself, why is she here? What does she need? What do I need? I'm here for a reason. You have to come to grips with my presence. You have to pay attention. You need to exercise curiosity or this isn't going to go well."

Her sternness softened but she wasn't joking around. I felt bad for dismissing her, for taking her lightly, though I honestly didn't know what to think about her serious tone.

"I'm sorry," I said. "This is seriously confusing. I'll try to pay more attention. I promise."

"Good," she said. "We can start paying more attention right now. Why am I here? Why did I ask for a sundress?"

"I don't l know."

"But you do know. The answer is in you. You're smart. Speculate. Do you need more attention?"

"I don't like attention." I found attention tortuous. Even good attention. Attention made me sink into myself even though I felt smothered and claustrophobic inside.

"Yes, but liking attention and needing it are not the same thing. You don't like it because it makes you afraid. But deep down your ego, your inner self, needs love, some affirmation. Maybe?"

"I don't know." I shrugged my shoulders. She seemed to know the answer so why bother asking me. She could tell me.

"*I don't know* is terrible speculation. This 'I-don't-know' crap is you afraid to look inside. Afraid to even think about it. We'll have to work on looking inside. You'll have to work on that when I'm not here too."

I nodded. "Liberation isn't free, is it?"

"Nope."

"Bam. Bam." The dreaded banging on the wall. "Hurry up, I have to piss," yelled BJ.

"One sec," I yelled back. Where did he come from? I hadn't heard him come back down the stairs. Every time I thought I could get a moment of peace in this overcrowded house, someone came out of nowhere and ruined it.

I had a precious few seconds to think since he had pounded on the door instead of barging in like normal. He probably thought I was one of the girls. He didn't dare barge in on the girls, but little did he know.

"Go away," I whispered to her.

"No," she replied and flashed me a defiant look, still upset. "Let's see why I am here."

"That's a bad idea. Please go." She shook her head again. She wasn't leaving. I didn't have time to argue, so I would have to deal with the fall out. I needed an exit strategy. How to slide by BJ without attracting his attention? I grabbed a towel and put it over my head. I could burst out pretending to dry my hair even though I didn't have much hair to dry, which would never occur to him anyway. Keep my head down and slide past him.

He'd be standing right at the door. Blocking the way because he was a jerk. Like one of those terrible TV movie bullies who always received a good comeuppance. I don't remember him ever getting his comeuppance though. Life and karma aren't quite so simple. I could choose to stand up to him. Standing up to him never went well. Standing up brought repercussions. Usually physical. Bullies are cowards they say, and if you stand up to them they'll back down. A nice theory. I usually got punched.

I slid open the crappy accordion door. I put my head down, rubbed at the towel on my head and turned sideways to slide past him. He shoved me as I came out. "Get out of the way, Sprout, ya loser."

"Hey, knock it off," I yelled back. My voice came out high, higher than usual. Not squeaky. A young girls voice. Nice, I thought. One more thing to deal with. But BJ didn't notice. He had to pee badly after all.

I ran down the hall to my bedroom and pulled the crappy accordion door shut. Couldn't Dad at least put a lock on the damned bathroom door? Was that asking too much? I felt like I had been cast in some ill-conceived psychological experiment where the goal was to destroy all my personal boundaries and see what happened to my psyche. What it did was put me on guard all the time, everywhere. Thanks Dad.

I tossed the towel on the bed and plopped down next to it in my not-so-private room. Besides BJ, the basement still sounded empty. I had time to collect myself.

"What the hell are you thinking?" I lashed my hands into the darkness of the room. "Shouldn't you stay in the mirror or make yourself scarce? And now I sound like a girl? What the hell? I can't go around sounding like a girl. It's hard enough disguising these breasts. I can't do this. You can't do this. This is dangerous."

"I'm sorry," she said. "I was mad. I know it's awkward, but I can't help it. It's not solely my fault though. You're part of this too. I'm you. You're me."

"You keep telling me that. But no way. This is not my fault. I like being a boy and doing boy things. What do I have to do with being a girl? I don't even know if this is real. I don't want to go all crazy."

"This is real. I'm you. It's not about being a girl." She fell back on to the bed. Curled up in the fetal position. "We're you," she whispered.

We sat quietly on the bed for a while, staring out at nothing. I didn't want her to be right. I didn't want her to be here at all. I didn't know how to handle this. This was not normal.

"You like it when you're me," she said. "I know you do." She spoke with a more conciliatory tone. "I can feel it because I'm you. You feel free and confident when I'm around, don't you? And I like being you too. Don't be mad at me." Tears appeared on her cheeks. "Don't be mad at me."

"I'm not mad. Don't cry." I wiped away the tears. "This is new to me too. I'm trying to understand." I sat up. I stared out across the small dark room at nothing. "It's okay. We'll be okay." I squeezed her leg to assure her. She nodded her head.

"What are you staring at, Loser?" BJ again. Caught me off guard. See what I mean about privacy.

Startled, I looked down. No breasts. She had retreated.

"Shut up, ya fat head," I replied.

"Whatever, loser," he said and grabbed the towel off the bed. He stepped back and whipped the towel at me a couple times. He liked that trick. He could torture me without doing any real physical damage. What a jerk.

I grabbed my shoes from under the bed and ran out the door. "Fuck you," I said when I had reached the stairs. I felt cowardly for that but better than pointlessly enduring another punch.

CHAPTER 6 – TAKING ROOT

SPROUT. BJ saw me as nothing more than the pathetic nickname he gave me. I wasn't a person to him. He viewed me as a thing, an object deserving derision, or at best the pet he never wanted. Based on our strained relationship, you might have thought he was ten years older than I. I was headed into my sophomore year, and he was going to be a senior in high school. Shorter than average, almost diminutive, I disappeared completely in my brother's shadow, who was tall, extremely athletic, competitive, and aggressive. The key difference between us didn't come down to our size difference but to our attitudes. While I liked to run, I had no interest in competition. He fancied himself an adult. I fancied myself a child. He wanted the perks of adulthood: independence, choice, responsibility. I had no interest in those perks. I wanted the perks of childhood: innocence, carefreeness, naivety. While we had some stark differences he could have called attention to, he seemed to define our relationship by my lack of manliness. To be manly you needed to ignore pain, not take shit and always win.

I wasn't self-aware of a lot of things, but I knew I wasn't competitive. Competition ranked you. I perceived ranking as both a personal need to bolster your ego and a societal need to measure, weigh and categorize people. I didn't want any part of that. I didn't want to be ranked. I wanted a uniqueness outside of social norms, possessing a quality society couldn't measure and probably wouldn't like.

Still, I daydreamed about having superpowers that would befuddle society, like the heroes in the fantasy novels I read, where the normal person finds they have a unique ability and it's the right ability at the right time to save the day, which would befuddle society. While society still would have not been able to weigh, measure and find me wanting for something they didn't understand, I would have drawn attention to myself. While in my fantasies I wanted to have a special skill people noticed, in real life I didn't want people to recognize me at all. I didn't want anyone gazing at me. I wanted to be a ghost, not a witch they burned at the stake.

Recognition, even acknowledgement made me uncomfortable. I felt it as a deeply visceral invasion of my private life. I drew back into myself whenever it occurred, an instinctive, protective reaction. I dreaded attempting to explain myself or even having to defend myself, which I couldn't do anyway without stumbling through a nonsensical, disconnected narrative.

As a toddler I hid behind my mother's legs during social interactions like so many toddlers do. But you can't hide behind your mother's legs forever, so I found other ways to create invisibility. In a world of self-absorbed people, I became invisible by becoming silent. People would quip about still waters running deep. I wasn't deep. I was just overwhelmed so I became a mirror.

To my silent inner wall, I added a defensive shield of aloofness. I projected a sense of nothingness. I was a cipher. I so wanted to be a ghost. Well-practiced facial expressions and body language created an effective barrier that kept people away. The aloofness didn't always stop the attention, but it kept it short lived. When I had no option but to break the silence, I spewed gibberish to confuse people, sometimes intentionally, often not.

The shield of aloofness worked but it came with a price: misinterpretation, an often unflattering interpretation where others thought I thought I was better than they were, which made me sad. I didn't think I was better. Entirely the opposite. Aloofness simply protected my inner self. Aloofness also buried and neglected my ego, an ego that wanted me to feel good about myself but never had the chance.

My brother noticed me though. He yelled "Sprout" often enough, so I know he noticed something. He didn't notice me as an equal, but he didn't have a choice but to notice me physically as our bedrooms sat right next to each other. No escaping. Like many older brothers he liked to torment me. Once he hit puberty and become more manly, he became more aggressive toward me. I presumed his aggressiveness started as a need to prove his manliness, to create distance between him the adult and me the child. When he was a junior, he turned from distancing to a more proactive effort to make sure I became manly as well, forcing me through a rite of passage. Tough love was his favorite weapon.

While I suppose his desire to guide me through a manly rite of passage was well intentioned, he still needed to remain alpha male. I should behave manly but not more manly than he was. He always needed to be in front of me, the leader. He needed to express his dominance over me. He needed to achieve this physically even when he didn't need to. Even his opinions demanded they be taken as fact. If I made the mistake of expressing an opinion, he quashed it. "Only girls like that music." Girl and pussy constituted his favorite insults any time he disapproved of me.

If we had to line up anywhere, even line up for dinner in the kitchen, he used force to maintain his alpha position. A shove, a punch, a hip check, a head lock. Establish dominance. He had both a need to put me in my place but also to make sure others saw him do it. He wanted me to resist or push back because a man was not to take crap from anyone. He expected me to be manly in all things. He wanted me to push back physically and verbally. Then he crushed me when I resisted. He wanted me to gain strength but to also remember my place. I slowly learned the confusing game, such as knowing verbal push back couldn't come across as complaining. Complaining wasn't allowed, certainly not in front of the other siblings. When I did complain, he applied extra head locks.

BJ liked to punch me in the shoulder, his preferred method of punishment. The ambiguous messaging frustrated me, as I never knew whether I should take the punch stoically or give a punch back. He never tired of it. Any proximity to me required a shoulder punch. Getting in the car. Shoulder punch. Getting out of the car. Shoulder punch. In the kitchen together. Shoulder punch. They varied in range of ferocity. I thought of it as a perpetual display of dominance since he couldn't actually mark his territory by peeing on me. I didn't like the game, but I understood the familiar goal of making me tougher while keeping me in line.

BJ turned the shoulder punching into a ritual we had to play out. He would decide when the ritual would occur. I think he thought of it like manliness training, like going to the gym. We stood face to face. He punched me in the shoulder. I punched him in the shoulder. The punches started out light enough then escalated until one of us gave in. I begrudgingly understood his tormenting as manliness training, but this wasn't a game I wanted to play. When the game first started, I would only take a few punches before running away, which came with a barrage of disparagement. "Cry Baby!" "Pussy!" He loved to insinuate I suffered from behaving too much like a girl. If I actually didn't run away, I had to cry uncle and profess my girliness. I never won. It was a no-win scenario.

After my freshman year he noticed my aloofness and didn't like it. "You think you're better than I am, you little pussy" often proceeded a punch now filled with anger. I sometimes decided to stand up to him, show him I wasn't a pussy. I wouldn't run or cry uncle. I planned to outlast him, hope he would become bored and quit. He could clearly punch much harder than I could, so I knew I had chosen significant pain if I didn't give in. The game always played out the same, ending when I gave in, not if. It was a stupid game.

One day he stopped me coming out of my room. He informed me it was time to play the punching game. He looked in a foul mood. I heard warning bells whenever a foul mood exuded from him. The game could go from teaching me a lesson to taking out his aggressions and frustrations. I don't know what triggered this outburst. I rarely understood what triggered the outbursts, though once in a while, I pieced together a motive, like when he was told he couldn't go to a party or to the lake with his friends.

"Hey Sprout," he shouted. "Punch me!" He used to laugh a lot during the game because he knew he wasn't going to lose. He wasn't laughing or smiling now. The game lacked playfulness. Playful or not, I didn't want to play the game. I had become weary of his bullying. I decided no more running away. I would wear him down out of sheer determination.

I started with a harder punch than usual. He was taller than me, so I had to punch upwards. I raised up on my toes to give it a little extra oomph. No more holding back.

"Oh, tough guy," he said and punched me back harder than usual as well. It hurt. So what? I wasn't going to back down, and I wasn't going to cry uncle. I punched back. I hit him as hard as I could, which wasn't hard at all. You have to actually practice punching to acquire the skill. I didn't want that skill, but it would have come in handy.

He noticed my strain to hit him hard. "Nice girlie punch," he said and laughed but not in a funny laugh. He wound up and leaned into the next punch. I flew into the hallway wall and fell down. That punch did hurt. The wall hurt me. The floor hurt me. I knew it hurt but the shock of how hard he had hit me pushed the pain down inside me. My pride rose up in me, determined I wouldn't back down.

"Come on," he yelled. "You fucking baby. Can't take a real punch."

My stomach cramped from the adrenaline running through it. I wanted to run. Instead, I stared up at him. What the hell was wrong with him? His anger bore down on me like a live ogre. I hadn't even mouthed off to him. I had taken the punch like a good subject. But fuck his anger. I stood back up and faced him. I hit him as hard as I could. I leaned into it like he had. I hoped it hurt him a little. He didn't show any pain, but he could see how hard I tried. He could see my determination, my defiance. He didn't like that.

He snarled at me. I think he meant to laugh but he snarled and growled. The snarl of a tormentor. He didn't say anything. He didn't call me a baby or a girl or pathetic. The snarl turned into a determined grimace. He swung at me like I was his sworn enemy who had killed his family. But I wasn't his sworn enemy. I was his brother. I had stood my ground like he wanted me to. But now when I had finally stood up in a manly fashion, ignoring the pain, he boiled over in infuriation. My insolence would not stand.

He wound up and stepped into the next punch. I watched his contorted face in slow motion as he roared at me so violently, I didn't notice the punch coming until I flew hard into the wall again and slumped to the floor.

"Fuck you," he yelled. "You lose again, pussy." He stepped over me and marched down the hall and up the stairs.

A thick, dull pain pulsed on the side of my head. My ears rang. He had violated the rule of the shoulder punching game. He had hit me in the head. He had hit me right above the ear with all the might his anger could conjure. Game over.

Crumpled to the floor like a broken doll, I might have even seen stars. I don't remember. I had never been hit in the head so hard. I couldn't remember where I was. I wasn't sure what had happened. I slowly recognized the basement hallway. I became aware of my bedroom door. I pushed myself up on all fours and crawled through the door to my isolation.

I dragged myself onto the edge of my bed. I put my head in my hands. I shook from the fear, the anger, the pain, the rush of the adrenalin. I kept my eyes closed. I didn't want to open them. I wanted to retreat deep inside, to hide, to become invisible. I no longer felt the pain. I felt the humiliation, the crushing defeat, the helplessness.

"You can cry," she said.

I shook my head. I didn't want to cry.

"I want to cry," she said.

I shook my head. He would have wanted me to cry like a girl. Even if he couldn't see me, I wouldn't give him the satisfaction. I wouldn't give in and add to my humiliation.

"Let me cry. If not for you, then for me."

I shook my head again.

"It doesn't make you a pussy." She gave the middle finger in the direction of my brother's room.

"I know."

"No, you don't. You think you're weak if you cry. He's bullied you into thinking that. Fuck him."

"I know. I don't want to think like that, but I can't help it."

"You can help it. I'll help you. You're not weak. You're human. And being human is good."

"I know."

"Then, please, let me cry." She wrung her hands. "I'm afraid and angry and scared. He's a monster and he hurt us."

"He's such an asshole. Fuck him." Now my head throbbed, the pain no longer masked by the adrenaline. I felt helpless. I wanted to run away. I wanted nothing to do with him, with this home, with this family. I felt all alone. Trapped. I didn't know what to do.

She hugged me. "I know." We started to rock back and forth. I squeezed my eyes together and trembled. The tears started to flow, eking out slowly at first. Our body began to shake as the tears began in earnest.

I wiped the first tears away. "I wish this was a dream, a bad dream."

"I do too."

We sobbed. I had never sobbed before. My whole body convulsed as my chest heaved. I covered my face with my hands. "I hate him," I muttered in between sobs.

She hugged me tighter. "It's okay. Just let it out. Don't hold back."

So we sobbed and rocked back and forth. We rolled down on our side and grabbed a pillow to hug. We sobbed and shook. I don't know how long we cried. Time faded and there was only the crying.

"It's okay," she cooed at me at me as we wept our fill. My chest slowly stopped heaving and I felt release. A seal had been broken. The pain and frustration leaked out. When the pain had all leaked out, I felt empty, still and calm.

"Thank you," she said.

Exhausted from the crying and the pain, I fell asleep and slept for hours. When I woke up my head hurt, and I remembered what had happened. But I felt renewed. I felt the strength to walk out of my bedroom to face my brother without fear. I couldn't beat him, but I didn't have to be afraid.

CHAPTER 7 – WATERING

"HI," SAID SPROUT, her usual greeting. I usually noticed when she had appeared because I could feel her, but she always announced herself. Just in case I might not have noticed, I suppose. I must say I appreciated the warning since she liked to show up at the most inopportune times. This time I sensed her. I felt the liberating drip of her into my blood. A little euphoria. A little fear.

When she showed up in the park or under the bridge, I had time to assess the situation. While almost all social situations made me feel uncomfortable, I could often warm up to the environment and feel safe if not interactive. I could find comfort in my own silence. And even though I liked her, I needed warm-up time with her too.

"What are you doing here? Crap. Not now. Not now." This time she appeared in church, a place where I never warmed up, and I always assumed was hostile territory. No amount of time would help me acclimate here. My euphoria slipped into panic, a much less reasonable drug. The anxiety made me hyperaware. I felt like I sat in a courtroom where guilt swirled around me as ghostly infractions I couldn't quite make out.

Lately, I had violated family protocol by not sitting with them. I exercised my rights as a moody teenager and sat as far from them as I could, which wasn't far, the church containing only a dozen pews. I sat in the back row of the church sitting right at the edge of the pew, as far from the front of the church as I could, anything to maximize my isolation. The only person in my pew was a young man I recognized but who didn't seem too interested in my existence, which was fine by me. Perhaps he had an actual interest in the proceedings, who knows?

My fear of interacting slipped into neurosis at church services where people intentionally gathered to socialize. The awful thought of socializing drained me of energy. I counted on my aloofness to save me, a handy trait when I didn't want to interact with people. Most people could read my aloof body language well enough to see they should leave me alone. Other people couldn't read the iciness and approached me anyway. Sometimes I think they felt bad for me and approached, a misguided effort since church was the last place I wanted to receive sympathy, a place where everything came off as contrived and judgy. I shouldn't have been so hard on them. They gathered in the name of community and my presence signaled I too wanted that. Bad form on my part since I clearly had zero interest. My presence wasn't optional though, so I didn't accept all the blame for the mixed signal.

"Hi." She smiled, always happy when she arrived, like a dog let out of her kennel. Any freedom was good freedom. I understood that. I could feel her pleasant energy running through me only to crash into my anxiety. I didn't want to waste feelings of liberation she brought but enjoying them in church wasn't going to happen. Irritation crept into my awareness and overrode the drip, drip of euphoria.

"I'm in church."

"I know. Shouldn't you be praying, or worshipping or something? It's terribly serious in here."

"It is."

I knelt down and hunched over to make myself smaller, arms folded in front of me, hands up in prayer to block my face, creating a deep-in-religious-fervor look, which I thought was good disguise.

"This is not a good time to show up. These people, of all people, will not understand you. They'll think I'm possessed. Call an exorcism on me or worse."

"Or stone you to death. Always a good way to deal with the unknown." She laughed.

"Don't laugh."

"Whatever. They already don't understand you." She looked around the church. "And no one is looking at us. They don't care." She was right. They didn't care.

"When service ends, someone will look, even if they don't care." I looked harder into my hand and shrunk a little more into myself. "Maybe we should leave now. Mom will yell at me if I leave early, but I can handle the scolding."

"When service ends, we'll worry about it." She knelt up nice and straight. Let her arms sink down, looked around the church.

"What are you doing? You're ruining our deep-in-prayer disguise."

"Just taking a look around. Staring at my hands was kind of boring." We looked to the front of the church where the priest performed his ritual. I had no idea where in the service he was. We saw my family on the other side of the church, all paying attention to the service except BJ, who lounged back into the pew, nonchalantly gazing around the church. If he craned his head enough, he would have seen us, but he was too lazy to do that, so I knew I was safe.

Sprout noticed the young man at the other end of the pew. Looked at him long enough so he felt the stare and looked our way. She smiled and winked. He nodded slowly, almost knowingly, maybe almost smiled and looked back to the front of the church.

"What are you doing? Don't draw attention to us."

"They're going to notice eventually." She looked down the pew again at the gentleman and gave him a good looking at, but he wasn't playing any more.

"Stop that. Someone is going to notice."

"Oh, if they look, they'll notice. Bound to happen eventually." She tapped a rhythm on the back of the pew in front of us. "Let's go to the bathroom. I'll show you. If someone accosts you, you'll have to be me. Act like absolutely nothing is wrong. Bluff our way out. Let's go."

"Right now?" I'd said I could handle the scolding, so she had run with that. I'm not sure why I was resistant to go since I knew it was the best option.

"Yeah."

"Okay." I wasn't paying attention to the service anyway and going to the bathroom provided a way to kill time. "Let's go look. See what I'm up against." We eased out of the pew and walked out the back door to the entry way. The stuffy hall was empty. We walked into the women's bathroom without hesitation. She controlled the situation now.

"Don't worry." She brushed off my resistance before I could speak. "You'll see."

The too warm, empty bathroom smelled stale and antiseptic, a bare-boned place with bad lighting and institutional white walls. I broke into a sweat immediately from my anxiety and the warm room, which only increased my anxiety.

"Look," she said. She stood in front of the faded and scratched mirror. She ran her fingers through my short hair, whether wishing it was longer or liking the feel, I didn't know.

She ran her hands over our full and soft cheeks. But I didn't have full cheeks. I was a lean, angular teenage boy with a straight jaw line. But there they were. Soft, full cheeks.

She ran her fingers over our full lips. But I didn't have full lips. I had narrow thin lips. But there they were. Full red lips. She pulled the corner of the lower lip down into a plump pout. She let go and smiled. Big wide smile.

"See, look how pretty you are." She ran her fingers over our face again.

I agreed. She looked pretty. She was definitely a girl. We smiled. She looked much more like her than me now. Was she more her every time she showed up? Seemed like it. How about mentally and emotionally? Was she

34

more her? She was more assertive without a doubt.

"You're more girly than the last time I saw you." I looked down at her breasts. "Where is this going? What's going to happen to me?"

"To us," she said. "We're us. I'm you. I keep telling you that."

"This is not me." I pointed at us in the mirror. "I may have accepted this psychosis because I can't seem to shake it, but I still don't understand, if you can understand that."

She shrugged. She patted our cheeks. "I understand and you will, eventually."

"You didn't answer the question. Where is this going?"

"I don't know. Does it really matter? It's going where it needs to go. Down a path we can't see. All we can do is follow it."

I still didn't understand, and this wasn't the place to figure it out. I stood there still looking like her, still in church, still under her influence.

"Is this what we looked like to the guy at the end of the pew? Jesus, he probably thought you were flirting with him."

"I am sure he did." She winked at us in the mirror.

"You can't flirt in church." I frowned at her. She smiled back, raised her eyebrows. She was definitely more her.

"Why not? He doesn't know who I am. I was simply being nice, being social, being part of the community."

"I don't want to be part of this community."

"Not like it's my scene either. A little too serious."

"I don't want to be part of any community."

"All community isn't bad. You have your community of runners."

"That's different."

"It's not. It's a community you like so you don't think of it as community."

"Whatever. You shouldn't flirt in church. He might reach the wrong conclusion."

"What kind of wrong conclusion would he reach? That we're both humans. Probably made his day."

"Good grief. One minute you are all deep on this 'I'm you, you're me' and the next minute you are totally clueless about what could go wrong by flirting with a guy in church. If this gets weird, I'm the one who has to deal with it."

"Yes, you'll have to deal with it." She mugged at me in the mirror. "It's a good thing, right? If you can deal with being me, you can learn to deal with being you. Maybe that's where this is going."

Her smile calmed me down. Or more accurately, she calmed us down. She knew how to stay calm.

"We have to get out of here. No way to hide you if you're wearing my clothes. They'll be totally confused."

"Why do we have to hide?" She ran her hands over our shirt and pants.

She sighed.

"Don't go on about the clothes," I said.

"Maybe if you had clothes I liked, I could blend in better. You could buy me some, you know."

"What then? Do I carry your clothes with me wherever we go? Geez. Can we not talk about clothes right now?"

"Okay. But you do like us, don't you?" She looked back in the mirror. I saw her soft cheeks and full lips and doe eyes. The euphoria welled up over the fear. I could fly away to a mountain meadow and run through the clover and wildflowers with her. Free, weightless, soaring. She could wear anything she wanted away from here.

I heard bells ring and knew service was almost over. Fear.

"We have to go."

"You didn't answer the question."

"What question?"

"Do you like us?"

"Yes. Yes, I do," I said curtly, only concerned with escaping. I regretted it immediately. I saw her flash a pout. I liked her. I wanted her to know I was sincere, so I added, "And you're pretty too."

"I know." She smiled. "What should we do?"

"Nothing. We're still in church." No soaring would occur in the stuffy bathroom. What we needed was an escape. We opened the bathroom door slowly. Peeked out. The empty hall stared back at us. All clear. No reason to go back into church now. We opened the front doors and started down the steps. We kept our head down. Out of the corner of our eye we saw a neighborhood boy I knew at the bottom of the steps, headed our way. We weren't friends but I'm sure he would recognize me, though I'm not sure why since I had just seen how much I looked like her in the mirror. No matter how weird the situation, I couldn't ignore him. I was shy, not rude.

"He won't recognize you," she said. "I'll be nice to him. Trust me." I didn't have much of a choice.

We lifted our head. Our eyes met. My stomach leaped, caught for sure. I wanted to look away and rush down the steps. But she slowed down and looked into his eyes. Locked in on him. She smiled a knowing smile, an 'I know something' smile. Her eyes followed him as he walked up the stairs and passed us. He looked back. You could see his eyes scrunch up in confusion but soon fell prey to her smile. He nodded at her, smiled and kept looking back. She gave a little knowing wink. She stopped on the stairs.

"A little late," she said. He stopped and looked back confused. "Service. It's done." What was she doing?

"I was working," he said.

"Ah, I'll have to use that excuse to bail out of going to church. Wait, I better get a job first." She laughed. "But you're too late to even pretend you made it."

"I'm picking up my grandma. She needs a ride home."

"Oh, how nice. What a good boy." She reached out and touched his arm. He blushed. "I wish I was such a good boy. I skipped out before it finished. I'm bad."

"I'm sure you're not," he said and continued up the stairs.

My heart raced. I sweated even more. We walked quickly away.

"See, he didn't suspect a thing," she said. "Wasn't that fun?"

"Fun. Seriously? I'm not so sure. And do you have to wink at everyone? That's not helpful." I wouldn't wink at anyone. I wouldn't even make eye contact let alone flirt. But she would and she did. What else was she capable of doing when she was in control? I didn't want to begin to imagine. Looking like her brought enough risk already. Now I had no idea how she would behave. How I would behave. "You can't flirt with everyone."

"Why not? I really wasn't flirting. I was just being nice, making him feel better. It's a good thing to make others feel good, isn't it?"

"You were flirting."

"Okay, maybe a little. But you don't have to flirt. You can just be nice. You need to learn to interact with people. Even if you don't like it."

"I don't like it and I don't want to."

"Boo hoo. You need to learn especially if you don't want to."

"I'm not going to flirt."

"You don't have to flirt. Start with an acknowledging smile. Or at least thaw out your icy stare a bit."

"Okay. I can smile. But no flirting. Flirting scares the shit out of me".

"I know."

CHAPTER 8 – PHOTOSYNTHESIS

THE BIRTHDAY PARTY in Jimmy's basement started out uncomfortable. Even the poor lighting couldn't provide enough cover to set the awkward bundle of teenagers crammed into Jimmy's basement free. The room with the low ceiling, cheap paneling, aged shag carpet, frumpy brown sofa, and poorly placed lamps at the edges of the room kept the crowd subdued.

The loud party music strived to shake up the crowd, but it blared so loudly it dampened social interactions. Conversations were limited to short phrases shouted back and forth. Not the most chatty person in a crowded room, I preferred the diminished conversation. I could observe and listen, though the music volume made it hard to hear much of anything. An actual conversation was impossible or pointless. If you were aggressive, loud and self-centered, you could shout a monologue at people. I could see Jimmy's older brother on the other side of the room valiantly trying to hold court. Good for him.

I stood next to Danny on the edge of the room, staring into the empty middle of the room where we supposed kids might eventually start dancing. We were too young to have blatant alcohol at the party, and the invisible alcohol wasn't yet plentiful enough to loosen the awkward teenage inhibitions. Sugar and caffeine were available, though, and worked valiantly to animate us into inevitable motion. It just took a little longer.

Jimmy was the social one in my small circle of friends. Extroverted, he had no end of topics he would expound upon. I liked listening to him. He had an easy charm I thought I wanted. You could talk to him too. He wasn't a great listener, but he wasn't judgmental. I could open up to him on certain topics.

I had arrived at the party early so I could talk to Jimmy without a throng of kids around. In the empty basement he busied himself setting up his stereo equipment and organizing the music he was going to play. I grabbed a chair and sat down and watched him.

"Hey Theo," he said as he started telling me about the awesome songs he planned to unleash on the kids. "This one is sweet," he said as he started up a song. "They'll be shaking to this one." He did a couple twisty dance moves then looked at me. "You been acting a little strange lately? What's going on?"

"Haven't been myself."

"Yeah, you been pretty moody. Are you depressed?"

"I suppose I've been moody. But I'm not depressed. Not at all. But I feel like I'm someone else." I squirmed in my chair. I usually spoke easily with Jimmy but talking about her was difficult. "I'm not sure who I am."

"Well, we're growing up, boy. It happens. You're not talking about getting boners, are you? Because boners are natural. Though I know your parents would shoot me for saying that." He shaped his hand into a gun and pointed at his head. He laughed.

"No. I think I figured the boner situation out." I squirmed in my chair, thinking that discussing this topic would be a lot easier if I could talk about her outright, but I couldn't do that. Talking about her without talking about her posed a challenge. "It's like I have another person inside me who has different ideas about the world, who thinks I should act and think different. She makes good arguments, so I don't know what to choose." Crap. I slipped up. Press on like it didn't happen.

"She? What?"

"He, she or whoever it is. What are the right choices in life? What do you do?"

"Kind of like having an angel on one shoulder and a devil on the other. Hmm. What do I do? Well, I don't have an invisible girl telling me what to do, but if I did, I would go with it. Would depend on the situation. On my mood. Maybe there's no right or wrong. Like you said, just different. You can listen to your new girlfriend when you want. You can choose." He poked me in the chest and chuckled. "Don't overthink think it, man. Life's weird." He turned back to his stereo and turned up the music. "This song. I'm telling you." He saw a few new kids come into the basement and wandered over to greet them.

Jimmy planned almost all the social activities I attended. He loved organizing. He liked people and people liked him, so the party had a good attendance, a good mix of boys and girls. I noticed the girls, of course, but I didn't hang out with any of them. I knew a few of the girls from track and cross country, though that was much more of a sisterly relationship. My social circle didn't include girls, so I didn't have much experience with them. I found girls attractive, but I was too naïve to know what to do with the knowledge and thought I didn't care much either way.

The sugar and caffeine kicked in and the crowd became more active. We started to move around without actually mingling. The music exploded and a pop song came on everyone knew. That's where the girls came in. They wanted to dance, and since the boys made it obvious they weren't going to initiate the dancing, the girls bound into the center of the room. They promptly started bouncing around in the small space in the center of the room, slowly expanding into the crowd, which was gobbled up into the dance or pushed out to the edge of the room. I found myself plastered against the wall to avoid the fray.

I watched the girls dance, their infectious movement stirred new feelings in me with which I didn't know what to do. I didn't know much about dancing, despite or in spite of the square dance and swing dance classes we had to take. But I could feel the energy and pop music was nothing if not energy. Pop music didn't care if you could dance. If you jumped and gyrated in the vicinity of a girl or boy or even alone, pop music was happy. Music gave you permission to move. You just had to accept the invitation.

The girls took over the center of the room not wanting to waste time as their favorite song ran on. Bouncing, twisting, spinning, flailing. The boys near me looked at the girls and then at each other and then back at the girls. We didn't know much about dancing, but we knew we liked to watch girls dancing.

Jimmy had broken the ice. He controlled the stereo and he had played a song he knew people liked. He knew what would happen. He burst into the fray of girls in the middle of the room. He knew how to dance or was good at faking it. He hopped and jumped from girl to girl. No inhibitions. His swirling and twisting energized the room. A girl shrieked. Another boy jumped into the fray, imitating Jimmy. Another boy jumped in and soon the dance circle was dense and expanding. The whole room moved with dancing, jumping and twirling kids. Even I danced. I mimicked whatever Jimmy did. Lots of bouncing, which I loved because bouncing was jumping, and jumping was freeing. A haze of people doing the same enveloped me.

Arms all over the place. Bumping into each other. Bumping into the girls. I hadn't experienced that before. Physical contact, even if not intentional or personal was still physical contact. I liked the feeling but not sure I understood it. The dance floor turned into a mosh pit. Everyone jumping, arms above their heads, flailing and jostling each other. The poorly lit basement with the low ceiling and the bland couch became a poor man's Dionysian festival with a little help from the sugar, alcohol and hormones, a mass of spirits immersed in ourselves as individuals and as community.

After a while I became used to the commotion and the dance floor seemed less of a blur. I could see individuals in the sea of people. I noticed Tammy near me, a cute girl I liked but knew by name only. I looked at her. Looked into her face. We made eye contact and she smiled. I turned my eyes away in embarrassment but fought the urge to escape and stood my ground.

I kept bouncing and spinning. But Tammy's smile energized me, and I jumped even higher as I found a place to express my joy of jumping. I came down after a particularly satisfying jump and could taste the euphoria Sprout brought with her. She had arrived, sprouted breasts and all, jumping in front of Tammy.

"Hi" said Sprout. "Oh, look, Tammy." She smiled and looked at Tammy, right into her eyes and held them longer than I ever could have. Tammy smiled back again. Tammy didn't freak out. She kept dancing as if everything was normal.

I freaked out. Tammy had looked at me. What did she see? A scared little boy faking it on the dance floor? I couldn't stay near her. I wanted to run but compromised by slowly backing away, edging to the outside of the dance floor, all the way to the wall. I stood against the wall, bouncing a little less energetically, trying to pretend everything was cool. Gave a nod to Danny, one of the few kids who hadn't run out onto the dance floor.

"What are you doing?" Sprout grabbed our face and gave it a shake. "We were right where we wanted to be."

"I'm sorry. I freaked out." Now I felt stupid, ashamed for giving into my fear. I had ruined everything. I began sinking behind my defensive walls.

"We're fine. Just a minor setback" She grabbed the soda we had left behind and took a big drink. "I can fix this. I shouldn't have let you run. We'll talk about it later. We're going back in." She set the empty soda can down and nodded at Danny.

We slid back into the dance crowd. The song ended and the crowd lulled. We spied where Tammy stood on the far side of the room. Another pop song came on and the crowd perked back up. We jostled our way back into Tammy's circle. She saw us bouncing across from her and smiled. We moved a little closer.

'Here we go," said Sprout as she moved closer to Tammy. "Just let go."

"No winking," I said.

"Whatever. We'll give her a little twirl then. Even better than a wink."

"No way."

"Oh, you big baby." Sprout surged forward and grabbed Tammy's hand before I could intervene. She gave her a twirl like we had learned in swing dance class. Tammy let us twirl her and laughed.

"See, this isn't so bad."

We laughed. The laugh distracted me, stopped me from panicking. Magically, we found ourselves dancing with Tammy, not simply dancing next to her. Knowing the darkness shielded us, I relaxed and smiled and laughed at it all. I could feel the drip, drip of euphoria. Unfettered. Tammy smiled back, no idea why we were laughing. We twirled Tammy few more times. We felt her hand in ours. We brushed against her hips. We felt her hair whip across our face.

The song ended. Silence. All the bouncing and twirling stopped. Tammy jumped at me, hugged me and pecked me on the cheek. I blushed. I felt bliss.

Oh my god, she's going to notice our breasts. I could feel hers. How could she not feel mine? She's going to freak out.

"Don't panic." Sprout made us hold our ground. "She wouldn't have been expecting them. She wouldn't believe it anyway."

"Thank you," said Tammy and she ran to the other side of the room. The dance floor cleared as I hesitated in the middle of the room, unsure of what to do next.

"Oh, I liked that," said Sprout. "Got a kiss from Tammy, ooh, la, la."

"Shut up. It wasn't a real kiss."

"It felt real. And you liked it."

"What are you doing here anyway? You don't have to show up everywhere."

"I didn't want to miss out on the party. You needed my help anyway."

"You're lucky it's dark."

"I know. But you're enjoying it now, aren't you?"

"I am."

"Well, that's why I'm here. So you can learn to enjoy."

We moved back to the edge of the room with my friends. Would they notice? Maybe not. The inadequate lighting made it hard to see. I wrapped my arms around my chest reflexively to hide our breasts just in case. I hugged myself a bit too much and Jimmy mocked me for giving myself a big, lovey-dovey hug. I dropped my arms and gave him a push. He pushed back. "Dancing with Tammy," he said giving me a push back. "You go."

I blushed. He laughed and ran off, didn't notice a thing. One disaster averted. What did I look like though? I needed to see what I looked like. I needed to know how obvious we appeared. She had been obvious at church. I wasn't wearing a baggy shirt this time, and her breasts clearly pushed my shirt out, certainly not disguised. And what about her pouty lips and full cheeks and big eyes. Were they there? What had Tammy seen?

I made for the bathroom, hunching over to shrink my profile. The bathroom looked empty, so I rushed in and closed the door. A mirror hung above the sink in the well-lit bathroom. Sprout looked back at me. Her round cheeks and softer features. I was definitely a her.

"Hi," she said and laughed.

"Oh, you're funny," I whispered. I wanted to tell her to go away and stop embarrassing me. I also wanted the trickle of liberation she brought to stay. I held back my admonition. I knew if she left, the liberation left.

I needed to look down. I need to know what people had seen, what Tammy had seen. I closed my eyes and prepared myself. I didn't want to look down. But I needed to know what I was dealing with. I opened my eyes and looked down and there they were, as noticeable as I had thought.

"Are they bigger?" I said.

"Maybe. They can be as big as you want them to be, I suppose. They look good though, don't they?"

"Uh, sure." I reached up and touched them. Not a sexual touch but a sizing-them-up touch. Definitely bigger. "What the hell?" I said looking Sprout in the eye.

She shrugged. "Yea, they're still real."

"Do I still have my penis?"

"I don't know." She laughed. "I haven't looked. Why? Are you worried Tammy might notice?"

"Shut up!" I said. Was she right though? I knew this happened, and I knew my penis would come back, but now, all of a sudden, I cared. Maybe because of Tammy. I didn't know. This wasn't the time to contemplate the feelings Tammy had evoked. All I knew was I had to check. I closed my eyes. Slid my right hands down my side, down over my pants pocket and over my zipper and pressed. Nothing. "Oh shit, shit, shit."

"What?"

"It's not there."

"Don't worry. You know it comes back. No one is going to notice you don't have a big bulge anyway. Unless you were planning to show Tammy."

"Jesus. Shut up," I said as I double checked. "That's not funny."

"Oh, it is."

Bam, bam. A knock on the bathroom door. "Hurry Up!"

I looked in the mirror. "What am I going to do?"

"Nothing. You were fine before you came into the bathroom." She was right. No one noticed before. No one will notice now.

I turned toward the door and unlocked it. I opened the door. Chad was at the door, Jimmy's older brother, a friend of BJ's, supposed party chaperon. "Quit clogging the doorway, Sprout," he said and shoved me in the chest as he walked by.

He shoved me right in the breasts. Shit. Chad might actually notice those. I reached my hands to my breast as a defensive reaction as I stumbled by. The breasts were gone. She was gone.

Relieved, I kept on moving. If Chad noticed, I'm not sure whether he would've groped me or beaten me up.

She had spared me. But when she left, so did liberation and the euphoria. I could feel it seeping out of me as I walked back across the room. She was like a drug. A drug I liked and terrified me at the same time. She was addicting.

CHAPTER 9 – CHLOROPHYL

I RODE as far out of the city as I felt necessary. Not as far as I could ride but far enough to find solitude. Far from prying eyes and ears. Far enough to feel safe.

I rode a lot. My bike bought my ticket to escape. Escape from a house and family a little too densely populated. I needed only a few things in life and one of those things was seclusion. I found seclusion on a bicycle. Even now I am puzzled by how little my family cared or understood about the stress of perpetual togetherness. And even now the topic never arises.

I moped about and kept my distance from my parents and siblings, like so many teenagers. My siblings could act all moody and self-isolating too, but that didn't stop them from eventually and perpetually gathering. I didn't want to gather.

I knew the need for solitude long before my teenage years. Craved it. When I was a preschooler, I would escape the perpetual togetherness by hiding in the shoe closet, crawling over the lumpy shoes and making a nest where no one would look for me. The smell of leather and sweat still reminds me of crawling into my secret lair of aloneness. The desire to escape increased with the perpetual need of parents and siblings to know where I was escaping to. What are you doing? Where are you going? Why are you going there? Why are you doing that? I wanted acceptance and understanding of my decisions. What I received in return was constant questioning.

The constant monitoring of behaviors and actions oppressed me, but the family's persistent need to know why, to know the reasons for any behavior, tortured me. What a terrible thing to demand from a child. Why? Why did I need to have a why? Why would I even know the why? Why would I understand the why? Why ask me an unanswerable question? I am sure a reasonable why existed, but I was a child. How would I know? Maybe if they had stuck to asking what and accepted the answer, we could have peacefully coexisted.

I struggled with personal sensitivity, the perpetual breaking of boundaries and their requests for explanations gnawed at me. I began to respond to questions about where I was going with a curt "Nowhere." To questions about what I was doing, "Nothing." When asked why, I responded curtly "To be alone." And silently I responded, "and to be left alone."

I rode out of town along the river. Thank the gods we lived near a river and corresponding river valley. Because a river valley meant trees, which are deeply important when you live out on the prairie. Outside the river valley you found a lot of nothing. The nothingness of the plains, the fields, the wind. I know people come to appreciate the prairie. I did not. The trails along the river served as a sanctuary, a different world, and I found myself subconsciously drawn there again and again.

I rode several miles out of town toward a state park along the river with walking and biking trails. The summer foliage dominated the river valley. A thousand shades of green. Legions of leafy shields against the sun. The trees and river oscillated between smelling fresh and a little too organic. Certainly more alive than the city.

The sun had moved slightly past peak. The heat grew quickly but the river and the shade provided relief The movement on my bike provided a constant, cooling breeze. I rode a mile or so into the park and locked my bike to a small tree near the walking trail. The park was sparsely populated on a weekday, so I had it mostly to myself. I walked from the biking path up away from the river, a hundred yards or so until the trees and underbrush obscured a view of the path. I wanted isolation, minimal chance of interruption.

"Hey Sprout," I called out. "Are you there?" Silence. I had never called her before. She showed up when she wanted. Showed up at the most inopportune times. I presumed not by accident. She said she showed up when I wanted her to. I didn't buy that. Why would I do that to myself? She said it was a subconscious thing, which didn't exactly answer the question.

I pulled my backpack off and sat against a tree. I looked down toward the trail and the river. I couldn't see or hear the river. I was alone. I waited. I picked a stone up and tossed it at neighboring tree. Whack! The only sound in the park. I threw another stone. Whack!

"Hey," I said. "Sprout. I brought you something. I think you'll like it." More silence. More nothing. I suppose she had a mind of her own. A life or her own. Wherever that might be. I had no idea. I pulled at the grass at my feet. Pawed at my backpack. This is crazy. I stared out across the park, at the sun filtering through the leaves. How long should I wait? Maybe I needed to stop encouraging her anyway. I endangered my own mental health at this point by encouraging her. But I wanted her to show up. While my desire to give her a present was real, I also selfishly wanted the drug she released into my veins when she appeared.

I stood and grabbed my backpack, where the present was tucked away.

The stolen present. I had to steal it because I certainly didn't own one, and I didn't have the courage to buy one. So it was a stolen, used present. So kind of a crappy present, I guess.

"Hey, here's this crappy gift I stole" wasn't exactly the best enticement for her to show up, I suppose.

The taking part had been the easy part. The choosing to take it was the hard part. That was the conscious acknowledgement of her existence. The agreeing to believe she was real. As real as anything in my sheltered and short life. I had chosen to actively engage. I had no idea what engagement would bring. But she had said to be nice to people. It made them feel better. I wanted to be nice to her. I wanted her to feel better. I wanted me to feel better. So now I actively engaged her, and perhaps against my best-self-interest, I had accepted her.

"Sprout," I called again after a little while. I didn't know how long to wait. Didn't want to be a fool in the rain. I swung the backpack around my shoulder and looked around. I started down the uneven ground, back to the walking trail.

"Where are you going?" she said. "I like presents."

"Hey. I didn't think you were going to come. I was almost relieved I wasn't going to have to go through with it."

"Well, here I am. Go through with what?"

I looked down. I could feel the sense of freedom she brought with her. I smiled. I always smiled more when she showed up. Her drug kicking in. I don't know what kind of drug it was, but it felt good. It gave me the courage to go through with the gift giving.

"I have a present for you."

"So you said. Well, let's see it."

"Okay." I walked back up to the tree I had been sitting against. I pulled the present out of the backpack and shook it out and held it out in front of us. "How do you like it?"

"It's a sundress." She held it out and spun around. "You did this for me? I can't believe it. You said you wouldn't."

"I said I wouldn't buy you one. I stole it from my sister."

"Obviously wasn't yours." She gave the dress another shake. "Willing to steal things for me, are you?"

"I guess. She's the same height as me so I thought it might fit. I don't know about these things."

"You didn't try it on?"

"Are you crazy? At home? No way. I'm not stupid."

"Not excessively stupid, anyway." She held the dress against us. "Well, let's put it on."

I hesitated. I wasn't even sure how to put it on. "I don't know how."

"Here. Let me do it." She took over. She knew what to do. We took my

46

shirt off and tossed it on my backpack. There we stood half naked, breasts exposed. "No one can see us." She pulled off my running shorts. "It's a pull over. Like putting on a t-shirt." She rolled up the bottom of the dress until she could stretch her hands into the arms and her head through the neck hole. Her head popped through, and her arms punched out. She let the rest of the dress tumble down to our knees. She smoothed it out.

"See. Easy. The clasp in the back here is to fasten the collar." She adjusted the collar. Smoothed out the dress again, running her hands down the sides and the front. "It's a bit wrinkled," she said and laughed. "Just teasing. It's wonderful." She twirled around. We floated away. Drip, drip into my blood.

She twirled again. The lower part of the dress wafting up. I kept looking down at the dress. White with a light yellow and green pattern of flowers. I could see her breasts, our breasts, filling out the front of the sundress. Our bare arms and legs spinning through the air.

"This is nice," I said. "I see why girls like to wear these. Light and airy."

"See. I know what I'm talking about." She pranced around the park, spun around the trees, jumped a stump, swiped at the branches of a bush. She found a patch of sun and stopped. "Ooh, quite nice."

The sun bathed us in serenity. We closed our eyes and stared up at it. We spread our arms to catch all the sunlight, accepting the life it gave. She twirled in the opening, spinning the dress outward.

"Now I'm hot. Let's go put our feet in the river to cool off."

"Let's do it." I acquiesced, her confidence flowing through us now. She could take control. We trotted, almost skipped, back down to the bike trail and another fifty feet to the edge of the river. Still no one around. We climbed down the short drop of riverbank. We looked for a place to dip our feet. We found a big rock on the water's edge large enough to sit on. We took our shoes and socks off.

We sat on the rock and dipped our feet into the water. Cool enough to startle us but soothing after a few seconds. We looked out across the river, no more than 30 feet, and surveyed the other side of the river. Covered in underbrush and trees leaning out over the water. Secluded. The only civilization you could see was an old wooden pedestrian bridge peeking through the foliage downstream. We watched the sun rays bounce off the middle of the river and disappear into the shadows of the trees along the banks. We leaned back and put our arms over our head. Relaxed. Forgot to worry about passersby, the world, everything. Gazed into the tree branches above.

"You like this?" she asked. "This is nice, isn't it?"

"Yes. It's nice."

"Even in a dress?"

"Even in a dress."

She ran her fingers through my short hair. "That was nice of you to give me a dress. Now we need longer hair and we'll look about right."

I laughed. "I don't think that's going to happen."

"It could." She sat up abruptly. "Let's go for a swim."

"What?"

"It's hot. What better time to go for swim? We're pretty much naked under the dress anyway." She stood up and started to pull the dress off.

"Whoa." I stopped her pulling on the dress. "You mean skinny dip? Like naked?" My stomach tightened. Naked. Exposed. Vulnerable. I was so used to constant monitoring and being obnoxiously interrupted, I feared being busted, caught out, in the middle of nowhere.

"Yes, skinny dip. Naked. But what does it matter? There's no one here."

"I'm here."

"Whatever." She stopped listening to me and pulled off the dress. She set it on the dry rock behind us. Before I could object, my underwear came off. She dropped those on top of the dress.

Splash, into the cool water. Floating on our back looking up at the sky.

"You're crazy," I said.

"I'm not. I'm normal. You need to become accustomed to me. You need to get used to me being you."

"That might take a while."

"Whatever." She floated on her back and kicked us out to the middle of the river. The weak current tugged lightly on our legs. She stopped floating and treaded water once we reached the middle of the river. The river was shallow in most places but here in the middle we couldn't touch the bottom.

"Thanks," she said.

"For what?"

"For the dress. For swimming. For everything."

"You're welcome for the dress. But I don't think I was in control of the swimming."

"Oh, you were." She splashed water into my face. Laughed.

"Very funny. You're only splashing yourself, you know."

"I know."

We looked back at the riverbank. Looked different from the middle of the river. The sundress looked small and abandoned. A breeze kicked up and fluttered the sundress, as if to say "don't forget me." Out of the corner of my eye I could see a couple people walking along the trail.

"Oh shit," I said. What if they know me? What if they know my parents? I couldn't get busted skinny dipping. The embarrassment would humiliate me. Explaining skinny dipping would be hard enough. Strangers talking about my boobs would wreck me.

"Oh, don't' worry. The only thing they can see is our head."

A man and woman came into view along the path right across from us. They looked in our direction. I wanted to duck in the water and disappear, avoid them altogether. She waved at them instead. They waved back and kept going.

"See," she said. "They just waved. They don't care."

"I saw." I felt my heart slow back down. She had countered my instincts and actually succeeded in not panicking. I had tried for years to overcome my scaredy-cat reactions and had always failed. She didn't let us fail.

We floated around for a while gazing up at the blue sky. We heard more voices. My fear returned. "Let's go back to the bank." My muscles twitched with discomfort. I couldn't let go of the fear.

"Don't be so nervous every time another human shows up. You think everyone cares so much about you. They don't. Trust me. It's not like they're your mom."

"I'm sorry." I had survived the first couple but was unprepared for multiple assaults. I felt I had disappointed her when I had panicked. I wanted to be carefree like her but I wasn't.

"It's okay. You did good. You actually tried. You need more practice is all."

I had tried. I would never have skinny dipped without her. Maybe accepting her was a bigger decision than I knew.

We swam back to the bank. It wasn't far. The river shallowed out quickly so we had to stand and walk the last few feet. Naked of course. I hurried up to the rock and grabbed the sundress and my underwear. I wanted to exude her confidence but my nakedness still made me nervous. I walked to where we left the backpack. I pulled my shirt and shorts out and started to pull my underwear on. I heard more voices and quickly grabbed my shirt but couldn't pull it on in time as another couple walked by and waved. Shit! I looked down.

She spared me. She was gone. Yet I noticed the joy of her presence, the sense of freedom and liberation she brought, had lingered. It had never lingered before. I liked that. It was nourishing. Now if I could only channel her confidence on demand and take advantage of the liberation.

CHAPTER 10 – SKYWARD

FOR AS ALOOF as I appeared to others, my aloofness wasn't driven by confidence. As much as I wanted it and we worked at it, I didn't have Sprout's confidence. To protect my sensitive nature, I detached myself from the world. If I didn't hear the whisperings, I wouldn't know about them. Ignorance was bliss. A terrible strategy of avoidance, I know. When I lived in my own world I behaved as I wanted, and no one was the wiser. Which was all well and good until you went out into the real world where we are all judged by appearances as well. While I didn't put much effort into my looks, and I pretended I didn't care; I couldn't escape the plague of other people's opinions about that.

In the eighth grade I didn't pay much attention to my hair. I woke up in the morning, dressed for school, and didn't give two seconds of thought to my hair. I didn't care if it was a mess. I remember Gary Jensen commenting one time how I looked like Alfalfa from the Little Rascals with spikey, oily hair going all directions.

"You could wash and comb that mess, ya know" he said, a mild insult at best but it penetrated my defenses. I felt its sting, embarrassed, inadequate, judged. I didn't care if my hair was messy. I cared if someone noticed it. If Gary noticed, other people noticed. I felt stupid. I wanted to shrink away and disappear from people's perception. I didn't want anyone to notice me at all. Gary's comment spurred me to cut my hair short, buzz-cut short. Harder for people to notice nothing. Move along, nothing to see here. I wanted a carefree nature, but I could only fake it. I had simply created another defensive layer and locked myself inside my sheltered prison.

"Let's go roll in the meadow," Sprout said, pointing to a grassy field one day while walking through Maple Street Park not far from the city zoo.

"This is hardly a meadow," I said. "A glorified field with a bit of grass and clover."

"Don't be a downer. Use your imagination. You're the one who imagined the back yard was a racetrack. You're the one who reads science fiction and has to imagine fantastic worlds. It can be whatever we want."

"I want it to be field of Willy Wonka candy."

"Don't be a jerk. It'll be alike a roll in the hay, but with ourselves."

"You don't even know what that means."

"Whatever. Let's do it."

She occupied me now. Drip, drip. If she wanted to frolic, we would frolic. I could see no reason to resist, so we stepped off the walking trail into the meadow. The meadow hadn't been mowed recently and the grass and clover bent lazily over, making it soft and bouncy. I looked around to see if anyone was watching.

"What are you doing?"

"Looking to see if anyone is watching."

"There's no one around, ya big baby. And who cares?" We walked further into the field. I could feel the softer ground underneath our feet. I could smell the clover. A light breeze flopped the long grass back and forth.

"May I?" she said and took a little skip.

"What are we going to do?"

"Just let go and trust me."

"I always trust you."

"Do you now?" she said.

I wasn't sure what I had agreed to except the vague notion she had of rolling in the hay, which I suspect she had intentionally misinterpreted.

"Ready?" she said as she started to run.

"Yes. Yes. Let's do it."

She started skipping then broke into twirling with her arms out. "Whirl, whirl, twist and twirl. Like Bugs Bunny, right?" She leapt like a ballerina into the air and let herself fall all the way to the grass with no resistance. Rolling and rolling until we stopped on our stomach and buried our face in the thick grass and clover. "Smell the grass. Breathe deep."

We breathed it in. Warm, moist, earthy. The soft clover felt soothing on our skin, but the grass tickled, a pleasing sensation I had never before slowed down enough to enjoy. And so simple. She knew what she was doing. She knew how to take it in. To enjoy the moment.

Jumping up to her feet. Arms reaching high. Leaping once and twice and coming down into a somersault. Back to her feet. More twirling and skipping. "We like to skip, remember?"

"Yes, I remember." Skipping was freedom. Skipping was liberation. Skipping was dipping your toes in euphoria. So we kept skipping and jumping. I felt free and unencumbered yet connected to the Earth. Mother

Earth. I immersed myself in the moment and didn't notice when a handful of boys came riding their bikes along the nearby path. I ignored them. But I had to work at it. I didn't want people's attention but skipping about was going to draw attention.

"Hey, you crazy bitch! What are you doing? You look like a Tasmanian devil." The boys all stopped on the edge of meadows. Howling at us.

The yelling broke the spell and I noticed them noticing me. I stopped and looked at them. My fetters had reappeared. Self-conscious and embarrassed for scampering around, I ached to run across the field and into safety of the city streets. My head sunk and I looked away.

"No," she said. "Don't do it. Don't let them dictate what we do. Keep skipping." She lifted her head and stared at them defiantly. "Ignore those dopes. Keep going." I didn't move. Frozen. I could feel a tear welling. Embarrassed for being noticed, for being not normal. Much worse than having messy hair. Messy hair might have been noticeable, but frolicking was weird.

"Come on," she insisted. "You can do it. Wave and skip away. They don't mean shit to us." She stuck her chin out and up into the air. She waved and skipped back to the middle of the meadow, where she jumped as high as she could. We fell to the ground and rolled around. We laid on our back spread eagle. "Woo hoo!" she yelled and stared up at the sky. She rolled on her side and propped her head up in her hands. She stared defiantly at the boys. She waved.

The boys hollered at this and rode off the path onto the meadow and circled around us. "Crazy bitch. Crazy bitch," they yelled. They circled closer.

She jumped to her feet and stared to twirl, like a ballerina, round and round, faster and faster, moving out towards the circling bikes, getting closer and closer, reaching out to them. She brushed the shirt of one of the boys and screamed out "Weee!"

The boy stopped his bike. Let it drop to the ground. Stepped into our face.

"You think you can touch me," he yelled as he shoved us in the chest. "Do you like it when I touch you?" He shoved us again in the chest.

She didn't back down. She stood her ground even though he was much bigger than she was. She held her head high. She stared silently back at him. She didn't justify his bullshit with a response.

"I asked you a question?" He thrust his arms out to shove her again.

She spun out of the way. He stumbled by. "I heard you," she said as she stepped back toward him. She raised her eyebrows at him. "And?"

"Are you crazy? Do you want me to beat you?" He leaned into her. She held her ground again. He raised his right hand into a fist. As he cocked his arm back, one of his friends rode by and grabbed his shirt and tugged him away.

"Come on, you idiot," his friend yelled at him. "You gonna' beat up a girl? Let's go."

He stumbled away and picked up his bike. "Super crazy bitch," he yelled. "What a whack job."

"Super crazy bitch," the boys all yelled together. They rode off jeering at us and disappeared into the city streets.

"See," she said. "They don't care." We plopped down onto the grass, shaking, exhausted, dizzy. "Maybe they care for a moment, but then they get bored. If you react, they get worse. Keep doing your thing. They don't know what to do if you're just bat-shit crazy."

"What were you thinking? He could have beaten the crap out of us. And I don't want to be bat-shit crazy."

"Be bat-shit crazy when you need to be. That's all I'm saying."

"You're just trouble." I wanted to pin the blame on her for drawing attention to us.

"Maybe. But I didn't do anything to them. They started it. We were doing our own thing. Having fun. I'm not going to apologize for that. Not going to not be us."

She was right. We shouldn't have to apologize. They were looking for trouble. Not that she seemed to make much effort to avoid trouble.

"I'm sorry. You know I don't like calling attention to myself. I'm easily embarrassed. And obviously it can be dangerous."

"I know. It's so worth it though. And you know it." She sat up. She thrust her hands down into the grass and clover squeezed a handful. "When you feel embarrassed or self-conscious you need to reach down into the Earth and let Gaia give you strength. Gaia loves you and doesn't care what those pimply boys think."

"You come up with the weirdest shit."

"It's not weird. Listen. I hear what you're saying. You don't want to be noticed. Understandable. It makes you uncomfortable. You react by freezing. You become paralyzed and stop being you."

"I can't help it. That's who I am."

"But it's not who I am. And I'm you. It's not who I want to be. It's not how we want to be. It's not how you want to be. You don't want to be like that, right?"

"Right."

"I'm not going to freeze. So you're going to have to learn how not to freeze."

"How? I don't understand."

"You can't always understand these things. We'll fight through it. You'll see you can change, take control. We'll work on it. Remember Gaia. Gaia is earth, nature, life. We're part of Gaia, and Gaia is part of us, and she doesn't care what anybody thinks. You understand?"

"No."

"You're shy. You're afraid of attention. Fair enough. But Gaia is nature, and she wants you to be natural, to be you. When you shut down and hide with your fear, you feel safe, but it's safe like a prison is safe. Instead of shutting down when you feel fear, she wants you to push back, to take a stand. Be you and to let go. Because the fear is in you, not in them. She wants you to choose, not fear. You can choose. Do you understand that?"

"Maybe. But seems easy for Gaia to say. She's not the one getting beat up."

"Just trust me. Gaia doesn't want you to get beat up. But better they mock you for being you than to be mocked for being nothing. They'll mock you anyway. Being carefree doesn't come without risk. We're learning how to navigate out in the world. We had our first lesson. We did good."

"But that was you. You're the one who stood up."

"But I'm you. You need to let me out. Learn from me. Practice choosing to let go of fear when I'm not here. You'll figure it out."

"It's not the same when you're not here. I don't have it in me."

"I'm in you. Channel me when you need me. We'll do it together."

We fell onto our back, still exhausted, and stared up at the sky. We waved at the sky.

"The sky doesn't care what people think," she said. "Be the sky."

CHAPTER 11 – VERDANCY

AT FIFTEEN, I was Peter Pan, more child than adult. Perhaps willfully so. I didn't want to enter adulthood. I didn't want responsibility. I didn't want a beard or rugged features. I was a child and a child I wanted to stay. Innocence, I suppose, is what I clung too.

At fifteen years old I found myself on the battlefield between the forces of innocence and the forces of puberty. Innocence imbued me with the energy of playfulness, imagination, naivete.

The forces of puberty made me a typical teenager: moody, difficult, rebellious, distant, reclusive, unpredictable and swinging between knowing everything and knowing nothing. The forces of puberty are strong.

Sexuality, of course, was scary. I perceived the unknowns of sexuality as a threat to my childhood. It was especially scary since I was offered no guidance on my growing sexuality. My mother, who had plenty of children, somehow didn't or wouldn't or couldn't acknowledge sexuality at all. Well, it existed for her because sex before marriage was a sin, which apparently meant you just didn't acknowledge it. Not much for guidance and not helpful. While I might not have understood my sexuality well, I knew it existed. I wasn't entirely stupid, and nature taught me a few things on her own.

While my sexuality grew whether I liked it or not, my attitude and approach to the world remained childlike. At home when I had the choice between hanging out with adults and hanging out with children, I didn't hesitate to hang out with the children. I was a child. I enjoyed and was proud of my childlike behavior. I enjoyed playing with my younger siblings and my nieces and nephews. They enjoyed it because in me they found an adult who still had imagination and who could still play. They liked it because I wasn't pretending, and they knew it.

One day my oldest brother, Darrin, and his four-year old daughter, Marti, came to visit Mom. My brother and Mom sat at the kitchen counter chatting. I didn't want any part of the small talk, so I took Marti down into the basement where all the kids' toys were stored.

We started by playing tea. We set up a little table with cups and saucers and other miscellaneous items apparently necessary for tea. We had guests of course. Doll, bear, giraffe. In fact, my niece and I had stepped aside. She was Doll. I was Bear and Giraffe.

"I say, I could use a spot of tea," said Bear.

"I could use a spot of tea, too," chimed in Giraffe.

Doll poured out the tea. "Would you like cream?" Doll asked.

"Of course," said Bear.

"There wouldn't happen to be any cookies," asked Giraffe.

"No cookies," said Doll. "But we have some cake." The cake looked suspiciously like Lego blocks.

"I like cake," said Bear and proceeded to eat the Lego block cakes as if he were Cookie Monster. "Nom, nom, nom."

Doll didn't approve of this terrible display of manners by bear. "No more cake for you." Bear was upset and fled the table by means of being tossed over my shoulder. Giraffe soon followed to check on his friend. Tea service devolved as my niece channeled the Red Queen, barked some orders, and swept the tea setting to the floor and announced, "Tea is over."

I turned to fetch Bear for the next adventure. I crawled over into the dark corner where Bear had landed. I turned to look around for Giraffe when she said, "Hi." I was used to Sprout showing up, sort of. I didn't panic as much anymore, but I always felt a quick sliver of fear twist in my gut. Frequently, we were alone, like when she showed up while biking or walking or alone in my room. We could chill and talk with minimal fear of discovery. We could talk about family, friends, school.

Things got weird when other people were around. Adrenaline started pumping. Initially, I thought all the adrenaline is what made me feel good when she was around. But the adrenaline would wear off and the drip, drip of her special essence still flowed through my veins. The intoxication gave me strength.

I held Bear in my hands as I pondered what to do. My niece may have been young but even she would notice. I looked at my chest. Sprout was definitely there. I knew I couldn't just stay in the corner of the room.

"Not now, Sprout. I can't not crawl back. What's Marti going to think?" I didn't have a mirror so I couldn't tell what we looked like, but we had breasts so I had to assume her full, glowing cheeks and lips had come along for the ride.

"She's young," she said. "She might not even notice."

"Might not. Kind of wishful thinking. Kids notice everything."

"She'll think you're still playing," she said. "So play like you always do. Be confident in who you are. Be the playful, caring, nurturing person you are. We'll keep playing and we'll be good."

The plan, to plow confidently ahead, didn't seem like much of a plan. Though as always, Sprout was confident we could power our way through it. I trusted her confidence more and more, but wasn't sure I trusted it that much. I didn't have a better plan. Running up the stairs and out of the house wasn't going to work. I guess we would bluster through it.

I crawled back with Bear and sat cross legged across the table from my niece. I placed bear on the table in front of me. I was still Bear, and Bear could block a clear view of my breasts, but Sprout's round, beaming face had nowhere to hide.

"Bear thinks we should go to the beach," I said. "Let's find some shovels and buckets. And maybe a beach ball."

"Yea, let's go to the beach," yelled Marti.

We pushed the table out of the way, found a towel by the washing machine and pulled a small play bucket and shovel from a box of toys. Found a bouncy ball, a rubber ducky and a few other toys. We sat at the edge of the towel. Instant beach party.

"The sun sure is warm and nice," said Bear.

"Yes," said Doll. "Let's lay down and sunbathe." So Bear laid down on the towel next to Doll to enjoy the sun. Marti laid on her side of the towel and propped her head up with her hand. I laid on my side of the towel and propped my head up as well. Bear and Doll took in the sunshine in between us.

"The sound of the ocean is nice," Bear said. "I can hear the seagulls."

"I see some seals," said Doll. "They're so cute."

"Yes, they are," said Bear. "It's getting warm. Maybe we need refreshments to cool us down."

"Maybe grandma has some pop for us," said Marti.

"She might. You can ask your dad if you can have some."

Marti looked at me intently. Her eyes narrowed as she focused on my face. She had noticed. Before I knew it, she leaned over the towel, reached out a hand and touched my face and rubbed my cheek. She gently touched our breasts.

"You're a girl," Marti said matter-of-factly, her eyes wide and wondering.

"Now we're caught." So much for her not noticing.

"Don't panic. She isn't freaked out. Keep playing."

"Sometimes we're a girl," we said. "Like when we pretend to be bear or giraffe."

"You're pretty," she said, unphased by the situation, passed her hands over our lips.

"So are you, sweety," we said and brushed our hand over her hair, tousled it.

"Your hair is too short." She gently rubbed my head.

"I know. It needs to grow out. Why don't you go see if your dad can find some pop."

My niece stood up, grabbed Doll and headed up the stairs. "I'll be right back. Don't go anywhere."

"I'll wait," I said. I collapsed onto my back and watched Marti walk up the stairs. "Holy crap! What are we going to do about that?"

"We're fine," she said. "She thinks were pretty, which we are. She's not freaked out at all. It's just more play to her."

"For now," I said.

"She's innocent. She accepts us," she said. "She still sees us as innocent too. She doesn't know that but it's what she feels. It's enough for now, isn't it? Isn't that good? We won't be innocent for much longer. We may as well enjoy it."

"Doesn't any middle ground exist between innocence and knowledge? Can't I retain my innocence?"

"Yes. But there's a price. Innocence is naivete that leaves you vulnerable to people who would take advantage of that. It's the pain that makes people lock up innocence in the tower. I guess it's whether you can handle the pain and not lock yourself up."

"That doesn't sound like a great trade off."

"There are no good trade-offs. Nothing is free."

"Shhh!" We heard her upstairs talking to Mom and Darren.

"Theo's a girl," said my niece.

"No, honey, Theo's not a girl," her dad said.

"But I touched her boobs," she said. "She's so pretty."

"Are you talking about one of the dolls?" Darren asked.

"No, I touched her boobs and her face," Marti said adamantly. "But her hair is too short. She should have longer hair."

"Okay honey," said her dad, placating her obvious nonsense. We heard him to the fridge. "Well, you can have this can of orange pop to share with her. It's Fanta. She'll like that."

"That's great," I said as we listened to the exchange going on upstairs.

"Don't worry," said Sprout. "Kids talk nonsense all the time. Your brother won't think twice about it. He's used to nonsense. He's just humoring her."

"Except she's planted a seed that something's amiss. Then he'll start joking about it with me. I don't need him poking round there."

"Whatever, let him have a joke. It doesn't mean anything."

"Yeah, not until my brother catches us off guard and sees you and it reminds him of what my niece said. He'll think I'm a freak, looking like a girl. He's not a real enlightened guy."

"We'll make sure it doesn't happen. I promise."

Marti came back down. "Dad found a Fanta. It's orange. He said you'd like it."

I picked out a couple of scattered tea cups to drink our pop. I opened the can and poured our tea.

"Bear likes orange soda," Bear said. "And so do I," I said.

"Daddy says you're not a girl," said Marti. "But I know you are."

"I'm only a girl when we're playing," I said. "Just make believe."

"Just make believe," she said. We lounged on the beach and drank our soda. Everything was normal. My niece, the innocent child I wanted to be, had accepted me. But the breasts I could feel under my shirt told me I couldn't stay innocent much longer. I had no idea of what to do with that.

Eventually her dad called down. Time to go. We cleaned up the toys. Marti grabbed my hand to walk me up the stairs. She smiled up at me.

"No getting out of this without freaking everyone out," I said to Sprout.

"We'll be fine."

"You always think we'll be fine."

"And we always are."

We walked slowly up the basement stairs. When we reached the top, Sprout had gone.

"I hear you're a girl now," my brother needled.

"Nothing wrong with being a girl," I said and winked at Marti. She winked back.

CHAPTER 12 – NOURISHMENT

BOYS EAT A LOT. I was a teenage boys who ran and rode bike all day. I ate a lot. An insatiable amount. I don't have many memories of eating so much that I couldn't eat more. Though I remember a few times when my insatiability did me in. I once ate an entire pan of cinnamon apple crisp. I don't know why anyone even let me eat the whole thing, but no one stopped me. I made the terrible decision to go for a ride afterward. The cinnamon-coated apple chunks burned my nose at they came up and passed over the handlebars. I apparently needed to learn enough was enough. I didn't eat apple crisp for a long time.

One afternoon I stood in the kitchen staring into the fridge looking for an eating inspiration. I spent a lot of time as a teenager looking in the fridge, looking in the freezer, looking in the pantry. I usually ate whatever I could find because I was simply hungry and didn't care what I ate. Sometimes I looked for an undefined something. What to eat? Cheese, milk, cereal, salad, sandwich. I'd already scoured the cabinets for a quick snack but had come up empty. I closed the fridge door and opened it again. I may have missed a hidden gem.

Dad walked into the kitchen to refill his coffee mug. He knew the drill of kids staring in the fridge. "Warming all the food up isn't going to fill your hollow leg. Pick something and close the door."

I closed the door without choosing anything. I leaned back on the counter and stared at the now closed fridge. Dad wandered off. I opened the fridge door again. Peered even deeper. Past the milk and the juice on the front of the shelves, looking for a hidden nugget of satisfaction in the back. I wasn't much of a cook at fifteen so if the food wasn't immediately edible it wasn't going to make the list.

Dad walked through the dining room and saw me looking in the fridge again. "Mom's making macaroni and cheese later if that even remotely matters." He kept walking.

It didn't matter. I couldn't wait for the macaroni and cheese. I craved something now. The craving frustrated me because I had no idea how to satisfy it.

"Hi," she said.

"Hey, be careful. Dad's lurking around."

"Not to worry. He won't notice."

"You never think anyone will notice."

"Well, do they?" She possessed an endless well of confidence. She splashed it around like it was water. She often doused herself in so much confidence she got cocky. When she was cocky, she made me nervous. Who knew what she would do? Did she do it on purpose? Probably.

"I think he might notice."

"He won't. You're generic kid number five to him. I think he guesses at your name most of the time. He'll just think I am one of your sisters."

"Let's not test your hypothesis." Dad had a lot of kids to keep track of but even he wasn't completely clueless. "He knows a boy from a girl."

"A hawk from a handsaw."

"What are you talking about?"

"Never mind. Keep your head stuck in the fridge if he comes in."

"Solid plan."

"Hungry?" She had already forgotten about Dad. She moved on to the fridge.

"Uh yep, that's why we're looking in the fridge."

"Cut me a wee bit of slack. I just got here. This stuff looks pretty boring."

"Well, this is what we have to work with. Salami, cheese, bread. Begging you to make a sandwich."

"Nah. There's nothing here. What are we actually craving? Hmm. I know. We need ice cream."

"It's three in the afternoon." I'm not sure why I argued about the time. I was always ready to eat. I guess I needed to push back on her surety. She was always so sure.

"So, who cares what time it is? Didn't know we had rules around when to have ice cream."

"I need something healthier."

"Oh, that's crap. If that were true you could make a sandwich or eat an apple."

"Maybe I will."

"But you won't. We've been staring in here for ten minutes. Could have made a sandwich by now."

"I still could." I pawed the loaf of bread and pretended to ponder it. Once she latched onto an idea, she persisted. She liked to get her way. I wanted to make her work.

"But you haven't and you're not going to. You're looking for the right thing. You're craving something."

"For what? You have any ideas, smarty?"

"I told you. For ice cream."

"How do you know it's ice cream?

"Because I want ice cream. I know. Our body is telling us. Listen to your gut. It knows what it's talking about. We know what we're talking about."

"If that was it, I think I would have figured that out by now. But I haven't. So it could still be anything."

"You clearly haven't figured it out. Because it's not just anything, it's ice cream."

"Why?"

"We'll have to talk about the why because it's not always about knowing why. Oftentimes it's simply knowing that it is."

"You and your mumbo jumbo. Crap. Here comes Dad." Dad was walking from the dining room into the kitchen. He'd yell at me if I he found me still moping about by the fridge. He might ask a question. He might expect a response. If I answered, I might sound like a girl.

"Close the door and run into the basement. We don't want any of this stuff anyway. He won't notice anything. Here, I'll show you."

She closed the door. Drooped her head down. Stopped at the utensil drawer and grabbed a spoon. Spun around Dad. "Hi Dad, bye Dad," she said, racing around the corner toward the basement.

"Slow down," he yelled. "This isn't a racetrack."

She bounded down the stairs. Ran to the basement pantry filled with canned and dry goods. I thought she ran in there to look for a hiding spot, but I realized the pantry also contained the freezer. She opened the freezer door. Scanned the contents and found a half gallon of ice cream on the bottom shelf. She grabbed the ice cream, bounced into my bedroom, and sat on my bed. She opened the half gallon of Rocky Road and plunged the spoon in.

"I love ice cream," she said as she spooned a large scoop into her mouth, savored the creamy flavor. "Mmmm." She would have been purring if she were a cat, and a cat wouldn't have enjoyed a bowl of cream any more. We reveled in the act of eating ice cream far more than I ever would have. I would have wolfed it down with a vague sense fulfillment. She ate every spoonful like it was like a little taste of manna from heaven. I liked that, enjoying the manna.

After a couple spoonful's she sighed and said, "See, this is what you wanted. This is what you were craving. Right?"

"Maybe." I didn't want to admit I thought this was exactly what I wanted.

Or how her slow savoring of it made the experience even more satisfying. She was feeling cocky enough already.

"Don't maybe me." She waved the spoon in the air. "We weren't simply craving food. We were craving comfort, pleasure, escape, a reprieve from the world. That's the why if you need to have one."

"You're just making shit up. When wouldn't ice cream make me feel better?"

"Good point. But I'm not making this shit up. Come on, admit this is what you were craving."

I hesitated. I couldn't let her always be right. She spooned out another scoop. Savored it.

"Admit it," she repeated. She banged my hand with the spoon.

"Okay, yes. This is hitting the spot."

"I know. Now you're in touch with yourself, see. Looking inside, paying attention. Listening. You're always go, go, go. Consume. Do shit, go some more. Consume some more. You eat food like a car consumes gasoline. The food itself isn't important."

"I'm always hungry. So that's what I do. I eat."

"I know. You're a boy. It's what you do. But I, you, we, need to slow down. Reflect. Pay attention to our inner voice, our gut. Learn to understand the voice. That's your intuition. You. Us. Your soul."

"I don't understand what you're talking about." I stared at the ice cream to distract her as she exuded deep seriousness. I didn't want to be serious so I said, "Who cares anyway?"

"We care," she said forcefully. "Pay attention and you'll understand. But the goal isn't to understand. The goal is to sit and listen and observe, to feel. Slowly understand what your inner voice is saying, and eventually understand why it's saying it. This isn't about wanting ice cream or other physical things. This is about paying attention to what your body and soul need. Sometimes, do you just know, yet can't understand why you know?"

"I suppose. Like when I feel uncomfortable around someone and can't explain why."

"Exactly. You have to pay attention to the vibe people give off and be able to interpret it. You can learn to understand why you're feeling what you feel. Like noticing you're uncomfortable around someone and knowing it's because they don't respect boundaries. That's huge. That's a survival skill. You can know when you are safe and when to be on your guard."

"Like avoid them or know to keep them at arm's length?"

"Yes. See? You understand. You have to work at it. Be aware and try to decipher it. Sometimes you'll be wrong, and that's okay, but you learn by being wrong, so that's good. Eventually you'll be right more and more often. Today it's ice cream but tomorrow, it might be a walk alone along the river. You like to walk along the river. Well, you have reasons for that, even if you're not aware of them, or don't even understand them. Ponder what the reasons might be. Your soul can tell you things you haven't noticed before. You need to slow down and be still and listen. It's like learning a language. It's surprising what you can learn if you know how to listen."

"That's a little deep for craving ice cream." I think I understood what she had said at a conceptual level, but I wasn't sure how I would use it in the real world. Her earnestness alerted me she was probably planting a seed of knowledge that might take some time to germinate on me. Even my undeveloped gut instinct told me so much. I asked, "Are we doing that now, by eating ice cream?"

"Well, I am. You, not quite yet. You're learning a language exists. And now we're talking about learning it, so you're starting. We'll keep practicing. But you can practice when I'm not here, too. Listen to your intuitions, your gut." She rubbed our belly for emphasis. "You'll learn things about yourself you didn't know. You'll even learn about things you didn't think you could possibly know. It's like a superpower if you know how to use it."

I agreed I would try to pay attention. I could use a superpower to battle the outside world. It wasn't quite superhero power, but it was something I could control.

We looked at the half gallon of ice cream. We'd eaten half of it. We felt comforted, content. She was right. We had satisfied the craving.

"I think that's enough for now," I said.

"I don't know. We could probably eat all of this. But maybe we should leave some for others."

CHAPTER 13 – FLOURISHING

THE MAD RUSH of students out the front doors at the end of the school day resembled a prison break. The suppressed energy in the kids bubbled over as the pressurized cap was removed from their daily sentence. A daily running of the bulls out the front door. For me though, the release allowed my energy to start to rejuvenate after being trampled all day long by the togetherness, to quickly rebound on the solitary walk home.

One day as I walked out the front door with the throng of students, I saw Tammy, the girl we had danced with at Jimmy's summer party. Shoulder length, blond hair. Full cheeks. Petite. I suspect I had a crush on her. I perked up when I saw her walking in the halls or in the lunchroom, and she was in my history class.

History class had assigned seating. Tammy sat in front of me to the left, enough inside my field of vision to have a clear view of her if I turned my head a little. I mean, it's not like I stared at her all the time. But I did notice her. I was still young enough to think she was cute without tying it to sexuality, though I am sure my biology made the connection.

I doubt she connected me with the person she had danced with in Jimmy's basement. She had been dancing with Sprout after all, and while we looked similar, Sprout was definitely a girl, and I was definitely not. Or perhaps Tammy made the connection. How would I know? I assumed she hadn't, and that was okay. I preferred to think she didn't make a connection, or at least I told myself I did.

I saw Tammy walking back into the school as I walked out. I decided I would be bold and look right at her. Practice confidence like Sprout had preached. I made sure I would pass right next to her. I kept my eyes on her as she came in. If she looked in my direction, she'd have no doubt I was looking at her. She looked up and at me. She didn't look away. Our eyes met. She smiled in seeming recognition. I might have smiled too. I don't know. I turned away as fast as I could, startled at succeeding in looking into her eyes, startled like a frightened animal, visceral fear overriding everything. In a blink the interaction was over, and I found myself outside.

Once outside on the sidewalk I stopped and backed up against the school building to recover. I felt warm all over. I'm sure I had turned a bright red. Flustered, I balled my fists and slammed them into my thighs. How could I have been so awkward by someone flashing a casual, passing smile? A weight crashed down on my spirit. How could I possess so little confidence, or manliness as my brother would say?

Like a good teenager, I walked home overanalyzing an interaction that had probably flitted in and out of Tammy's consciousness within seconds. Perhaps the interaction hadn't registered on her radar at all. Or maybe it had. I had turned away so quickly I couldn't know. My behavior had registered on my radar though, leaving me depressed.

I walked over one of the bridges crossing the river that snaked through town. I bent over the railing to look down at the slow-moving water. I liked to stop and stare at eddies on the way home to clear my mind. "To the sea" is what I always thought about the water below that would one day join the ocean.

"Hi," she said.

"Hi."

"To the sea," she said.

"Yep."

"So Tammy smiled at you."

"Maybe."

"Maybe nothing."

"Doesn't mean anything. I passed a girl in the hall who smiled at me. That's pretty nothing."

"Well, I don't know. Maybe."

We leaned over the bridge railing and looked straight down. The water swirled more around the footings of the bridge. The swirls had a hypnotic effect. The swirls took me away. I replayed Tammy walking by. I imagined her saying "Hi." I cringed at how I had reacted.

"You shouldn't have looked away so fast," she said. "Like a scared rabbit. You might've seen more. You'd know if it was nothing or if it was something."

"You sound like my brother. Be more manly. A ladies man."

"Shut up. I don't sound like that clown. I'm not saying you should've leapt over and kissed her. I mean, you did good at least trying. I'm saying you didn't have to be a scaredy cat. You could have been more open and receptive. You'd already done the hard part. Accept it. Go with it. You can't interact with her if you turn away."

"I can't help it. My body takes control. It overrides everything."

"It's natural to feel fear. The courage comes from acknowledging the fear and moving forward anyway. You have to work at it."

"Making eye contact is weird. It makes me so uncomfortable." I'd look anywhere but into someone's eyes. I'd look at my hands, my feet, their feet, at the ceiling, into the distance.

"Don't think of it as weird. It's a fairly natural thing. It's boundary thing. Your boundary. If you're looking into a person's eyes and they look back, they're looking into you now. That can be scary. Letting someone look in. You need to build confidence. Become familiar with it. Take control of your mind and body."

"Like a ninja."

"No. Like a human being. We can practice in the mirror at home. You can look into my eyes. I'm as pretty as she is. Except for my hair. She has better hair."

"Don't say stuff like that. It's weird."

"Okay. But you can still practice looking into my eyes, into my soul. The eyes are the portal to the soul."

"Whatever."

"Seriously. Maybe you're afraid of what you might see. Or maybe you're afraid of what she might see."

We walked home and slipped into the basement and into my bedroom.

"We're going to do it," she said after we dropped my backpack on the floor. She steered us to the bathroom. "This will be good for you."

"You mean this will be fun for you."

"That too." She laughed. She liked to use her guidance to torture me, as if she believed in the old saying "this is going to hurt me more than you." Or "no pain, no gain."

"If you want others to be more receptive to you, you need to be more open too. Opening yourself up is scary. You have to let your defenses down. Who knows what will creep in? That's why you have to practice. Understand how that feels and not be afraid of it. Learn when you need to be open and when you need to close it up."

We stepped into the bathroom and closed the door. I stood rigidly in front of the mirror, like I was getting a mug shot. My eyes shot around looking at everything but the mirror, everything but her face.

"Okay, look at me."

I looked in the mirror. I saw her pretty face. Full cheeks, pouty lips, soft eyes, round nose.

"No, you're looking at my face. Look into my eyes." She pointed at our eyes. Pressed her fingers right below her eyes. "My eyes are up here, as they say."

I looked up. I looked into her eyes. Soft blue eyes. I drifted down again to look at her cheeks and her full lips.

"Hey focus. Look into my eyes. Concentrate but try not to tense up. Be calm and see in."

"How can I not be tense with you barking directions at me?"

"I'm sorry. I'll chill. We'll ease into it. Shake your shoulders out. Shake your head around. Now let's be still. Soften your eyes. Good. Now try it again. Look into my eyes."

"What should I see?"

"You should see me."

"Are you looking back at me?"

"I am. Relax. Look past my eyes and into me. Don't tense up. You'll look intimidating, intrusive. Now a small smile." She patted our cheeks. "Come on. You can do it."

I smiled.

"See. Now you're relaxed."

I chuckled and felt self-conscious. I looked down, unable to face myself.

"Hey, up here. You have to keep at it. You're only looking at me. I'm not going to hurt you. No one else is here. We're looking at each other, at yourself. You're not kissing me or grabbing my ass. Just looking. Next time she looks at you, don't look away. Look back. You'll be afraid, but don't panic. Maybe even smile. Use your smile as a weapon against fear. Fend it off. You can even smile with your eyes if you want. You know that, right?"

"No. That doesn't make any sense."

"What do you know? Smile with those wonderful blue eyes. Right now."

"How?"

"Lots of different ways. Mostly let it happen. But it's less about how and more about letting your feelings shine out through your eyes. Tell your eyes you're happy. They'll do the right thing. Maybe they open a little wider. Or maybe your eyebrows will raise a little."

I tried. My eyes opened wide.

"Okay, maybe a bit much. You're not a startled deer. You're happy, aware of a pleasant human interaction."

I tried again. My eyes crinkled like lie I was staring into the sun.

She groaned. "Be calm. Be at peace. Pretend you're happy to see a friend. Maybe happy to see me."

I shook my head to ease the tension. I thought about the euphoria she often brought. My eyes flashed a little more open.

"Better. You can practice on anyone. Doesn't have to be for Tammy. It's good to be able to do this with anyone. But we'll have to practice more. Don't want you scaring small children."

"Yes, thanks. Very nice."

"And for Tammy, next time we won't look away. Right? I'll help you out.

We'll be chill."

"She can't see you. That would be bad."

"I mean I'll be with you in spirit. Not like I'm going to jump out and kiss her."

"No, you won't."

She laughed. "You mean you wouldn't like to kiss her? Why not? Even I want to kiss her."

"Don't talk like that."

"What? What's wrong with wanting to kiss her? Nothing. It's normal."

"I wouldn't want to force it."

"Of course not. But if opportunity arises, you might at least try."

"She might not like that."

"Perhaps not. But we'll know. We'll know how to look into her eyes, and her eyes will tell us. You have to pay attention to her eyes, which is why we have to practice looking into my eyes. So you can look into hers when it matters. Do you want to keep practicing? Or do you want to practice kissing?"

"No. You're weird."

She laughed. "No one would know. Or you can practice kissing your old teddy bear. Smooch. Smooch."

"Very funny. Go away now. I'm not sure what's weirder. You acting silly or you acting like Dr. Freud."

"Smooch, smooch." She receded and was gone. I stared at my own face in the mirror. I walked back to my bedroom. I didn't want to stare into my own eyes.

CHAPTER 14 – UNFOLDING

BABYSITTING. You make a buck where you can. Not old enough to find a real job, but old enough for people to entrust you with a child. The logic there escaped me. Parents must have perceived me as responsible and capable, though I certainly didn't feel endowed with any caregiving skills.

I could handle toddlers. We operated on the same wavelength. I was playful and silly, a giant toy. I could be calm when needed though, stern and disapproving if necessary. I didn't have to be the parent. I only had to keep them alive.

My sisters babysat a lot. When better plans came along and they didn't want to break the commitment, they called on me. None of my friends babysat. But they didn't have a bunch of sisters. No one ever asked my brothers to babysit either. Babysitting was a girl's job as far as they were concerned. BJ let me know I was a pussy for doing it. "Hey, nanny girl" he would mock. "Hey Sprout, practicing to be a mom. You're such a pussy." He already tagged me as a wimpy girl, but the babysitting gave him extra fodder.

My sisters relied upon me as a trustworthy back-up plan as long as the children weren't too young. No infants. Infants could be easy to babysit, since they would sleep most of the time, but they were fragile and fussy, and you needed to know what to do with them when they weren't sleeping. I didn't know what to do with them except stare at them. I could change a diaper and feed them a bottle, but I didn't want their lives in my hands for a few dollars.

I eventually discovered the beauty of babysitting meant I wasn't home. One more way to escape the perpetual familial togetherness. Not that that it didn't come with a cost. I had to endure the deathly fear of that first interaction with a new family. Apparently, I put on a good face. My insecurity didn't shine through and make them nervous.

The kids liked me because I would play whatever they wanted. I could animate the stuffed animals or the dolls. I invented the game "Throw Barbie from the Roof." Barbie would climb to the top of a structure and for an inexplicable reason propel herself off with a squeal. The kids laughed and called "Again!" I suspect the parents would have frowned on the "Throw Barbie from the Roof" game.

Once we tired of throwing Barbie from the roof or played halfway through several board games, we had a snack. We watched videos of their favorite show until they wore themselves out. They were ready for bed. After tucking them in, I was essentially alone.

Alone to read. To daydream. To do homework. To watch television. To do nothing. To be left alone. Glorious.

One night I watched my oldest sister's son, a toddler of four named Cooper, while my sister and her husband attended a concert. We played Legos. We played stuffed animals. We played dinosaurs and monsters. I played scared, hungry, sleeping, and dead. Eventually, Cooper exhausted himself and was ready for bed. I read him a story and he fell asleep.

I wandered through the living room looking for a distraction. I grabbed an old encyclopedia, M for mammals, meteors and medieval cities. I sat at the dining room table with a can of soda and opened the encyclopedia. Lots of good pictures. I had my backpack with school work in it I should have worked on, but I lacked the motivation to think too much.

"If you're bored, we should write a diary," Sprout said. "Lots of people do that."

"Oh hi," I said. "And no, I don't think I want to write a diary. Your nemesis always finds those, and embarrassing shit ensues."

"That only happens in the movies." She paged half-heartedly through the encyclopedia. "You can write in code or metaphors so if anyone finds it, they won't know what the hell you are talking about. Anyway, we're pretty interesting. Tell a story about us. Or how we feel about us?"

"I don't know how I feel about us."

"Ding, ding. You make my point for me. You write stuff down and see what comes out. You know, work out your feelings. You can write whatever you want in a diary. You can say things you wouldn't say to anyone. You can be honest about shit. If BJ was being annoying, you can write "BJ was being a bitch." Or "Jimmy thinks he's all that." Or you think I'm crazy. Whatever you feel."

"Whatever, Dr Freud."

"Sure, I'm the doctor. Dr. Sprout. I'm saying it might be good for working stuff out. Like giving yourself emotional support."

"I'm not sure I want to work it out."

"You could refer to me as "trailing clouds of glory." I think that would be a good way to describe me."

"I don't know what that means."

"It's Wordsworth. We read it in Mr. Thompkins' class."

"I don't remember any poetry. What does that even mean?"

"I think it means we bring knowledge into this world that is a part of us we can't explain. We understand things we haven't yet experienced. We know without knowing why."

"Sounds fishy."

"It's not fishy. You've experienced knowing things without knowing why. I know you have."

"You mean like the intuition you're always going on about?"

"Yes. A lot of intuition comes from the trailing clouds. It's like universal human knowledge we all have access to if we know how to look inside for it."

"Oh, good grief. You spew a lot of serious mumbo jumbo."

"It's not mumbo jumbo." She stopped paging through the book and stared across the room. "You're already tapping into it. Like I said, I'm your trailing clouds of glory. I'm like proof it's real."

"I still don't want to write a diary."

"Okay, but you have to admit it's a cool idea" she said and picked up the encyclopedia. "Trailing clouds of glory."

"You like to say that because it makes you sound mysterious."

"I am mysterious."

"If you say so."

"We're not reading this, Jesus." She tossed the encyclopedia back on the bookshelf. "We're not at school." She looked around the room for anything more interesting. Shuffled through the books. Came across a collection of romantic era poetry.

"We should read this," she said and thumbed through it. "Might be a little Wordsworth in here."

"I'm definitely not in the mood for poetry, Miss Trailing Clouds of Glory."

"Bit of a spoilsport tonight, are we?" She looked around the room. She put the poetry book back. She fingered through a few more books. She walked around the room touching objects on the shelves, a vase, an old lantern, a photograph of my sister. "Oh, I know what we could do. We should put on your sister's make up. I've never worn any."

"What? How do you go from poetry to make up? And, no way." I folded my arms around my chest in defiance. "She'll find out."

"She won't find out. Why would she even suspect it? She probably doesn't use most of it anyway. "

"No." Her diary idea shone in comparison to her makeup idea. I should have agreed to that.

"Oh, come on. Do this for me. All you have to do is wash it off when you're done. No one will know."

"I'll know."

"What will you know? If you don't do it, you'll know you're a big chicken shit. That's what you'll know. You'll have some juicy behavior to write about in your diary." She laughed.

"Ha ha. Very funny. Shut up. Peer pressure isn't going to work."

"Good thing I'm not your peer. I'm you."

"I know. You keep reminding me. But you don't always seem like me."

"That's the whole point. You need to come to understand me. I'm your trailing clouds of glory. I'm who you could also be."

"Oh, enough of you and the trailing clouds of glory. I get it."

"Okay. But the idea is to leave the sheltered comfort zone you've created and discover new ideas and feelings. It's an act of creation, of expression, or exploration. You like exploring. It doesn't mean you're girlie, as BJ would say."

"I don't need a motivational speech. I don't want motivation to do something I don't want to do."

"Okay then. Do it for me. It's a little thing. And anyway, no one will know. Come on." She pouted and plopped down on the couch. "Otherwise, you're going to start reading that stupid encyclopedia."

I didn't want to give in to her motivation speech crap because I didn't want to admit I might agree. Even if she was right, putting on makeup wasn't the first thing I would have thought of doing to leave my comfort zone. Was she right though? Maybe you weren't always in control of when you left your comfort zone, which I suppose was the point. If I couldn't leave my comfort zone when alone, when could I? Maybe she was right. We could put the makeup on, clearly leaving my comfort zone, when no one was watching. I needed the practice, as she would say. "Okay. As long as we wash it right off."

"Deal." She jumped up from the table. "Let's do this."

We ran up the stairs into my sister's bedroom. She had a small wooden vanity with a chair in front of it. The vanity had a small mirror and light to check yourself out. Makeup, lotions and hair products occupied the bulk of the surface.

We turned the vanity light on. She sat down and started to paw through the accessories, lipsticks, rouges, foundations, eye liner, makeup I didn't understand. She picked up a tube of lipstick. Pulled the cap off and looked at the color. "Oh, look at this color. Passionate red or something sexy like."

"Do you even know how to use that?"

She looked in the mirror and smiled. "How hard can it be? We've seen other people do it." We leaned our head toward the mirror. She pressed the lipstick to her full lips and pulled it across. Nothing much seemed to happen. "Hmm." She said.

"I think you have to push harder."

She leaned in again and pressed harder and as she pulled it across her bottom lip. Now the color came out. Her full bottom lip had a smear of blood across it. Her lip exploded red into the world. She sat back and smiled. "Ooh, look at that."

"It looks a bit ragged. You have no idea what you're doing."

"And why would I? And who cares? This is how you learn. And we're not done yet, so shut up." She leaned toward the mirror again and pulled the lipstick across her upper lip. Another slash of red. "Now we smack our lips or smoosh them together. Like this." She pressed her lips together and made smacking sound as she popped her lips open.

"Look at that," she said. "Aren't we pretty?"

"Well, it looks a little better." The red streaks ragged across her lips, but they were bold and bright. You wouldn't miss them. I'm not sure what my expectations of what we would look like were, but I suddenly realized I was wearing lipstick. I blushed.

"Oh, don't get all embarrassed. I'm the one wearing the lipstick."

"I can't help it. It's weird."

"It's only makeup. But do you like it?" she asked.

"Yes, I suppose." It seemed a bit much, but I didn't say anything. I started thinking if BJ found me like this he would beat the crap out of me. Even if I was a girl, would I put makeup on? Seemed like a good way to call attention to yourself. I knew I didn't want that.

"You suppose, do you. Well, I like it." She smiled wide. Her white teeth contrasting against the deep red. She turned her head side to side, assessing the different views. "See, this isn't so bad. It's like wearing a mask. You can highlight parts of who you are. Or you can be a totally different person for a little while."

"I don't want to wear a mask," I said. Unless a mask completely obscured my identity, I didn't see the value. I wanted anonymity, not attention.

"Then think of it as putting on armor, allowing you to go out to do battle with the world. Gives you confidence. You see, everyone wears a mask in public, whether they wear makeup or not. It's a buffer between you and everyone else. Some people have subtle masks and some have obnoxious ones. A little red lip stick can be a subtle mask."

"I think I feel stupid."

"Good. At least you're feeling something. Maybe it's a bit much though. Too bad your sister doesn't have a wig. I could look like a proper girl."

"Oh yes, a proper shame we don't have a wig." I'd taken the step and let her put lipstick on us. I wasn't having anything to do with wearing a wig.

"Maybe a little eye shadow. Make these beautiful eyes pop out."

"Just don't poke my eyes out," I said.

She ignored me and looked through the cosmetics on the vanity. "Look at this dark green stuff. A nice color. Not sure how to put this on. I don't see a brush or anything." She opened the drawer in the vanity. Found a brush that looked like it would work. She applied a bit of green material on the brush and pulled it across our upper eye lid, an unevenly applied swatch of color. She dabbed at it with the brush to fix it, but the dabbing only made it blotchy.

"Now we look like a bug. That's terrible."

She laughed. "Okay. Might need to practice applying the eye shadow." She looked back down at the vanity and sorted through more of the cosmetics. "What else can we try? I don't know what some of this stuff is. I wonder if she has some rouge. I know what rouge is. I could make my cheeks rosy."

"Your cheeks are fine."

"No, I need little more red to match my bug eyes."

"Why not put on some green rouge. It will complete your bug look."

"I think we'll stick with a more natural red color." She found the rouge. Brightened up her cheeks. We looked like a poorly drawn harlequin. We laughed. She jumped up and danced around room. "Look, I'm Jo-Jo the bug-eyed girl." She sang and laughed. "See, this isn't so terrible. You didn't die leaving your comfort zone, did you? You have to work at it though. Nothing's free."

We sat back at the vanity. I looked in the mirror and saw a clownish girl looking back at me. I chortled. We would need more practice if she ever convinced me to venture out in makeup, which seemed unlikely. I relaxed when I realized the world hadn't crashed down on me for wearing makeup. I felt less stupid. How different was this than the aloof look I wore all the time? It wasn't. People wore makeup as a mask. I wore a smirk.

Sprout started digging through the vanity for more makeup when we heard the front door open.

"Theo," my sister called out.

"Shit. We have to get this shit off." I wasn't expecting my sister home so soon. My calm understanding of masks flew out the window the moment I thought I might be caught. My comfort zone had flown the coop.

"Okay, don't panic." We scrambled to the bathroom next to the bedroom and turned the light on. "It'll wash right off." We grabbed a bar of soap, wet our face, lathered up and started to rub our face. The rubbing only managed to spread the make up around and now we looked like a squished bug. "It's not coming off. How does this shit come off?"

"I don't know, probably make up remover but I don't see any. Rub harder." We rubbed harder. The make up slowly started to give way but our face was ruddy red by the time the makeup had all been removed. "Now you have to go. I don't know how but you gotta go."

"Fine, I'll try," she said, drying our face vigorously with a towel. "There, all clean."

"I look like a beet."

"Nothing we can do now." She patted our cheeks with her hands. "At least no makeup, bug boy."

"Theo," my sister called my name again, though not too loud knowing Cooper was probably sleeping. We opened the bathroom door. "Up here," I called out.

We walked towards the stairs slowly. Took a deep breath. I looked down at our breasts. Still there. We walked down the stairs and into the entry way. I could hear my sister in the kitchen. We started that way but we nearly jumped out of our skin when the front door opened. My sister's husband burst in. Shit.

"Hey Theo," he said. He grabbed my shoulders and gave me a shake. "How did Cooper do?"

I looked up. "Hey," I said. My heart was pounding. "He was fine." I looked down. She was gone.

"Hi," said my sister as she walked into the hall from the kitchen. "Wow, your face is all red. Looks like you have rouge on."

"Ha, no," I said. "Just scrubbing it real good to keep the zits at bay."

"Might not want to scrub so hard"

"I know, I can be a little overzealous."

CHAPTER 15 – WEEDING

I SOUGHT TO LIVE in my own world, deep inside where I was alone. No one to disturb me, make me uncomfortable, make me interact. I enjoyed quietude, often wandering through my inner world not thinking at all. I possessed a nemesis when it came to maintaining my isolation: the outer world, the providing-constant-interruption-world that didn't care about my boundaries.

I didn't have to be alone, only left alone. Engagements and distractions forever harried me in a large family, and the big bad world wasn't any more forgiving. I struggled against the onslaught. I needed weapons, defenses, strength and stamina. I used my body language and facial expressions to ward off people, but many people couldn't read the language. Some people didn't even know a language existed at all. Others just didn't care.

People assaulted my inner world relentlessly, but they composed only part of the onslaught. The world itself, a world absolutely disinterested in your need for solitude, bombarded me with, noises, visual distractions and expectations. Random event after random event assaulting me with a demand that I pay attention. Overwhelming, unnerving. The universe doesn't care. I tirelessly worked to stop the world from trampling me. I used the tools I had available: aloofness, defensive body language, warning facial expressions, diminutive behavior, silence. Sometimes they worked. Sometimes they didn't.

One day in the kitchen making a bite to eat so I could take it to my room and be alone, I encountered a bombardment. Two of my sisters wandered jabbering in and out of the kitchen and dining room, the most popular places in the house. I had acclimated to people constantly milling around. I could prepare myself for it, set my guard. My siblings and I could all do a good job of ignoring each other most of the time, but not always.

I had finished making a sandwich and dumping potato chips on my plate when BJ came into the kitchen. He didn't know such a thing as body language existed, or any other forms of signaling. He didn't know what a boundary was and certainly didn't care about aloneness. He was my own personal nemesis.

He walked by as I grabbed a glass for water. He had plenty of room to walk by but he bumped into me and pushed me into the countertop. A show of dominance without acknowledging me. A friendly reminder of the pecking order. Like I needed a reminder. I didn't care about the pecking order. If he needed to sit atop of the pecking order, he could sit atop. I wouldn't fight him.

Off somewhere in my own world when he bumped into me, I felt him crash not only into my body but into my inner world. I found myself ripped back into the kitchen, back into his presence. I spilled water all over the countertop. My hands tightened up and my face hardened. I stood still. I had been through this before. I ignored him despite an intense urge to lash out. The beauty of ignoring him was he felt like he had succeeded in reinforcing dominance. Satisfied in his successful play, he moved on.

I noticed the water had also soaked part of my sandwich and chips. "Shit." I reached for a towel to and soaked up the water. I noticed how wet my sandwich was. My eyes twitched. My hands curled into fists. My protective defenses crumpled and failed me. I twisted around and yelled at him. "What the hell? Watch where you're going. Why can't you leave me alone?"

He didn't bother to turn from the fridge and look at me. "Leave me alone," he replied in a whiny, mocking voice, his favorite tool for disrespecting people. Repeating back to you what you said in the stupidest, whiniest voice he could muster. "Boo hoo hoo." Finding nothing he wanted in the fridge, he headed back out of the kitchen. He looked down at me as he passed. He shoved me back into the counter again. I knocked my plate and sandwich and chips over the countertop.

He never failed to be a jack ass. I know he had his own problems and probably worse than mine, but I didn't, as far as I knew, terrorize others because of my own personal issues.

I stood still, quiet. I had already fallen into his trap when I told him to leave me alone. Don't make it worse. Put the food back on the plate and get out of the kitchen. Don't engage. Let him think he won. The jackass both wanted and didn't want resistance. If I took it, he felt he was dominating me. If I resisted, he saw it as the opportunity to crush me even more. The universe had constructed a win-win for him and a lose-lose more for me.

I gathered my food back on my plate in its damaged state. I swiveled to walk out of the kitchen. I kept my head down, slightly hunched over my plate. He should have liked my submissive display. A clear sign of victory. I had recovered from my poor choice. I could still escape. Instead, as I headed out of the kitchen, he reached onto my plate and grabbed half of my sandwich and took a big bite. He started to put the remainder of the sandwich back but changed his mind and walked away. "Thanks Sprout," he mocked as he looked back at me.

"Okay, fuck that," I thought. I was tired of his abuse. Tired of everything about him. Tired of his superiority. Tired of his mocking. Tired of his face. Anger I had swallowed from every one of his demeaning, belittling and derisive acts swelled up in me. I couldn't swallow anymore and the hate came vomiting up.

I followed him into the dining room. I grabbed him from behind and spun him around. He looked down at me in amazement, stunned at my unexpected behavior. He stared at me in wonder.

"Hey, give that back," I yelled, and I never yelled. My sisters turned to look at us. Surprised by my outburst as well.

My brother's eyes narrowed. He scowled. He laughed as he raised the sandwich high above his head. "This sandwich?" he said, shaking it around. He took another bite and held it above his head again. "Come get it."

"Give it back. You can't do whatever you want. That's shit."

"Wah, wah, wah. Theo can't take it," he mocked. He took another bite. The sandwich mostly devoured now. At this point it wasn't about getting my sandwich back. I would stand up to him whatever the cost. But besides asking for my sandwich back, I didn't know what else to do. I could physically confront him but that would end terribly.

"Give it back," I repeated. I would at least stand my ground. We had a crowd watching us now. I could have witnesses to his jack-assery. I would take the small win. I saw him quickly glance at my two sisters watching from the other room. He looked back at me with a scowl. Perhaps he suspected he had lost the public relations battle and needed to end the confrontation.

"Eat that, dick." He took the remainder of the sandwich, shoved it in my face, rubbed it around and let go of it. I watched it drop to the floor. I didn't reach down for it. I wouldn't give him the satisfaction of seeing me retrieve the scraps he had left me, like a lion leaving the scraps for the hyenas.

"Loser. Wah, wah, wah." He stood defiant. "What are you going to do about it?"

I stared at him. The adrenaline released. I shook from head to toe. The anger burst out of me. I shoved him in the chest. "You're the dick," I said as firmly as my shaking voice could muster. "Don't treat me like shit." ·

He stopped laughing. He shoved me hard in the chest. I tumbled and twisted in a heap to the floor, sprawled out on my stomach. Too angry to notice the pain, I pushed myself to my hand and knees and paused. I couldn't see what he was doing. Would he pounce on me? Walk away? Just laugh?

"Hi," said Sprout as we trembled on our hands and knees.

"Oh my gawd, not now." I couldn't stand up looking like her. My life as

I knew it would end. Why did she show up now?

"Don't get up," she said. "I know he's an asshole but it's not worth it."

"You can't be here, Sprout."

"This isn't a good time to fight back. Crawl away."

"I can't. I have to stand up for myself. I don't care if I lose. He's going to have to work for my defeat."

"Don't do it, please. Just run away."

"Not this time. I have my pride too. You have to go." Now I was angry at her too. I was angry at everybody.

"Please." She pleaded. I could feel her dripping into my blood. I could feel her wanting to take control and run. She wanted to help. I wanted to run with her. I looked at the hall to the basement stairs. I could get to it before he could stop me. End this mess. Not let a soggy sandwich ruin my day.

My heart pounded. I clinched my teeth. I wouldn't back down. Not this time. "Go." She pouted but then withdrew.

I jumped up and lunged at my brother. I was a terrible fighter. All I wanted to do was land a few blows. I hit him in the stomach before he understood what was happening. I swung my other arm at his side but I hit his shoulder. He shrugged off my attack and muscled me into a head lock, dropped all his weight on me and crumpled me face first to the floor. He landed on my back with a thud. I heard one of my sisters swear. He punched me several times in the back of the head. I felt my face pounded painfully into the floor.

"You're a dick," I yelled. I resigned myself to whatever else he would do, powerless to stop it. I had witnesses though, however silent they may have been. He was a dick.

After a few more blows fell, Mom came up from the basement. "Knock that off. Get off him." She gave BJ's hair a yank. My brother pushed my head into the floor as he stood. He stepped back and didn't say anything. He was a bully, but he wasn't stupid.

My chest heaved in and out. My head pounded. I didn't want to move up, but I couldn't stay on the ground. Mom would freak out if I didn't stand up. She'd think I was dead. I pushed myself to my hands and knees and stood away from my brother. My head hurt. My face had butter and cheese stuck to it. I wiped off what I could and stood in silence.

"What's going on here?" Mom asked. She looked hard at him and then at me and then back at him.

"Nothing," we said in unison. And it was nothing because no logical reason would explain it. You couldn't explain it. Mom looked at my sisters. They shrugged their shoulders and walked away. They weren't going to commit to a side unless forced. They had witnessed though. They knew.

"Go to your room," she said to my brother. "Go outside," she said to me. She knew we weren't going to explain anything and knew enough to put distance between us.

I picked up my scrap of sandwich on the floor and threw it away. I collected my plate with half a soggy sandwich and remaining chips. I walked slowly on my shaking legs out to the picnic table in the backyard and plopped down. My hunger had abandoned me. I sat staring at my plate. I rubbed at my bruised head.

"Hi," said Sprout as soon as I sat down. I didn't respond. Still angry and humiliated, I didn't have anything to say. We sat quiet for long while. She reached up and touched my cheek. "I'm sorry. I was trying to help."

"I know." I wanted to be mad at her. I wanted to let her know she couldn't do whatever she wanted even when she had good intentions. But I knew I wasn't mad at her.

"He could've knocked our teeth out." She was right. I could feel the cuts in my mouth where my teeth had torn at the cheeks when he smashed my face into the floor. I could taste the blood. I felt the lump on my forehead, swelling larger by the minute.

"I had to stand up to him."

"I know."

"He's a real jackass. I had to do it. I'm so sick of him. I'm tired of him stomping all over me. Tired of being afraid. Do you understand that?"

"I do now."

"You keep telling me I need to be confident. Believe in myself. That's what I did."

"I know. You did good. I shouldn't have made you doubt yourself. You needed to stand your ground."

"I did. And my resistance lasted a whole three seconds."

"But you stood up to him. Right? That changed you. You don't have to win to change. You needed to stand up for yourself."

"Why did you tell me to run away then?"

"I was afraid too. Because I need to learn too. I don't know everything. I'm glad you stood up to me, too."

"It did feel good to fight back. Fight him, I mean." I touched the lump on my forehead. "But it wasn't free."

"It never is."

"You did good."

"I don't know if I did good or not. What good did it do? He won't change."

"Probably not. But I get it now. Standing up to him was about you, not him. You chose to be strong, confident. You can control that. You can't control him."

"I want to believe it matters. But I wonder what's the point of getting beat up if nothing changes?"

"For those times when it does make a difference. And when it does, you'll feel good you made the effort."

"I don't think I can take getting beat up too many more times. Shit. Here comes Mom." Sprout flew. I didn't blame her.

"Are you alright, Theo?" Mom asked as she sat down.

I didn't say anything. I stared at my mostly empty plate.

"Honey, are you okay?"

"No. No, I'm not okay. My own brother beat me up. That doesn't make any sense."

"He does have a temper."

"He doesn't have a temper, Mom. He's an asshole. You do know the difference, don't you?"

"Watch your language."

"Whatever. He's an a-hole, then."

"You need to avoid him. Not set him off. He'll grow out of it."

Mom was the queen of avoidance, rationalization and denial.

"What am I supposed to do in the meantime? His room is right next to mine. How do I avoid him? Should I accept getting beat up? Should I live in constant fear?"

"No, I don't mean it like that. He's going through some hard times."

"So am I. Don't defend him. You can't wait and hope time will make him a better person."

"I know. I'll talk to him. Until then try to be a little extra careful around him. I can't be there to protect you all the time."

"I don't want you to protect me. I don't want to have to be protected from my own brother. I want him to not be an ass. But I'm not dumb enough to think he'll change. I only want to protect myself."

"Honey, you're fast. You can outrun him."

"You have no clue, do you, Mom? I have nowhere to run. Not in the hallway. Not in the bathroom. Not even in my own bedroom." I knew an easy answer to my problem didn't exist. I knew she certainly didn't have one. If I wanted a path forward, I would have to find it myself. I wanted to protect myself, defend myself. Then I thought, self-defense, that's what I need. "Let me take karate lessons, please. Maybe I can at least put up a fight."

"I don't like that kind of sport. It's violent."

"The butthead slamming my face into the ground isn't violent?"

"Violence won't stop violence."

"Easy for you to say. You're not getting beat up."

She clearly didn't like the idea. She shook her head back and forth.

"Just let me do it. You won't have to protect me anymore. How can it get worse?"

She looked off in the distance. I have no idea what was going through her head, but she looked back at me and nodded. She didn't have anything else to offer so she stood and reminded me to take my plate into the kitchen.

I dropped my plate in the kitchen as fast as I could. I ran out of the house and walked off towards the river.

"What was all that?" Sprout asked as she broke into a skip. "She isn't much help. Does she seriously think he's going to all of a sudden stop being a jerk?"

"Apparently. But we know he's a jackass and he's not changing."

"Probably not. She's letting us take karate lessons though. That's cool. We can put up a fight."

"Maybe. He's still a big moose."

CHAPTER 16 – FLOWERING

"DON'T SIT THERE, NERD." Bully Steve waved me off from sitting in the back row because he had saved the seat for his bully friend Rod. It's not like I wanted to sit in Rod's desk. I had a choice between three desks. I didn't want to sit next to the cute girl or in the front row. I had to choose one and it apparently belonged to Bully Steve's friend Rod. I wanted to sit and be invisible. That was all.

Seating assignments. Half my classes in sophomore year had them. The other half adopted the first come, first served method. Apparently, half the teachers thought we were adults now and could handle choosing a seat, and the other half thought we were children who would make a mess of it and didn't want to deal with the chaos. I always figured the teacher made or broke the control of a class and the seating arrangements had little impact either way. But I'd never been a teacher so what did I know.

As a socially awkward introvert I oftentimes liked seating assignments. I liked the comfort of not having to choose. I didn't like the daily panic of having to choose to sit by a popular kid or a bully or a cute girl, feeling the full weight of everyone watching me make a choice. Bully Steve harassing me if I made the wrong choice was bad enough. He had to keep going and mock my appearance and nerdiness, making me the butt of a joke for picking the wrong seat.

In junior high most teachers used assigning seating, so back then I escaped Bully Steve's attention. I'm not sure if teachers ever thought of it as a social issue, but they controlled school life tightly. Except curiously at lunch, they allowed a free-for-all to break out. In 8th grade I picked up my tray of food and stared into the cavernous lunchroom of wild animals, having to make a life or death choice. If I saw one of my few friends at a table, I hit the jackpot, no difficult social choices. But since the lunch period spread out over two hours, I didn't always find a friend, so I wandered alone into the Serengeti hoping to avoid the lions.

If I couldn't spot a friendly face, I would search for the most isolated table I could see. The lunchroom always bustled, so an empty table was rare. I searched for a table where I could find at least one space between me and the next person, preferably with no one sitting across the table. A futile search most of the time. I looked instead for the least menacing person I could find. I hunched over my food and tried not to make eye contact. I didn't want Bully Steve making fun of the way I ate. I remember kids mocking me for hunching over my food too much. Why did I need to be mocked for that? Thanks to that I carried my anxiety of finding a seat to high school and even beyond.

Anyway, assigned seats worked to my advantage when I didn't know anyone in class. I welcomed open seating when I had a friend in class. I tried to arrive at class early and sit in the back and save a seat for my friend and hope to avoid Bully Steve's evil eye.

Mr. Thompkins attempted open seating in his English class. My friend Jimmy was in the class, and we usually sat together. One day I knew Jimmy had stayed home sick, so I arrived early and was able to find a seat in the back.

Mr. Thompkins liked to believe we were adult enough to pick our own seats. Mr. Thompkins also didn't have enough control to maintain order in class. Students perpetually interrupted him and created chaos half the time, though he didn't seem to mind. I figured open seating was a bit like a rite of passage. Maybe Mr. Thompkins did too. He wanted you to prove you could handle it. We clearly could not.

Mr. Thompkins maybe should have reverted to assigned seating. He had clearly lost control of his class. On bad days, Bully Steve and Rod and other tough kids would come to class and rearrange the desks in the back of the room to face each other and play cards. He let them do it. They were less disruptive if not learning. Maybe he figured it was a win for everyone who wanted to learn.

Mr. Thompkins had the unenviable task of teaching us *Romeo and Juliet*. The Shakespeare play they like to teach newbies. The tragic love story often gets presented and interpreted as romantic. I suppose you could somehow see a bunch of characters making rash decision after rash decision leading to tragedy as romantic as long as true love was involved. I suspect teenagers see undying love and the willingness to die for it as appealing when their hormones are raging. It seems a cruel trick to play on them. I hadn't bought into the squishy love stuff. Not yet. Maybe once I fell in love, I'd have a different take.

Mr. Thompkins asked for volunteers to read the famous balcony scene between Romeo and Juliet. Of course, no one volunteered. For as chaotic as his class was, Mr. Thompkins did know how to pick people trying ever so hard to avoid his gaze. He picked a girl in the front row, Cheryl, to read

Romeo. He caught my eye and pointed at me. I would be Juliet.

My practiced slouching had not saved me. The back of the room hadn't saved me, which, I should have known better, was probably the first place he looked for volunteers. I sat up straight. I comforted myself knowing I had actually done my homework and read the passage the night before. I cleared my throat. This would be a good time to channel Sprout, be like her, be confident. Practice what she preached.

Then there she was. I always knew she had appeared when she smiled. She smiled in a way I did not smile, full of life and confidence. And the drip, drip of liberation. I knew that feeling. I hadn't wanted to summon her like a genie, though, not into class. I had only wanted to channel her energy, her attitude.

I looked to my left and then my right. We remained so far undetected. I had what I wanted though. Sprout was excited to read, which I certainly had not been seconds ago. I peeked quickly at my chest. Yep, in the flesh. I needed visual confirmation even though I knew.

"Hi," she said. "Let's do this."

"Start with line 'But soft! What light through yonder window breaks?'" Mr. Thompkins called out.

We opened the book to the correct page. Romeo had the first line. Romeo's voice came out quiet and hard to hear. We called out to Mr. Thompkins, "I can't hear her."

"Turn your desk around to face the room, please. And speak up," said Mr. Thompkins. You could hear Romeo's desk scuffling as she turned it around. She began again. You could hear Romeo now. Thankfully, a handful of heads obscured her line of sight to me. I didn't have to make eye contact, not that Romeo was going to look up from her book.

"But soft! What light through yonder window breaks?" began Romeo.

"We got this," said Sprout. She beamed. She stared at the page as if she, Romeo, stared back off the page. I felt the dopamine rush of a crush. She was all in. Romeo finished her passage.

Our first line was simple. "Aye me." Then Romeo went on some more.

Now it was our turn for real. "O Romeo, Romeo! Wherefore art thou Romeo? Deny thy father and refuse thy name." Sprout read loud and strong, with conviction and passion. She meant it. Mr. Thompkins looked at us with a quizzical face. We didn't catch much of his gaze, but we saw surprise in it. We had read the assignment, so we were at least familiar with it. Or maybe we sounded good in contrast to Romeo, who had clearly not read the assignment.

Romeo's turn again. She spoke slow and hesitated often, which was totally understandable when reading Shakespeare for the first time. We weren't theater students after all.

"What's in a name? That which we call a rose By any other word would smell as sweet." We became more confident as we read. I could feel a few people looking at us now. This wasn't the Theo they knew. We kept our head up enough to project our voice but bent forward enough to obscure our face. We held the book up at an angle not only for easier reading but to cover our breasts.

Romeo started again. Sprout looked up and made eye contact with a few students even though I had resisted such a terrible decision. But I had channeled her to be confident and so we were confident. She even nodded at a few students. Bully Steve turned to us and smirked. "Nerd," he mouthed. She smirked back and mouthed, "Fuck you." She was in a mood. She didn't have time for any of Bully Steve's shit. Bully Steve chuckled at the audacity and turned away. Back to Juliet's turn.

"My ears have yet not drunk a hundred words Of thy tongue's uttering, yet I know the sound. Art thou not Romeo, and a Montague?"

"Okay, that's enough," said Mr. Thompkins. "Thanks Theo and Cheryl. Good job." He started his lecture on the scene. He called another student to give insight.

We remained sitting up nice and straight. I would have normally slouched back down to slip into obscurity. She sat upright, proud of how she had read. I was proud too.

"We did good," she said.

"Yes, we did."

"Did you see what I told Steve'"

"Yes. You're pushing the ballsy attitude a bit much. Bully Steve can beat us to a pulp any time he wants, you know."

She shrugged her shoulders. Her confidence seemed to grow every time she showed up.

She looked around the class observing who she could. The center of attention shifted away from us, and students were busy avoiding Mr. Thompkins' eye so he wouldn't call on them. She'd never shown up in class before. This was all new. A stranger in a strange land. I felt soft and relaxed as she looked around even though I knew I shouldn't have been. Thank god for the desk in the back row in the corner near the window. We gazed out the window. They were shut and the only thing we could see was a brick building across the street, but we could at least see the daylight, which shed a few good vibes into our prison world.

"I feel nauseous," she said out of the blue.

"What?" I said and looked in a panic around the room. I hadn't noticed any problems. No one was looking at us. "Are you okay?" I asked but immediately felt the nausea.

"Shit. No." She looked down between our legs. "My period has started."

"What?" I could feel the wet, warm flow of blood. "What's this? How can this happen?"

"It's called being a girl. You do know about this stuff, don't you?" She spat the words out sharply. My burst of confidence flew with the wind.

"I know what is," I said. "But I'm not a girl. I don't have to deal with this."

"You do now," she said. We looked down and could see my pants getting wet and colored. I could feel the warm, wet blood between me and the desk seat. This was real. The most real physical experience we had shared together. But I was squeamish, more afraid of fainting than the actual blood. Fainting would be beyond humiliating.

"Shit, shit, shit." I could feel the nausea grow. I felt warm. Don't faint.

"Sucks, doesn't it? Being a girl has a price."

"I'm not a girl."

"If I'm a girl, you're a girl. And we're definitely a girl right now."

"Okay, what do we do now?"

"We'll be fine." She had regained her composure. "This is part of life. We're not going to die."

I didn't feel fine at all and could only think of the unbelievable embarrassment headed our way. The laughter, the attention, the shame.

We sat quiet. I shook from the adrenalin, from the fear of fainting. I was lightheaded. I put my head down on my book. Clammy. Blood rushing in my ears. I wanted to cry. Don't faint. Don't faint.

"Don't panic," she said. "We'll be alright. A little blood's no big deal. It's normal. We're not in danger. Keep breathing. Breathe slow. Relax." I didn't have a better idea so I slowed my breathing down and began to feel less clammy. I raised my head and felt cool air on my face.

We sat breathing slow for what seemed like forever. The class bell rang. Thank god class was over, but now what. I couldn't move. How would we escape this? I hadn't fainted but I still had blood-stained pants. No amount of confidence was going to hide that shame. I waited until the other students cleared out of the class. When they were gone, I still couldn't move. What was I going to do? I couldn't walk the halls with a bloody crotch. I sat paralyzed.

Mr. Thompkins sat at the front of the class writing notes in his planner. He finally looked up and saw me sitting alone in the back. He walked to the back of the room and stood beside me.

"Good job reading today, Theo" he said. "Must have done your homework."

I nodded. "Thanks." I didn't move.

"Are you okay? Is something wrong?"

I looked up at his face. Still pale and clammy, I forgot about that while I worried whether we looked like her. I slowly put my hand to my chest. She was gone. I wouldn't have to explain the breasts, but the blood wasn't going to go away.

"You look a little pale."

I had the lying chops of a cherub, but I needed to give it my best shot. I couldn't tell him we had our period. Even if I was a real girl, I wouldn't have disclosed that.

"I have a bandage on my leg from a cut and it's broke open. My pants are all bloody now. I'm embarrassed by it."

He looked down and saw the blood. "That's a lot of blood."

"It's not as bad as it looks. I bleed easily." I didn't want him to panic either.

"Okay," he said calmly. He may have been a bad teacher, but he was a good person. "Let's take you down to the nurse and see what she can do."

On no. We couldn't have her exploring my crotch. The lie will fall apart. No explaining all the blood when no cut is found.

"It stopped bleeding now. It'll be okay. Really."

He looked at me dutifully. "That's a lot of blood. I think we should see the nurse."

"No, really, I'll be okay. It's fine now. It stopped. I just can't walk around like this. It would be super embarrassing." I pointed to the stain.

He chuckled. "I'm sure it would be." He gave me a torn look. "Are you sure it's not still bleeding?" I nodded yes. I assured him even though I wasn't at all sure. His look softened. "Alright, we'll get you a pass to go home. It's too late for you to go home and back so we'll say you don't feel well. But you have your mom or dad bandage you up good when you get home. Okay?"

"Yes. Of course. Thank you," I said, and we headed to the administration office. The nurse issued me a pass. I thanked her and walked outside where I immediately felt better in the cooler and fresher air. I leaned against the brick wall in the front of the school, took a deep breath and sighed. I felt my pants and winced. I felt the drying blood against my skin. Yuck.

"What the hell was that, Sprout? Do you have any idea how embarrassing that could have been?" I said.

"I know," she said. "Didn't see that coming. But hardly surprising. Had to happen eventually."

"Gawd, do I have to worry about those now too?"

"Probably. Our physical nature is a part of who we are, whether we're a boy or a girl."

"I just want to be a boy."

"I know. But this is where we're at. We don't have to let it define us, but we can't ignore it. It's part of being human. Whether it's having my period or you getting a boner when you don't want one, we have to learn about our bodies and let them be part of us."

"Can we not talk about this? I don't even have a penis right now. I have a bloody crotch."

"I know." We tugged at my jeans to pull the cool, crusting blood from my legs but it didn't help. It still felt gross.

"And I don't want to have periods."

"Neither do I."

We started to walk home. The cool air soothed and dried my sweaty face. My head cleared up. Her mood improved. She started skipping.

"But they're a small price to pay for having me around, right?"

"Not that small," I said.

"Oh, you baby. Women have to live with this. Consider yourself lucky."

"I do. I would've still been humiliated walking around."

"There are worse things. You'd get over it. You'd survive." She gave me tough love. I suppose I needed it.

We walked home with a bloody crotch but an escape from complete social embarrassment. I knew I had to learn the difference between channeling her and summoning her. Things could get awkward. I needed to find her confidence when she wasn't there. We had nailed the reading and the surge of confidence invigorated me. Could I do it without her? Was I addicted to her? I wasn't sure. I wanted her rush of confidence, but I didn't want to repeat the period debacle. Was this another price I had to pay for what she offered? Was I ready to keep paying it? I had no idea.

CHAPTER 17 – BLIGHT

MY SELF-CONSCIOUSNESS HUNG like an albatross around my neck. I could not escape it. If I noticed someone watching me, I froze, whether in action or in thought. Like ubiquitous stage fright, I saw everything as a stage and everyone as an audience.

My lack of self-understanding drove my insecurities and those drove my self-consciousness. I didn't want everyone observing me as I worked through those insecurities. Unfortunately, home life supplied plenty of constant, unwanted observers. Even if they weren't always an active, judging entity, they were an audience always waiting to happen, ready to break the fourth wall with commentary. Even when I was alone, I battled with the anxiety of when the aloneness would end. I had no way of anticipating when someone would burst in on me. I knew eventually they would, whether siblings barging in looking for company, or Mom perpetually checking in.

Escape is what I constantly wanted. Freedom. Freedom to do. Freedom to be me. Freedom to find me. Freedom from observation. None of that freedom existed at home. Even the liberation Sprout brought couldn't protect me in that prison. I turned to running or biking or any activity away from home. In a small city, places for escape were limited. I couldn't run and bike all the time. Sprout had lectured me on needing stillness in order to rejuvenate. I believed in this lesson, but while I could be still at home, I could rarely be alone and still for long.

The public library came to my rescue. The great escape. While others certainly mulled about the library, I was alone in a crowd. No one knew who I was and as long as a I didn't make a ruckus, no one cared. The books served up the icing on the cake. The books that took you away. Books for intellectual freedom and curiosity. Books often frowned upon at home. Books that sent you on journeys across the earth and the universe.

I gravitated towards science fiction and fantasy novels. Serious escape. I knew a few of the big authors, Asimov and Tolkien, but I didn't recognize and never remembered most of the others and it didn't matter. I disappeared off planet or into a different world when I stuck my nose in one. What more could I ask for?

I usually walked to the library, a couple miles from home, instead of riding my bike. I didn't need to hurry. The escape could take its time. I could follow a wandering path along the river, under the railroad tracks, across the main thoroughfare, up the hill to the library.

One fall day the turning leaves framed a cloudy, gray sky as I walked to the library. "Look around, Leaves are brown." And they were. The wind that endlessly raked the valley swirled the leaves around my feet and tried to pull me down into the coming dormancy. I resisted. The long winter would come soon enough.

I walked into the library's large atrium with its wall of windows across from the entrance. Even on a cloudy day the atrium washed itself in light. They used to make libraries like old train stations. Majestic. Awe inspiring. Destinations. I knew I was going to learn something when I visited the library. I had space to explore.

I walked into the stacks. The science fiction area. I dragged my hand across the spines as I walked down the aisle. I'd stop and pull out a book based on looks alone. I judged a book by its cover in those days. The cover art of fantasy books dragged me in, splashed with color and elaborate scenes. The saying was right though. The artwork was often better than the book. Still, unless I knew the author, I wouldn't pick a book with bad cover art. I eventually learned my lesson, don't judge a book by its cover, when I moved on from science fiction and fantasy to the classics, which often had no cover art at all, as if to say I will not be judged by anything more than what I am. An even better lesson.

I pulled out a thin volume. "The Left Hand of Darkness" by Ursula K. Le Guin. The idea of darkness lured me in. Darkness was good, exciting, mysterious. I knew nothing of darkness.

"Hi," said Sprout. "What's this?"

"Some science fiction."

"Is it any good?"

"I don't know. I've never heard of it."

"Hmm. Well, at least it's by a woman. Probably won't be filled with triple-breasted woman though, if that's what you are looking for. Hot aliens."

"Shut up. Not all science fiction has triple-breasted women."

"I'm sure not. Don't be all offended. We should definitely read the book by Ursula." She pawed at the books on the shelf without pulling them out. "But we should read something other than science fiction, too. Don't you think?"

"Like what?"

"Something deeper."

"Deeper. You think we need deeper? Well, this is about darkness. How much deeper can you go?"

"I don't think they're the same. Okay, maybe not deeper. Maybe more human, like real human experience."

"People in sci-fi are human, usually. Even if they look weird, they still act human."

"I mean human, like you and me. Just normal humans making our way through life."

"Okay, so like what? The human experience is a broad category."

"How about poetry?"

"Poetry. You mean like Shakespeare. I don't remember being overly excited when we read Shakespeare in class. Little hard to relate to. You must have been the one excited about that."

"Well, I was thinking of other poets. Though Shakespeare did poetry, lots of sonnets. Might be a little thick for us. I thought maybe something more modern. Might be a little easier to read."

"Probably." I was sure I didn't want to read poetry. I had even less energy for poetry than I had for the diary she had wanted me to write. "But why do you want to read poetry?"

"I think it's because people writing poetry are writing about being human. Trying to deal with the struggles, and the pleasures too. Like we all do. We've read poetry in school, remember?"

"Vaguely. Did we read that before or after Shakespeare? I don't think I understood any of that. People trying to say something without saying it. Like they're trying too hard."

"I know what you mean. But not always." She leaned against the bookshelf. "You don't have to understand everything anyway. That's not the point."

"What is the point?"

"Hmm. It's hard to explain. Maybe it's about gaining insight into other people's humanity. Or something like that. But it's like learning a foreign language. Takes time to understand the language. Maybe you understand it and maybe you don't, and that's okay. Sometimes you only feel it. And that's fine too. If it's too boring and stupid, we'll move on. It's not for everyone. Can we at least try? Humor me?"

I had a hard time saying no to her. She exuded curiosity, and I knew I needed more of that. We moved into the poetry stack. I didn't know what we were looking for. A little research on poetry might have helped me pick out a good poet. I did the same thing I did with science fiction and ran my hands along the spines until I liked the look of a book, which was rather pointless in this case since most of the books had no art. We started at the A's.

"Oh look. Maya Angelou. We've heard of her. Mr. Thompkins mentioned her. She's modern. Let's grab it."

"I don't remember that, but sure." I thumbed through the Maya Angelou, not sure what I was looking for. Maybe making sure the poems weren't too long. "Do we want more?"

"Yeah, keep looking. We'll find something."

We thumbed through A, B, C, D, F. Looking at names of poets who meant nothing to me. I didn't know anything about poetry. Picking books at random would have been equally effective.

"Oh, look," she said. "Robert Frost. We've heard of him. He's older but not Shakespeare old. Let's try him."

We carried Ursula K. Le Guin, Maya Angelou and Robert Frost to a table in the Atrium. We opened Maya Angelou and thumbed to a random page. We read a few stanzas of *Caged Bird*.

"See," said Sprout. She's not so hard to read. Talking about being a human."

"So? Who cares? We're all human. I get it." I didn't dislike reading the poem. While I struggled less than reading Shakespeare, I didn't understand what I was supposed to think or feel.

"So?" she said. "Didn't you feel like some of it related to you? Maybe a feeling you couldn't put into words."

"I guess." It was like drinking water. I had no real reaction to it, like I was reading the newspaper. I could take it or leave it.

"Boy, don't get too excited. Give it a chance. Let's read it again." So we read the poem again. I still didn't have anything to say.

"Well, I liked it. This person is telling us we're not alone. Telling us we humans have experiences in common. Isn't that reassuring?" She leaned back away from the table. She looked off at the big windows. She leaned back in and touched the book. "Or say the poem shows you a new experience you're never had to deal with. Might open your eyes to how they feel. Make you more empathetic, more understanding. More human."

"I am human." What I felt like was defensive and inadequate. Was Sprout saying I was a deficient human and I needed to read poetry to fix myself? That seemed harsh.

"I know. What I mean is seeing other people's humanity. Understanding how they feel. Knowing you might go through that one day as well."

"Shakespeare didn't make me feel much of anything."

"Let's not go back to Shakespeare. He's hard."

"Okay. I don't remember any of the poems in Mr. Thompkins' class making me feel more human. I didn't dislike this. At least I could understand it."

"Sure. Fair enough. Not every poem works. Not every poem speaks to everyone the same."

"Can't science fiction open my eyes to humanity? Why do I have to like poetry?" I pushed the book away. I didn't like having ideas shoved in my face, like when matchmaker friends have tried to set me up on a blind date. I immediately and viscerally withdrew from the idea. "You're always forcing shit on me. You need to do this, you need to do that. What do you know? Why would you know more than me? I'm not stupid, Sprout."

"You're not stupid. I know. I didn't mean it to sound like that. Remember, 'trailing clouds of glory?' I'm connected to a world you're not conscious of. That's why I'm here. To help you see it. To help you explore the world below the surface. I'm your guide."

"I don't need a guide."

"Then why am I here? Huh?" she said.

I shrugged. My annoyed frame of mind didn't lend itself to pondering why she was here. Poetry was boring was what I thought. I could explore the world without reading poetry. "I don't know why you're here. Why don't you tell me?"

"I'm here because you want me to guide you. Your inner self wants me to guide you."

"But why?"

"That's for you to figure out. I'm simply the medium, the guide."

"That's not an answer. And I don't always need guide. I'm okay being me, wherever I might take me. I don't want a lecture every time I don't do what you want. I'm human too. I've got ideas, feelings."

"I'm not trying to lecture you. I'm trying to help. You're upset because you're insecure."

"That's enough, Dr Freud. Keep it to yourself." I lost patience with her guidance. "How can I not be insecure with you pointing out my shortcomings all the time? I can think for myself. I do it a lot when you're not here." I leaned back hard onto the chair. I sat and stewed. "Why are you still here? Go away."

She stared up at the ceiling, silent. She leaned back in towards the table. She pulled back the Maya Angelou book and closed it. She sat up straight. "We'll put it back. It's not important." She picked up the book and stood.

I had never gotten angry with her before. I knew she wanted to help. Her confidence and passion got the best of her sometimes though. I struggled with criticism. She knew that. Why was she continually pointing out weaknesses? Poking at me? I was insecure about my insecurity. I didn't enjoy having the soft spot jabbed all the time.

I could tell she wanted to cry. But she didn't. I fell back into the chair, annoyed at allowing myself to get angry. We stared out at the big windows, out into the universe that befuddled me. I felt bad. I knew my insecurities are what made me mad, and so I lashed out at her. I couldn't blame her for everything, but if she was going to poke my wound, I was going to feel pain. I would defend myself instinctively. My silent anger gave me time to think. I could feel her suffering. That poked at me too. I knew she was trying to help. I wasn't always ready for help. She hadn't seemed to learn that yet.

She didn't say anything, her head drooped down. She started to stand again to put the book away. I could feel her unwilling yet persistent acceptance of her defeat. That poked at my empathy. I knew that feeling.

"Hold on," I said. I sat us down again. I couldn't allow our relationship to crumble because of my insecurities. "I'm sorry. I was being a baby. Let's try this again. We'll see what we can learn." If I wanted to defeat my insecurities, I needed to persevere. How else would I ever leave them behind?

"We don't have to do this. I know I made you mad. Are you sure?"

"I'm sure. Why don't you take the lead? You're a better reader than I am anyway."

We read another Maya Angelou poem, *A Plagued Journey*. Sprout read it quietly out loud, because you need to hear poetry she informed me. No one noticed.

This time I paid attention. Thought about the words. Maya understood humanity. I had to give her credit. I realized I didn't know much about chasing curiosity, or even much about being human. As a know-it-all teenage my insecurities didn't like hearing about my gaps in knowledge and experience, but that's exactly what they needed.

CHAPTER 18 – IN FULL BLOOM

I CAME OFF AS SECRETIVE, which may have implied I possessed some mysterious underside. I wished I had had anything mysterious to hide, any character idiosyncrasy or singular talent, but I didn't. I unintentionally created a secretive vibe by working so hard to mask my complete lack of understanding of who I was. When Sprout hung around, she was a mystery to hide, because in no way could I begin to explain her. She claimed she was me, which was one more thing I didn't understand. She was a different problem. How could I explain her when I couldn't explain myself to me or anyone?

Privacy. I think I mentioned I didn't find much of this. Well, no one in the house did, but the other family members didn't seem to mind. Maybe I desired privacy more than the others because I felt I needed privacy to find the answers to the questions about me. No matter how hard I tried, I found privacy elusive. Not even in my own bedroom could I expect it. Not even in my own bed. I sort of had a room to myself, dubiously divided off from the rest of the world by the ever popular, unlockable accordion door. The same sham of a door attached to all the basement rooms. An illusion of a door, which was worse than no door at all. The door may have blocked immediate view into the room, but it blocked no more than that. It kept no sound in or out. In a house that operated mostly as a commune, the door offered no resistance physically or socially from anyone entering. Knocking was a foreign concept. We shouted, "Can't you knock?" often enough, but no one did.

Despite not having much insight into myself, I wanted to feel interesting or special. Though at the same time I would have shuddered and retreated within myself if anyone suspected it. I certainly wasn't the one to judge whether I was special. I'm sure I wouldn't have known what that meant even if it were true. Maybe being special to me meant being anything but who I was, or perhaps being special meant choosing what unique talent I had, though obviously it doesn't work that way. I couldn't have pinpointed what talent I wanted to have anyway. I supposed the universe would reveal it to me in the privacy I couldn't find.

I certainly didn't think Sprout made me special. I instead suspected her of being the product of some mental illness. I certainly couldn't explain her existence, though as she often reminded me, my inability to understand and explain her didn't make her less real. However true that may have been, I didn't derive much insight from it.

In my daydreams I wanted people to suspect me of having a special talent but be unable to put a finger on it. I could play cool and reluctantly talk about it. I'd read too many fantasy books, where the hero always had an unsuspected power. I didn't want people to know I turned into a girl sometimes. If that was my superpower, I definitely didn't want to talk about it with anyone. Well, maybe I wanted to talk about it, but I could fathom no one I trusted to have that conversation.

At times lying in my bed at night with lights off and the accordion door closed, I would think I had found privacy. I knew, though, lights off behind a closed door did not deter commune members. I don't know what they looked for when they came into my room. A book or clothes or music or god knows what. I can't imagine they came to look at me. Though I am sure Mom peaked her head in at times to make sure I wasn't sinning. Though I'm not sure what she would have done if I had been sinning. I presume I was sleeping most of the times when people crept in. If I was awake and annoyed enough, I would protest with 'get out of here.' Yelling at them didn't seem to deter behavior so pretending to be asleep proved a better option than having an awkward conversation with my sister in her pajamas in my bedroom. I didn't want to know why she was lurking in my bedroom.

One night in bed, simply lying on my back staring at the black nothingness of the dark ceiling, I daydreamed about the day at school. I don't recall what. I lay in my stuffy room, stuffy despite the beautiful fall because my dad liked to heat the house like it was a sauna and complain about the heat bills. I wore a pair of underwear underneath a sheet to combat the stuffiness, and though I would have felt cooler without the sheet, I needed to feel covered in order to sleep, a carryover from the womb I suppose.

I must have been done pondering as I rolled over onto my side. I slept on my side or stomach but laid on my back when I was thinking. I couldn't fall asleep on my back, but I could relax and unwind. Every night I climbed into bed, laid on my back, bent my legs up and stared at the ceiling. My nightly ritual.

I rolled over on my side, tucked my knees up, adjusted my pillow and hugged my extra pillow against my chest. And then those breasts that hadn't existed a moment before pushed back against the pillow. I felt the soothing drip, drip of her presence into my blood. Her calm and airy peace of mind drifted into my awareness.

"Hey," I said.

"Hi," she said.

"Sorry, not much going on here. Time for bed is all."

"I know."

While I had yet to comprehend the why, she had told me often enough she showed up for a reason. I seldom understood the why even when she tried to explain. I think she knew more than she let on. While not exactly a game she played, I think she wanted me to figure it out for myself. I was often not particularly gifted at the game.

I rolled over on to my back and straightened my legs out. I pulled the sheet up toward my chin, perhaps to subconsciously make sure we kept our breasts were covered. "I'm not wearing a shirt. So we're mostly naked under here."

"I know We don't need to choke ourselves though." She pulled the sheet away from our chin. We looked up at the darkness. She wriggled our legs then settled back down. "But we probably won't be disturbed so that's good."

"Probably not. But who knows what my idiot brother will do."

"But probably not.".

"Probably not." I agreed though I knew from experience that that was a risky assumption.

We let the silence linger. I didn't mind the quiet. I guess she didn't either.

"It's good to do nothing, isn't it?" she said. "You should do nothing more often."

"So you keep telling me."

"I do. Because you suck at it."

"But we're doing it now, right?"

"Sure," she said. "But I was thinking of doing nothing besides when you're lying in bed before sleep."

"I do nothing sometimes."

"No, you don't."

"Yes, I do. I ride bike and do nothing, or walk and do nothing and go down to the river and do nothing."

"Okay, I'll give you credit there. But maybe I mean like not thinking. And not worrying. Just being. You're always thinking."

"It's hard not to think."

"I know, which is why you have to work at it."

"I don't know how."

"I'll show you. We can practice."

So we were quiet again.

"Don't think," she said. "Stare out into nothing. Be here with me. With your body. With our body."

I noticed her hands on her breasts. She held them gently. "No thinking," she said. She took a deep breath. She smiled. She lightly hummed. She softened and closed her eyes. She moved her hands down from her breasts and slid them slowly over her belly, swirled them around and around her belly button. She kept humming.

"What are you doing?" I asked as the pressure of her swirling increased, then slowed down and became more assured, a pulsing, probing massage. Around and around our belly button. The circling grew and caressed the bottom of her breasts. Drip, drip. A new drug slipped into the blood stream.

"It's nice, isn't it? We're here with our body. Listening to it. So shhh. No thinking."

She slid her hands down the sides of her soft belly, softer than my belly, down to her hips, fuller than my hips. She swirled her hands firmly around our hips and gave them a squeeze. Hmmmm.

She slid her hands around her hips to her round butt, rounder than my butt. She slid her hands down the sides of her thighs, smoother than my thighs, and back up and around to the front and started to pull them up.

"What are you doing?" I asked again.

"I'm feeling. No thinking now. Just feel."

"I'm not thinking. I don't know what to think."

"Good. Shhh. I'm exploring my body, our body. I never have a chance to know what's under those boy's clothes. I want to know how I feel. I want to know what feels good." She slid her hands up and over her vagina.

"It's not there."

"Shhh. I know what's there." She slid her hands back up to her belly and clasped them over her belly button, took a deep breath and relaxed. "Don't think about it." She smiled. "See, simply a nice feeling." "Not thinking, only feeling and being." We laid quiet, softened, relaxed and peaceful. I enjoyed the calmness as if sinking into a soft cloud, almost floating.

"You should explore your own body when I'm not here. You should be comfortable with who you are."

"You mean like masturbate?"

"No." She laughed. "I'm not talking about sex. I'm talking about being comfortable with who you are, with how you feel. Understanding how your body feels and what it likes to feel. How it responds to touch. How it likes to move and be moved. Because it's who you are. You'll learn things about yourself. If you're comfortable with being you, you don't have to be self-conscious or apologetic. But you have to work at it."

I struggled with self-consciousness, so she knew what she was talking about. I had never thought about doing anything about it. I had not thought emotional confidence could start with understanding my body. I had always thought of self-consciousness as mental problem.

"It's important. If you're comfortable with yourself, the world can't drag you down, and believe me, they'll try. One day it might be about sex. But not today and not always."

"What should I do? Feeling self-conscious isn't fun."

"No, it isn't. But you have to be comfortable with yourself. Everything starts with that. The world wants us to obsess on our so-called deficiencies. Fuck them. Obsession is a quick path to low self-esteem and depression. A tree doesn't obsess about a broken branch or a crooked trunk. It focuses on growth. Be comfortable with who you are right now knowing you will grow. The tree is confident in who it is."

"Gaia doesn't give a fuck."

"Right on. But it's more than comfort with your physical self. It's knowing what brings you joy and fulfillment, mentally or emotionally or physically, and being comfortable with those too so people can't take them away."

"I don't know what those things are."

"You don't because you don't pay attention."

"I don't even know how to pay attention, or to what."

"Oh boy. You're sad. Don't make me make fun of you."

"Hey, you're supposed to be helping me here."

She chuckled. "I won't make fun of you. Not right now. I have to figure out where to start. Now listen to what I'm saying."

"I'm not an idiot."

"But you're a bit sheltered and naïve when it comes to this stuff." She explained I needed to consciously take stock of when I felt good, or felt a sense of accomplishment or fulfillment, or anything positive. Consciously decide to be aware. Then ask myself what caused that. Ask what happened? What did I do? What did I experience to end up here? Can I or do I want to recreate the feeling?"

"But isn't that how people get hooked on drugs? I did this drug and it made me feel good, so I want to do it again?"

"Drugs are a short cut. They're cheating. They don't teach you anything about yourself. They take control away from you."

"So I shouldn't do drugs?"

"I'm not saying don't do drugs. I'm saying don't confuse the two activities. The whole world is full of behaviors that might bring you fulfillment and joy. You have to go look for them. Explore. Experiment. You never know what will provide a spark."

"You sound like a motivation speaker. Should I put inspirational quotes up on my wall?"

"Sure. It should say 'Listen to Sprout.' You know what I'm saying. I'm saying be self-ware. It's harder than you think."

"You mean be a brooding, self-absorbed teenager?"

"No. You already perfected that one. This is a step further down the road."

"Who are you talking to, butt head?" BJ yelled from outside the door. "Got your girlfriend in there?" He banged on the door but didn't come in.

Girlfriend. Little did he know. Even if I did have a girlfriend I would never bring her to the house. What a terrible idea. The walls had eyes and ears. I can't imagine anything worse than getting caught with a girl by my mom. Though maybe getting caught with a girl was better than getting caught masturbating, which was always like playing Russian roulette with ultimate humiliation.

She put a finger to our lips. "Shhh."

More banging on the door. My brother burst in. He couldn't help himself. "Who are you talking to, weirdo?" he leaned in and punched me in the shoulder. The breasts shook beneath the thin sheet.

"Talking to myself. Duh!"

He punched me in the shoulder again. "Weirdo. Like you'd have a girlfriend anyway, fucking Sprout." He ripped my sheet off and threw it on the floor. "Nice underwear, clown."

Naked and exposed, I tensed up as I prepared for a mocking or beating. I threw my arms over my chest. Maybe he wouldn't notice in the dark. But the breasts were gone. She was gone.

My brother threw the sheet back in my face. "Sprout with a girl. Ha!" He lumbered out of the room.

Alone, I jumped out of bed and closed the door. I sat on the edge of the bed. She was right. Butthead had provided a perfect example of why I needed to be comfortable with myself. No matter how hard I tried to cloak myself, I couldn't always escape exposure. Confident self-knowledge and self-acceptance would protect me from humiliation. I was going to have to work hard at that.

CHAPTER 19 – FERTILIZER

AT A YOUNG AGE I learned social tolerance is a skill that can be refined into a defensive tool. I honed my tolerance at the frequent large family gatherings where I, instead, should have been working on my social interaction skills. Sprout had taught me to smile so as to engage gracefully without speaking. A useful social too, but one I managed to turn into a double-edged sword that helped me survive but stifled my social development.

I remember one family gathering where I found myself sitting across from my mostly blind aunt. She spoke to me kindly but all I could manage was to nod and smile back. Mom came up and whispered in my ear, "She can't see you nodding. You have to speak up." That didn't help. I panicked and couldn't think of a thing to say. So I said, "Bye Auntie, I got to go." I jumped up and ran out of the house. My double-edged sword had turned on me and I simply ran away.

One fall weekend my Mom's sister travelled through town with her family, her husband and three children. A teenage daughter two years older than I and two boys, eight and ten. They hadn't been through town in years. I couldn't remember anything about them. They were essentially strangers.

Mom decided we should go to the park since it was a larger than the usual crowd. We could have a barbeque and hang out since the weather was unseasonably warm enough in late September to have a gathering outside. She invited my uncle who lived in town and his family, three girls and two boys. She invited other friends of the family as well. Another large family gathering. Too large for the house. Certainly too large to be enjoyable.

A sunny Saturday afternoon, I remember being able to wear running shorts and a sweatshirt. I rode my bicycle to the park so I could arrive late and leave early, engage on my own terms. I hadn't invited any of my own friends to see my social awkwardness on display with my family, though I did often invite Jimmy to smaller family gatherings to provide support and create a diversion. Jimmy liked social events.

I locked my bike on the edge of the park and walked up to main picnic table with all the food on it. My mom greeted me. No one else noticed my arrival, which was fine by me. I wasn't in the mood to interact. Like any good teenager, I would have rather been doing anything else, which wasn't unusual since I felt that way about almost all family gatherings. I tried and failed many times to explain to Mom that I didn't dislike the people, I disliked the crowd. She never came to understand the distinction. The more the merrier for her.

Dad cooked hot dogs and hamburgers on an old, deteriorating stone grill in the park. Side dishes lined one of the picnic tables. A group of adults sat at a nearby picnic table, while others sat in folding chairs or mulled around the grill where Dad was cooking.

I grabbed a Coke out of one of the many coolers. I surveyed the gathering. Most of the adults gathered around Dad and the grill. The younger children had run off to swing sets and slides a hundred feet away. A handful of my siblings and older cousins huddled around another picnic table, my brother BJ holding court. I saw the dessert section on the main picnic table, more interesting than anything else going on. Cookies, pie, cupcakes and more.

"Oooh, cupcakes," she said. "All different kinds. Nice."

"What are you doing here?" I asked. I immediately flipped up the hood of my sweatshirt and leaned over the table. "My family is here. All of my family."

"No one's paying attention."

"Do you ever listen to me? There's nowhere to hide."

"We're hiding in plain sight."

"I don't think so." I didn't want to agree with her, but she appeared to be right, or so it seemed for the moment. We stood as an isolated being in a sea of people. The "alone in a crowd" principle I've leaned on many times to feel comfortable. Being alone, after all, was as much a state of mind as it was a physical occurrence if you could master your inner world.

"Sure we are. Just watch."

"Oh wait, don't do anything crazy."

"I wasn't going to. I'm going to stand here and show you how no one cares. Look, we're wearing a baggy sweatshirt. Who can see me underneath this?" She tugged at the front of the sweatshirt.

"You're still a girl. You look like a girl. You sound like a girl. You walk like a girl. This is risky."

"Of course it is. Don't you like the thrill of getting away with it though?"

"No. You're the one who likes that."

"True. But I'm here because you need me to be here."

"Why?"

"Do you ever listen to me? That's not for me to say. Maybe I'm better at social situations. So I'm here to help you cope socially, maybe. We're placing ourselves in social risk so we can learn to handle the anxiety."

"I don't think I would do that to myself."

"I don't think you know what you'd do to yourself. Obviously, you wouldn't make yourself socialize. But here I am, another chance to figure out the why you won't or can't."

Sometimes she snipped at me right from the start, which put a damper on the good vibes she usually brought. I'd sometimes tell her to go away but she rarely left. Arguing with her then proved pointless because I was sure she knew something I didn't and was holding back. Or we both knew some issue lurked well below the surface neither of us could make out clearly. She was my alter ego, my devil's advocate, my better self, my worse self, all wrapped into one. I couldn't out argue myself.

"We'll take one of each, I think," she said, returning her focus to the cupcakes and effectively ending the argument. She was staying.

"Take whatever you want." I remained skeptical no one was paying attention. I hadn't actually looked around and decided not to look around and draw attention to us. I tried to remember the layout of the park. Where could we escape to?

She grabbed a plate and piled four cupcakes on it. "Four should do it for now. I took two chocolate ones for sure. I'm not sure what the others are but they look tasty. Mmm."

"Wonderful." Too distracted by devising an escape plan I didn't share in her enthusiasm for the cupcakes. "Let's go sit on the picnic table by the swings. The little kids won't bother us."

"Hot dogs will be done in a minute," my mom called out, pointing to my plate of cupcakes. "Those can wait."

"I'm good," I said as I walked away, ignoring the disapproving tone.

We sat on top of the picnic tabletop and put our feet on the bench. We set the plate of cupcakes down. We looked back at the people near the grill and the picnic tables. I couldn't see anyone paying attention to us, so I pulled my hood back to have a better view of the park.

"They don't pay attention to us, do they?" she said. "See, hiding in plain sight." She reached down, grabbed a cupcake and peeled off the paper wrapper. "But why don't they pay attention? That's what I want to know. What's wrong with them?"

"What's wrong with us is more like it."

"Nothing's wrong with us. We're awesome." She bit into the cupcake. "Good. Nom nom."

"I'm not so sure nothing's wrong with us. I am sitting here talking to you, after all. But better they don't pay attention anyway. Gives me more freedom."

"Sure." She wiped the frosting off her lips. "Maybe they don't notice because you spend so much effort trying not to be noticed. Maybe they grow tired of looking. And all this freedom is great, but you actually have to take advantage of it. If you're going to be free, be free. Take advantage of their disinterest. Get out and do more."

"I am free. I get out a lot. I run and ride all the time."

"Those are good but riding the same paths over and over again is not doing something new. I mean like do new things. Exploring. Remember?"

I remembered. You can't know if you like something if you haven't tried it. "Like what?"

"Well, like go roller skating."

"I don't want to go roller skating. I don't even know how. I suppose. I'll think about it."

"That was just an example. I mean, just be yourself whether people are watching or not."

Stage fright is what she was talking about, a familiar theme. I hadn't figured out that puzzle and didn't have time to think about it as my teenage cousin from out of town walked up to us.

"Hi, I'm Cynthia. Your uncle Eliot's daughter. Can I sit with you?" She sat down before she finished the question.

"Sure," we said. I vaguely remembered Cynthia. She was probably twelve the last time I saw her. Still a kid, sporting pigtails back then if I remembered correctly.

"I see you like cupcakes," she said and nodded at the plate. "A lot."

"Oh yes, we do, I mean I do."

"Cupcakes are good," she said and nodded. "Who do you belong to?" What clan did we belong to was the question. She didn't remember me or at least associate her with me. I would have been in grade school. A real kid. So what story should we tell? I hoped Sprout could weave a better story than I could. Time to practice our social skills.

"I'm a friend of your cousin Rachel's." Sprout pointed to the table of teenagers. Rachel was a fourteen-year-old cousin on my Dad's side of the family. "She has the long blond hair. She invited me for emotional support."

"You're doing a terrible job." Cynthia gave us a friendly push on the shoulder. "I met her earlier. She looks a bit abandoned over there."

"I know. I told her I'd be terrible. I come and sit around and eat cupcakes." Nice. Make a joke. Good way to keep it light without having to come up with anything real to say.

"At least you're honest about it." Cynthia laughed. "And she brought you anyway so she must like you a lot. I'm sure she didn't want you to miss out on the cupcakes."

We looked Cynthia over as she laughed. Tall and slender, light brown hair pulled into a ponytail. She had full cheeks despite her slenderness. You could see a family resemblance in her. She looked athletic but I don't know if she was or not. Two years older than I, but she seemed much more grown up than I did, much like my brother BJ. Maybe it was the way she carried herself, confident, self-assured. We noticed because that's what we desired.

"What's your name again?" Cynthia asked.

"Sprout."

"What kind of name is Sprout?"

"Just a nickname. Better than my real name." Sprout to the rescue. I would have fumbled through that explanation, but Sprout just powered through. Though if Cynthia mentioned the name Sprout to any one, they wouldn't know what she was talking about. Oh well.

"What grade are you in Sprout?"

"I'm a sophomore. It's okay, I guess. What grade are you in?"

"I'm a senior like your brother BJ, for what it's worth," Cynthia said. "Things get weird when you're a senior. Expectations start to develop. Everyone wants you to grow up. Become an adult on the flip of a switch. Enjoy your freedom."

"You want a cupcake?" we asked. Oh gawd, what an awkward and obvious way to avoid a subject. I blushed and bent my head down to hide my embarrassment. Cynthia was getting all deep, and I'm like all "are you hungry?"

"No thanks." Cynthia reached over and rubbed our head. "I like your hair." I forgot about the short hair. I could understand the intrigue. Not many young girls sporting buzz cuts. "I wish I could pull off that attitude. But gawd I would be mocked at school by all the rednecks. You're a regular tomboy so it seems."

"Only on the outside," we said. "I'm a girl on the inside."

"Oh, don't be embarrassed for being a tomboy. Nothing wrong with that. Gives you an identity, Sprout."

"But not much of an adult yet, I guess." We tried to salvage ignoring her comments on growing up. I knew I was still more of a child than I should have been. If I made a joke of it maybe she wouldn't notice how true it was.

"Oh, you don't want to be an adult yet. Trust me. The adult world will come in good time. You can be a tomboy as long as you want. As long as you're not an actual stupid boy. Gawd are boys stupid."

"Sometimes," we said. "Not all of them." I had to defend myself a little bit but didn't want to stop her from going on. We'd never received a girl's perspective on the world.

"Oh, you're right," said Cynthia. "The bad apples are what you have to look out for. They don't always look bad. You have to be careful. You interested in boys yet? You're old enough, even if you like to hide it." She rubbed our buzzed head again.

"I like boys. I'm not sure what to think about them yet. Mostly confused by it all. Sure you don't want a cupcake?"

"Oh, trying to change the subject. But be careful of boys. Always remember, you're in charge. Boys are always single-minded and often simple-minded. Always tell them the truth even if they don't like it. Keep them on their guard." Sprout smiled. Cynthia liked to speak her mind just like Sprout.

Cynthia had a lot of opinions about boys. I'm guessing from negative experiences. I didn't think I was simple-minded but what did I know. I knew she was talking about sex when she said single-minded. I wasn't sex crazed yet so at least I wasn't single-minded yet.

"You're in control," Cynthia continued. "You can still be feminine, but you always need to be tough. Take a stand. Don't take any of their crap. They won't be fooled by your tomboy look. So don't think the short hair will save you."

"I can speak the truth. I'll give them a piece of my mind." Sprout made a fist.

"Good girl," said Cynthia.

"I'm just myself. If people don't like it, they can shove it." Sprout shook her fist at the sky.

"You show 'em. You're strong. That's good. But they won't like that." Cynthia carried on about using our inner strength to retain control. We could feel her strength. She put her arm around our shoulders and gave us a hug. "We have to stick together, right? Strength in numbers." She made a fist and shook it at the world. Sprout made a fist too. They shook them together at the sky and laughed.

Cynthia mesmerized us. Like the caring older sister we didn't have. Well, we had older sisters but of course they thought I was a little boy. And my older brothers, well, we'd rather they not pay attention to us.

We enjoyed talking to Cynthia, a personal, one-on-one conversation at a family gathering. That never happened. Usually someone barged in on any conversation, whether you desired them to or not. I knew the opportunity with Cynthia was rare and didn't want it to end.

But all the while we talked, I kept an eye on the crowd. Eventually I saw my older brother BJ headed our way with his friend Chuck in tow. He was probably jonesing on the attractive Cynthia even though she was his cousin. He didn't care. He wanted admiration and to exert his manliness.

"I got to go," we said. We grabbed a napkin and wiped the frosting mess we had made on our lips. We didn't have much time to escape.

"What's the rush? Not going to abandon Rachel, are we?" Cynthia laughed.

"Oh, Rachel will be fine." We looked from her to my brother and back again. We frowned at Cynthia. We had to make a break.

"Ah." She nodded in understanding.

"One of the single-minded."

"I'll take care of him."

"You can have my last cupcake," we said. We jumped off the table and walked toward the edge of the park. "Nice to meet you," we called back.

"Thanks," said Cynthia. "Bye Sprout."

We waved back and broke into a run. Circled around the park to my bicycle. Unlocked it and rode away from the park.

"See. You could have a conversation at a family gathering."

"Only because we were isolated."

"Well, something to remember. Look for isolation opportunities."

"Easy to say, hard to do. Finding isolation is hard and keeping it is even harder. Some idiot always has to ruin it."

"Anyway, I liked Cynthia," she said. "She knows things."

"You mean like thinking boys are stupid?"

"No. I mean, like thinking all boys want is sex."

"Not all boys."

"I know. It's though boys treat you differently if you're a girl. Cynthia is bothered by that, not the sex. People treat you a certain way because of who they think you are, and what they want from you. They often don't know you and often don't care. That's annoying."

"How do you know that?"

"You know how I know. Trailing clouds of glory. And it's how you'll know. You need to work on recognizing it. Don't be fooled. Anyway. She treated me like a normal girl. I liked that."

"You are a normal girl," I said. "At least I hope so."

"Oh, I am. Trust me."

"And I'm not simple-minded. Or single-minded."

"Oh, I'm sure you're not. Yet."

CHAPTER 20 – PRUNING

WE CAME ACROSS as a rag-tag bunch of runners, but we were a team. The whole cross-country team treated each other as equals regardless of age or ability. Yes, we razzed the younger runners sometimes, but no terrible hazing like the football players did. They had a hierarchy, and they were mean. We acted like a collective and we had fun.

At a cross-country practice one day, a new runner showed up. Jerry. He was new to the team and new to the school. After coach introduced him, he greeted everyone politely but didn't say much as he dressed for practice. We all watched him out of the corner of our eyes to assess his character.

Tall, lean and blond, still tanned from the summer, Jerry jumped right into practice. A good runner. Confident. Fluid. He immediately ran in front of the pack next to Kevin, our de facto leader. Kevin's advanced physical maturity had turned him into our de facto leader. His sexual maturity may have played a role in his exuding his alphaness. We all knew Kevin was sexually active. We all knew the rest of us weren't. Kevin kept talk of his sexual exploits to a minimum with us, which I am sure he didn't with the tougher crowd he hung out with outside of practice. But Kevin was kind. He treated us like his childhood friends, and when necessary, as our big brother. He acted as our protector when he didn't have to.

Jerry was a man among boys even more so than Kevin. Jerry knew it. He was only a grade ahead of me but the disparity in maturity, if you want to call it that, showed even more than between my brother BJ and I, except Jerry didn't have the history of being a dick to me that BJ did. Jerry was much more like Kevin's other tough friends, a clique of the no longer innocent. Jerry and Kevin immediately bonded in that superior, alpha dog way.

Only one could be top dog, though. Jerry played it cool at first but soon began to exert himself. Kevin fought back for a while, but it soon became clear, Jerry's will outpaced Kevin's. Jerry became the leader and Kevin eagerly followed. Jerry didn't have the same understanding of social dynamics that Kevin did, and we weren't his childhood friends. We were to become his minions, his followers, his pack.

At first, we saw Jerry like a mentor. He knew things about life we didn't, and especially about girls. Unlike Kevin, who knew the rest of us were all virgins and didn't mock us for that, Jerry soon knew and jumped on any opportunity point it out. Once Jerry started to belittle us, Kevin joined in. Kevin jabbed at us, but he wasn't as mean-spirited as Jerry. But Kevin's desire to be in Jerry's good graces outranked his childhood friendships with us. Kids grew up. I understood that.

The rest of us didn't like the new dynamic in our group, but we tolerated it, knowing the situation could have been worse. The new dynamic brought the rest of us closer Most of us knew we weren't alpha dogs. Most of us didn't want to be alpha dogs. We knew we were misfits and used to the mocking of football players and toughs. Jerry and Kevin didn't mock us all the time so we usually all got along. We respected our leaders in as much as we didn't outwardly fight against the hierarchy, but it was now us against them.

Before Jerry had shown up, Kevin had treated me like a little brother, one who actually liked me, unlike my brother BJ, who did not. He put his wing over. Even more so than the others. God knows why. Instructed me on things to do and not do. Like the time a pair of my running shoes smelled so bad he told me I needed to throw them away. I didn't throw them away, so he threw them away for me. "No one wants to smell that shit," he said. He was right.

When Jerry became the not-so-de facto leader, he noticed Kevin's treatment of me and decided he would become my protector as well. He took a liking to me that didn't make any sense, except as a power play to take ownership away from Kevin, the alpha dog routine, take ownership of everything. I also suspected I was an alter ego he was drawn to. Drawn in a way he didn't understand either. He was loud. I was not. He was confident. I was diminutive. He was man of the world. I was bookish. He was manly. I was a nerd. A sense of pride bubbled up in me, flattered by the attention. Besides Kevin, who I had known forever, no one paid any attention to me, which I usually preferred. But being singled out by the alpha dog was a new experience. Especially since I hadn't sought it out. The rest of the pack kidded me about Jerry's attention, but they didn't hold it against me.

One day after practice I walked into the locker room and into the bathroom. I found a stall and stepped in. I sat down to do my business, blocking out all the commotion in the locker room.

"Hi," she said.

"What are you doing? This isn't the best place to show up. I don't need help going to the bathroom." I wanted to berate her some more but since we were safe in a stall, I waited for her to explain why she so urgently needed to be there. I'd worry about getting back to my locker after that.

"We need to talk."

"Right now?"

"Yes."

"Can't wait?" I would have liked to finish doing my business. I did feel a little awkward sitting on the toilet talking to her, yet I knew she wasn't going to leave until she had her say.

"I'm here now. We should talk."

"About what?"

"Jerry."

"Jerry. Why?" I imagined all different topics she might want to talk about: the communal showers, the hygiene, my clothes, but not Jerry.

"I see he's taken a liking to you."

"So, what's wrong with that? I'm a likeable person." I sensed another conversation about self-confidence coming. Trying to defend myself while doing my business would be uncomfortable.

"Yes, you're likable. I'm not talking about you. I'm talking about Jerry."

"Okay, so what about Jerry?"

"I don't like him. I don't trust him. I think he's sketchy."

"Sketchy? We hardly know him."

"Trust me. He's not a nice guy. He exudes jerk like too much bad perfume."

"What's he done wrong?"

"To us? Nothing yet. Besides his weird interest in you. But it's in him. You haven't noticed it yet. But I can feel it. He's got a bad vibe."

"You can feel it. Really? What a weak argument."

"It's not an argument. It's intuition. And it's good intuition. Remember our gut feelings. This time it's not about craving ice cream, it's about someone being a bad person. My gut's telling me, and your gut should be telling you that too. It's the way he treats people, especially girls."

"So, he's probably having sex. That doesn't make him sketchy."

"It's not the sex. Something more is going on there."

"I don't feel it."

"You should. I do. It's a wrenching feeling. And I'm you. You need to learn to feel it. You need to listen to me. You need to trust me, to trust your intuition."

"I do trust you, but I don't feel anything so how can I understand. How do you expect me to believe it without proof?"

"Do you always need proof? No. You don't always have time to find proof. You need to know you know. Everything doesn't have to be explained or can even be explained. Things aren't always on the surface."

"I trust you. But I don't feel what you're telling me I should feel. I'm sorry." I wanted to feel it or at least know whether I felt it or not. She wanted me to imagine what an eggplant would taste like when I didn't even know what an eggplant was. I couldn't do it. "I don't understand."

"Obviously," she said and sighed. We sat quiet for a while. I thought maybe I could finish my business but then she started up again. "I shouldn't have to prove it, but what if I do? What if I give you proof? What if I teach what his crappy vibe does to me? Draw him out. You'll feel what I feel, and you'll see what I see. You'll know what I am talking about. You'll know what that feeling is and you'll remember."

"Okay," I said. I could feel her ire boiling. I knew she meant what she said. I trusted my intuition enough to know something was eating her up. "So how do we do prove Jerry's an ass?"

"I have a plan."

"Of course, you do."

She explained the plan to me. After practice Jerry liked to hang out near the door of the gym, where most sports kids left after their different practices, most of which ended about the same time. Jerry liked to hold court by the door with Kevin and few others and watch people walk by, especially the girls. This, she explained, is where her gut feelings came from. Jerry and Kevin liked to banter with themselves and comment on the girls going by. We would draw the real Jerry out there. We'd expose him.

We would acquire a skirt form my sister and anything necessary to not look like me. We'd keep it in my backpack and change into when the right moment presented itself. Still new at the school, Jerry didn't know everyone yet so a new face wouldn't surprise him. If we put on a hat or a bandana to cover my hair, he wouldn't think twice. We'd be another a girl to flirt with. We would walk by and test him. "Let's see how Jerry treats a girl and see if your gut has any sense to it."

"That's the plan," I said. "Let's see if Jerry treats you differently than he treats me? Of course, he will. He doesn't know you. Sounds like a set up."

"Oh, it is," she said. She seethed with certainty at the prospect. She wouldn't let me rest until we tested Jerry. One day after practice when the timing seemed right, we slipped into a bathroom stall.

"Are you ready?" she said.

"I hope so," I said. "What am I supposed to do?"

"Nothing. Let me be me. Trust me."

I trusted her but I felt the butterflies multiplying in my belly. I pulled the sundress out of my backpack. The weather didn't exactly warrant a sundress, but it was all I could borrow from my sister, and Sprout would look fetching in it. We wrapped a silk scarf around our head that trailed off in the back, giving the illusion of hair. I wanted to see how we looked but we didn't dare stop and check a mirror. We needed a speedy exit. Didn't want anyone finding her in the boys' locker room. We ran to my locker and threw in my backpack. Jerry or Kevin might notice it belonged to me.

We snuck out one of the front doors to the locker room and looped around to the hall leading to the back door where Jerry hung out. Jerry leaned against the wall holding court, flanked by Kevin and a few other kids. They nodded at the guys as they walked by and looked the girls up and down. I could already sense the gauntlet we'd have to run.

Sprout waited for a lull in kids walking out so we could garner Jerry's undivided attention. She started down the hall. She knew how to walk like a girl, deliberate, a little swingy, maybe too swingy but she wanted to make sure he noticed. About fifteen feet from Jerry, she looked in his direction, made short eye contact, smiled with her eyes like she had taught me to do. She looked away. Jerry straightened up. Stopped leaning against the wall. Took a small step out to separate himself from his pack. Locked his stare on her.

Noticing his movement, she looked at him again. "Hi," she said, and put a little jaunt in her step.

"Hey, look at you," said Jerry and moved a little further into the hallway.

She smiled. Didn't say anything. Looked away haughtily. The trap snapped into position.

"Got some love for me cutie," he said.

She shook her head, looked at him again, crinkled her eyes. "Not today."

"Oh come on, sweetness," he said. "Look at that, Kevin."

"Looking good," chimed in Kevin.

She looked away again with a sweeping head motion. Cold shoulder.

"Tease," said Jerry and as we passed a few feet from him, he stepped further into the hall, close enough to touch her and touch her he did. As she passed, he gave her a little goose, a confident, practiced grabbing of her ass. "Maybe next time." He laughed and his wolfpack laughed with him. He had gotten a goose for free.

She stopped. Turned slowly around, faced him. Looked hard into his eyes. "There won't be a next time, jerk off." She slapped his face hard, stood her ground, leaned a little closer to him. She used her eyes again but this time she didn't use them to smile. She used them to sear a hole through his head. Jerry felt the burning gaze. He stood dazed, silent, teetered a bit. She looked at Kevin next and seared a hole in his head too. Kevin looked away, frightened.

"Don't ever touch me again or I'll trash your sorry ass." She wanted to slap him again, but she didn't. He might hit back. She swiveled to Kevin and gave him another searing look. "And fuck you too, Kevin."

She walked away from them. We walked to the back door and pounded it open with a bang. She looked back one more time with a Medusa-level scowl. "Who the hell was that?" we heard Jerry ask Kevin. Wouldn't he like to know?

The door slammed shut behind us. We kept walking until we turned around a corner of the school building. She stopped and leaned against the wall, breathing hard, heart pounding.

"Oh man. That was a ballsy display of confidence. Are you okay?" I said.

"Shit no. What do you think? He could have punched me or worse. What a jerk. He's never seen me before. I walk by him once and he gets all grabby with me."

"You encouraged him."

"Fuck you! I barely smiled at him. I didn't give him permission to touch me. Fuck that pig. Keep his grabby hands to himself."

"I'm sorry." Drip, drip. I felt her anguish pulsing through me, a terrible drug. No wonder she trembled. I had never experienced a violation like that before. A poison coursed through our veins that shouldn't have been there.

"Do you feel that? Do you feel that in your guts now?"

"Oh yeah." I felt the shaking, the nausea, the weak muscles.

"Does it feel good?"

"No." My voice trembled.

"Remember what this is like. Let that pain sear into your brain and your gut. Do you like me being treated that way? Do you want to be treated that way?"

"No."

"Do you want anyone treated that way?"

"No."

"Do you want to treat people like that?"

"No."

"Because when you treat people like a piece of meat, this is how they feel."

"I understand." I did understand but what a terrible way to learn. Feeling the poison course through me, inflicting pain on my body, my mind, my soul.

"Good. Don't ever forget it. But that's how Jerry treats people. It's how Jerry sees woman. It's how Kevin sees woman."

"I'm not like Jerry."

"No, you're not. But hanging with people like Jerry is saying it's okay. You're judged by the company you keep. And you pick up bad habits from them and you don't even know it. Do you see where this leads?"

"I do now."

"So was my gut instinct right?"

"Yes." Her gut instinct was right and strong. I wouldn't forget the lesson.

"Yes. Yes, it was. Pay attention and trust your gut. I won't always be around to help you."

"I know." I didn't want life to have these feelings. "It makes me sad."

"I hope so." We stood recovering our breath. Waiting for the shaking to stop. When we had recovered, she said. "Now we seriously need to go back to taking self-defense classes. If Jerry ever catches me, he'll beat the shit out of me. Or worse. Promise me we'll take more karate lessons. I'm not kidding. Being brave is good, being able to take care of yourself is better."

"I promise."

"Good. Now let's put some pants on. I'm freezing."

CHAPTER 21 – POLLINATION

SELF-EXPRESSION is a hard skill to master when you're a teenager. I vacillated between wanting anonymity and wanting an identity. That created a giant muddle, to say the least, incoherent to both myself and others, I am sure. As a teenager dressing to express an attitude seemed like an easier path than trying to explain it. But since I didn't understand my attitude, I certainly couldn't dress to express it.

The few times I thought of dressing to impress it collided with my fear of attention. Fear won. Fear won a lot. I remember in the second grade, long before I even understood the concept of identity, a classmate invited me to a Halloween party. My mom bought me a cool skeleton costume I am sure we couldn't afford. My Dad drove me to the party. He pulled in front of the friend's house. Terror of exposure took over. I couldn't move. I couldn't get out of the car. Whether my Dad should have made me go in or not, I don't know. He accepted my fear and we drove home. I hid in the basement and cried. I've never forgotten the intense fear of self-consciousness.

So I tried to dress neutral and blend in, which was signaling an attitude as well, even if I didn't understand it. I couldn't escape interpretation. Sprout had said everyone wears a mask in public anyway, so I put a bland mask atop my aloofness atop of my fear. Interpret that, people.

I rode my bike to the outskirts of town a lot, a good place to be alone. One day I found myself on the south side of town, near the edge where the prairie began to encroach upon the city, and upon you. The prairie. Talk about blending in. Earthy, neutral, blandly permanent.

I wore a white t-shirt and brown khaki pants, about as close to being the prairie's visual soul mate as you could get. No, I didn't like the prairie, and yes, I was aware of the irony. Still, I could have ridden out into the prairie and been swallowed by its crushing neutrality in a matter of minutes. No one would have noticed.

"Hi," she said.

"Hey."

"Kind of empty out here." She stared out into the expanse, at the sparse scattering of trees and buildings that could have just as well been a mirage. The ever-present wind blew in from the expanse and rippled our shirt.

"It might look empty, but it's not. Keeps its secrets hidden."

"Definitely does a good job." She shook her head slowly and looked around at the empty, earthiness of it all. "Kind of like you. Outwardly boring. Nothing to see here, move along kind of a look."

"Gee, thanks."

"It's true."

"True in a strange sort of way, I suppose."

"No. Just true. Maybe your outward self is a little too boring. You can blend in without receding into nothingness, you know. You can have identity without calling for attention."

"Where did that come from? You think I'm nothing?" My insecurity jumped up to take advantage of the opportunity. Was I so ambiguous, so doubting, so unsure I was essentially a cipher, nothing? Did I have no substance to my internal workings?

"No. You're not nothing. You try hard to come off as nothing but you're not. Maybe not try so hard. We should go shopping."

"What? For what?"

"Clothes. Maybe I could find something nice to wear. Your clothes are so boring. You could get an outfit, too."

"I'm not getting an outfit. The whole point is to be unnoticed." She obviously didn't know about the skeleton costume incident.

"Okay. But you could have an outfit without compromising your principles. You're not selling out your soul."

"Still not happening."

She tugged at my white t-shirt and stuck her tongue out. "You know you can buy t-shirts that aren't white. And I'm tired of wearing your sister's ill-fitting rejects."

"Hey, it's the best I can do. She might notice if I started taking her favorite clothes."

"Oh, it doesn't matter. They still wouldn't fit."

I shrugged. "What do you want me to do about that?"

"The mall's not far from here. We could at least go check for any cool stuff."

"I don't ever go to the mall."

"Why not?"

"What would I do there?"

"Buy things. We all need things sometimes."

"I don't. I'm a minimalist."

"Whatever. You're not a Trappist monk, you can have things. Everybody needs something sometimes, however small. But the point is I might need things even if you don't. We could go see what's there. Maybe you'll see things you didn't even know you needed."

"I doubt it."

"You doubt it, do you? Whatever. I don't doubt it. And maybe I might see something. Let's go."

"Seriously. You want to go to the mall and shop?"

"Yes. Don't worry, we don't have to buy anything. I mean, it's not like we're going into the war zone."

"I don't know. Maybe it is."

"Shut up. Do it for me then. I need a little love here."

"Okay. But not for very long. You're getting kind of needy."

"Oh, don't pull that crap on me. Having needs and being needy are not the same thing. You'll know if I'm needy and it won't look like this, I guarantee it." She tugged at my chin and gave my head a shake. "It won't be pretty. Got it?" I don't know if I got it, but I didn't want to see it.

We biked to the mall, which somehow managed to be even more bland than the prairie. At least the prairie had a hidden life. The Mall had no life. We walked in the cold and sterile front entrance into the cold and sterile inside of the mall. We wandered slowly along the store fronts. I noticed the terrible music and life-sucking lighting. The freezing air-conditioned environment blasted at me. Kept customers alert, I suppose. Don't want people drowsing off when you wanted them to spend money.

"This really isn't doing anything for me," I said.

"Shut up. Let me take charge here. I don't need all your negative thoughts floating around." She looked into the store fronts. Paused to look at stuff I had no interest in. We came to a clothing store geared to teenagers and young women. "Okay, let's do this. Don't be scared, ya baby. We'll be fine."

She walked into the store like a frequent customer. She started going through the racks like an experienced shopper. You could hear the shoop, shoop, shoop as she slid the hangers along the racks, quickly scanning, looking for the right thing to catch her eye. She pulled out a shirt and held it up to her chest.

"Do you even know what size we wear?"

"I've never had to know. I'll make an educated guess. I'll figure it out."

"What are you looking for?"

"Don't know. Maybe a nice shirt. Maybe a skirt. I'll know it when I see it."

"No one wears skirts anymore."

"They do. You simply don't notice. And I like skirts. Not afraid of expressing that. I'll wear what I like. Skirts can be perfectly pleasing and comfortable. Sure, maybe I wouldn't like them if I was forced to wear them all the time, but since I'm not, it's not a problem."

"How are you going to pick one?"

"You're an idiot. The clothes will speak to me when I'm ready. We'll see what there is. I'll let inspiration wash over me."

We walked around the store. She pulled out blouses and skirts and pants and held them up to us. Looked in the mirror. Twisted and turned around for a better look. Assessed if they would fit.

"I like these," she said. She held out a skirt and a blouse. "What do you think?"

"They're nice, I guess. What do I know?"

"You guess. You're a lot of help." She pawed through a couple more racks. Then stopped. "Okay, I'm ready."

"For what?"

"To try them on."

"Here?"

"Not right here, you idiot. In the dressing room, here. How else will I know if they fit or even if they look good? No one can see us in the fitting room anyway. We'll be fine."

She walked over to the fitting rooms, selected an empty one and we walked in. She hung the shirt and skirt on a hook. She started to pull off my t-shirt.

"What are you doing?" I pulled the shirt back down.

"I can't try it on over your clothes, moron. Let go."

"But you're not wearing a bra."

"No shit. You want to put on a bra?"

"No."

"Then shut up. And let go. This is the-you-being-me part. We'll be fine."

She pulled off my t-shirt and slid my pants down. She didn't hesitate. She put on the blouse, a slate blue color with a faint pattern. It seemed to fit well. Her breasts pushed out and the blouse accented the curves formerly disguised beneath my baggy t-shirt.

"I like it," she said. She nodded approvingly at the mirror, shifted to the side for another view. "Yes, this is styling." I nodded in agreement. She looked good in it.

She grabbed the skirt and started to pull it on. As we looked down, I remembered I didn't have any pants on. I felt exposed. "No one is going to walk in," she said. "Your butthead brother isn't next door." She was right. Thanks to my butthead brother I now fixated about anyone catching me doing anything, unusual or otherwise. "You're going to have get past that fear." She shook her head. "You have issues."

"Hey, be nice."

"Sorry. Sorry. You're doing good." She pulled up the skirt. A pleated wool skirt, dark gray with a dark ocher color in a checked, almost plaid pattern. The skirt hugged her hips. Rose up on her waist and hung down below her knees. She'd done a good job guessing at size. She swirled around and the skirt billowed up. She smiled into the mirror.

"That's more like it," she said. "I look good."

"You do. But looks like a kilt."

"Ha! What do you know? Anyway, kilts are manly. You should like that"

"Not with a blouse, they're not."

"Whatever. This is about me, not you." She turned slowly around peering back into the mirror. Taking a good look at the outfit. "Let's buy them."

"Seriously? I thought we weren't going to buy anything."

"Right. But I didn't know how much I'd like this." She flowed her hands down the side of the skirt.

"You tricked me. You planned all along to trick me into buying you some clothes."

"I wouldn't do that. They look so nice though. We don't have to buy them. It's okay." She started to unbutton the blouse. She flashed a sad smile as she worked her way slowly down the buttons.

"Okay. They're on clearance, right?" I said. "So they're cheap. Don't think I'm going to do this all the time."

She buttoned the blouse back up. "Thank you." She beamed a big smile in into the mirror. She ran her hands over the blouse and skirt. Pleased.

We changed out of the blouse and skirt back into my t-shirt and pants. We walked up to the cashier. We walked with our bag out into the mall. We strolled around the courtyard looking into different stores. She bubbled and bounced with contentment. I felt her contentment and was happy too, though my self-conscious monster clawed at me about carrying around a bag with a skirt and blouse in it. At least I didn't have to wear it.

We looked into a shoe store. She looked down at my worn running shoes. She sighed. I didn't have enough money left to buy any shoes We decided to take a look anyway.

"I need a pair of saddle shoes," she said as we browsed slowly along the shelves.

"Okay, I know nobody wears saddle shoes. You're a few decades too late on that trend."

"Maybe. People don't know they should wear saddle shoes."

"Well, thankfully, they probably don't have any."

The amount of shoes in the store overwhelmed me but she didn't seem phased by it. We continued along the shelves of shoes, picking shoes up and putting them down. We took a break from looking at all the shoes and looked across the store.

"Oh look," she said. "There's Tammy."

"Oh shit."

"Don't freak out. We're in a shoe store looking at shoes. Just being normal. It's not like we stalked her here. Let's go over and see what she's looking at. She won't recognize me anyway." She started to walk toward Tammy. "Unless you want to talk to her. I can leave."

"Are you crazy?" I stopped. I looked again at Tammy. I liked looking at her. I knew what that feeling was.

"Quit being a baby. You can handle it."

"No way."

"Resist if you want but I'm going. We'll practice confidence. It'll be worth it. It'll feel like this." She released a few drip, drips of euphoria into us. I felt lighter, floating, soaring, swooping. I felt warm and tingly. "Like that. How can you not want that?"

I did want that. But the fear, the skeleton costume, the paralysis. I couldn't move.

"It'll be easy. She won't even know who we are. We're nobody. We can be close to her without falling head first into embarrassment. This will be good practice."

She didn't wait for me to agree and walked to the other side of the store where Tammy sat on a chair, bent over trying on a pair of black dress shoes. We pretended to look at a pair of shoes nearby. Tammy stood and stepped in front of a mirror to check the shoes out. We watched her in the mirror. Her face said she didn't like the shoes, but she didn't notice us.

"Okay, here you go. I'm with you but you're on your own." She stepped closer to Tammy. We looked down at the shoes she had picked out. I looked down. "Talk to her about saddle shoes." Sprout was gone. Tammy noticed us. We were in the fire now.

"You know what would look sweet with your outfit," I said as Tammy looked at us.

Tammy looked at us and smiled. "No, what do you think?"

"Some black and white saddle shoes." I can't believe I said that but it was all I could think of. Why did Sprout have to bring up saddle shoes. This was not going to go well. Why did I listen to her?

"Oh, really," said Tammy. "I would've never thought of those." Of course, she hadn't thought about those. Who would have?

"They'd be sharp." I said. I had to keep going with the topic. I didn't know what else to say. "Make a bold statement. But they don't have any here."

"Too bad. Do you have a pair?"

"Not yet. But they're on my list. Looking for a retro look." What did that mean? I don't have a look. I didn't even want a look but apparently Sprout did.

"Now they're on my list too." Tammy laughed. "Thanks." She looked at me with a quizzical look. "You're in my history class, right?"

"Yes. Mr. Budinger's class." Like she didn't know that. "I'm Theo."

"I know. How do you like his class?"

"It's okay. Kind of boring sometimes."

"A little bit." She laughed. She turned her attention back to her shoes. She sat on a chair to pull off the shoes she had tried on. I watched her take the unliked shoes off. I blushed as I stood there like an idiot not with nothing to say. Flustered, I looked down at the floor. I didn't know what to do. I couldn't stand over her all awkward and lurking. I started to sweat. Time to make an escape. "See you in class," I said as I waved a wave she didn't see. What a stupid thing to say.

"Bye," said Tammy, but we didn't look back.

Outside the shop, we stepped away from the door and looked back in the window to catch one more look at Tammy. We couldn't see her through all the displays. My face flushed from the blushing, my heart beating strongly. I walked away from the store and sat on bench in the atrium.

"How fun. She even knew your name." Sprout clapped her hands together as if she had just witnessed a death-defying circus act. She bounced her hands off our thighs. "I liked that. Did you like that? Felt good, didn't it?"

"I was so nervous I'm not sure what I felt. But you were supposed to help me."

"I did help."

"Why did I start blushing then? You wouldn't have blushed."

"Maybe I would have a little. Takes practice to not blush. But you liked it. See, you can talk to girls. Maybe it takes a skirt to loosen you up."

"Funny." I certainly didn't feel loose. What a stupid conversation. I'm sure Tammy thought I was an idiot.

"You weren't an idiot. Not entirely. Next time you can flirt a little. Let her know you like her."

"Oh gawd. I'm not doing any flirting."

"Yes. Why not? I'll be with you cheering you on. You're this close. If I can do it, you can do it."

No flirting. I'd barely managed to spit out three sentences. Though three sentences were three more than I usually managed to sputter out when I spoke with strangers let alone a girl. So I guess she was right. We had made progress.

CHAPTER 22 – BEARING FRUIT

SCHOOL ASSEMBLIES. Throw a couple hundred pent up teenagers into a gymnasium and see what happens. I had to believe it was a social experiment of some kind. Perhaps a lesson in social dynamics. Why else would you invite such chaos except to force interactions between social castes, give a taste of unsheltered reality.

The assembly topics were irrelevant because no one paid attention. Maybe a few people attempted to pay attention, but by its nature the distraction of the social experiment undermined any attempt to do so. I failed to pay attention like everyone else. I liked assemblies because I wasn't in the stifling atmosphere of the classroom, and precisely because I didn't have to pay attention.

Whenever the principal scheduled an assembly, I always tried to find one of my few friends in the clusters of social groupings. Depending on when the assembly occurred, I might be closer or farther away from the gymnasium, so whether I could find a place near my friends was always a hit or miss. If I couldn't sit next to my friends, I found an isolated pocket, play the weird loner. I could sit and observe, fully knowing I was observed as well. Do my little part for the social experiment.

The assembly topic was *Veteran's Day* and several students had won a competition to give presentations that I recalled seeing a poster for. I already knew Jimmy was out sick so I wouldn't find him. I walked into the noisy gym. The raucousness immediately assaulted my ears, my being. I suddenly didn't feel like looking for anyone else. I surveyed the bleachers on the right side. The right side was my preferred location. About halfway up, a few rows behind the nearest bunching of students, I saw a large empty pocket, a good observation point where I could survey the crowd.

A bunch of tough kids sat a few rows below me. I'm surprised they had come at all. Skipping assemblies seemed an easy way for them to exercise their rebellious ways with minimal repercussions. Next to them the hockey players bunched together in the center of the bleachers. Half the hockey players were just toughs with skates who had enough discipline to make it to a practice. The toughs and the hockey players threw insults back and forth. I'd heard a few scraps had broken out between the two groups earlier in the school year. I suppose they had enough smarts not to start anything physical in the gym. A lot of verbal posturing would have to do.

Veteran's Day was a fine topic for a presentation, but as far as I was concerned you had to be ballsy to clueless to agree to give a presentation to this crowd about anything. Most of the crowd viewed you as a suck up if you agreed to present. The toughs and jocks pegged you as nerd, and hurled boos and insults at you. The teachers kept the crude heckling to a minimum but still a hostile atmosphere. Everyone else ignored the presenters or pretended that they weren't ignoring them. Another social lesson? How to soldier on when no one cares?

The history teacher introduced the first presenter. She walked slowly to the podium. She talked about Pearl Harbor, I think. I tried to listen since I would have wanted people to listen to me, but I lost focus immediately and started watching the crowd. The social dynamics proved much more interesting than any speech. Who was sitting by whom? Who was looking at whom? Who was avoiding whom? Who was quiet? Who was chatty?

The toughs heckled the girl, though more subdued than usual. Perhaps the toughs knew enough not to make fun of a topic like veterans. Everyone clapped when she finished. The principal thanked her, perhaps a little too heartily.

I didn't know the girl. She seemed familiar but I couldn't place her or even attach a name to her. When she finished, she walked away from the podium and walked up the right side of the bleachers toward me. Her head hung down, avoiding eye contact with anyone. Her shoulder length hair fell unkempt onto the collar of her faded red blouse, which I couldn't see much of as she clutched her notepad and her books close to her chest. She wore a long gray plaid skirt down to her shoe tops, which looked nice to me though it stuck out since almost no one wore skirts to school. She wore glasses so of course she was a nerd. She looked a generation or two behind with her skirt and glasses, the nerdy librarian stereotype, I suppose. The toughs and hockey players had clearly reached that conclusion and ran with it. The hockey players, purveyors of style for sure, apparently needed to show the toughs how crass they could behave, began to jeer her as she walked by.

"Nice speech, Mable." Mable was an old person's name so even the hockey players keyed in on her old-fashioned looks. "Couldn't find your comb this morning. Be careful some crows might nest in there."

She made her first mistake. She looked up at them and made eye contact. They had her now. "The library is the other way, Mable. You can check my book out any time." The insults were tame for teenager standard's. The teachers ignored any commentary that wasn't vulgar, too many to keep track of otherwise.

The toughs, needing to one up the hockey players, called out as she walked by their section. "Nice skirt, sexy nerd. What's under all that? Buried treasure?" The insults grew more vulgar but didn't become explicit. One of the toughs reached out and tried to flip the skirt up. The apparently heavy skirt only hiked a bit above her ankles, which would have barely been scandalous even in the Victorian era.

And though nothing had been revealed, her personal space had been violated. She ran the rest of the way up to the top of the bleachers. She didn't protest, and she didn't look back.

"We'll see you later, sweets. Meet you in the bathroom." One of the toughs yelled. They laughed. They found themselves terribly funny.

As she passed me, I looked into her face and tried to catch her eye, get a read on her. I saw her blushing face, her lips pressed straight and hard together, her eyes squinted straight ahead. She looked at me briefly and made no sign of acknowledgement as she and her skirt swooshed by. I looked away and didn't say anything.

I should have said something to the toughs. Told them to shut up. I didn't. I had a healthy fear of them. They didn't care about me. I wanted to keep it that way.

The next student came to the podium to give her speech. The assembly moved along now. No one noticed or cared about the jeering the girl had received. All in a day's work. I looked back to see where she had gone. All the way up to the top of the bleachers. Right in the center. All alone. Head down, eyes closed, notebook still clutched to her chest.

"We should go sit by her. Give her a little support," Sprout chimed in. "Those guys are such assholes. If we were bigger, I'd give them a piece of my mind."

"Jesus, Sprout. Let's definitely not give them a piece of our mind. What a horrible idea."

"I know. I was just kidding, sort of." There Sprout was. In the middle of a school assembly. Now I needed to hide. Luckily, no one appeared to be looking back up in the bleachers. I moved my backpack to my lap and hunched over it for cover.

She looked up at the girl. "Who is she?"

"I don't know. What are you doing here? You know school's not a good time. We're ten feet from Bully Steve. That's not good."

"Fuck Bully Steve."

"I agree. But what are you doing here?"

"She seems so sad. I can feel it." She looked back up at the girl.

"Yes, she does. I can feel it." My face tightened into a small grimace. My eyes felt heavy, a weight on them, the weight of shame, embarrassment. My fingers tingled with the slightest tremble. I felt how she felt.

"See, we have empathy. That's why I'm here to help her. We should go make her feel better."

"No. We can't help every person who gets treated poorly. We'd spend all our time doing that."

"Maybe we can't help everybody. But we can help a few here and there."

"I don't even know her name."

"Who cares? She's still a human being. How would you like if they did that to me?"

"I wouldn't like it." I wouldn't like it if it happened to me, which is exactly why I avoided those situations. I knew what she had gone through.

"And if it did happen, wouldn't you like it if someone had your back?"

"Yes."

"So we can make the world a better place one person at a time. Maybe this is an important moment for her. Maybe we change her life if we stand by her. Little actions can make a big difference."

I didn't move. I feared the interaction. And she was a girl. It might seem like flirting.

"It won't be scary. We'll be fine. You need to do this and you know it. You said you could feel it. Well, what good is empathy without action? Huh? No good to hold your empathy in."

How hard did I want to argue I shouldn't help a fellow human because I was socially awkward? No matter how you looked at it that position looked bad.

"Am I going or are you going?" I asked. I still didn't want to go, and I didn't want her to go either. Sprout was right that I shouldn't be afraid, but I was. My stomach twisted at the idea of addressing a stranger. I would have rather addressed the school assembly than walk up to a girl.

"We can both go, but even if you won't I will. Come on. We've been working on confidence. You can do it."

"I was thinking more about who she would see. You or me?"

"Oh, she'll see me. But so what? She doesn't know who I am, or even who you are. It's not how we look, but what we do, what you do."

I hesitated. I could argue more but I knew she would tell me my intuition knew what we should do. And I did.

"This is a good thing to do, you'll see. Come on."

She stood up and I could feel her in my blood. The drip, drip of determination. She was in control. She walked tall and confidently. I was confident too. Fake it till you make it.

Sprout moved like a girl up the bleacher steps, which I was afraid would call attention to us, but all anyone would see was the backside of my clothes walking up the bleachers. So up the bleachers we climbed. We bounced up the stairs and dropped onto the bench beside her. I looked down to see who was watching. I spied Bully Steve watching. I made eye contact with him. He scowled. Sprout smiled a fake smile and mouthed, "fuck you." She liked poking Bully Steve.

"Hi," said Sprout in her smooth and higher voice. "I'm Sprout. Don't pay attention to those guys. World class losers is all they are. I wish I had hair like you." She sincerely meant that as she rubbed my short cropped hair. "I had to buzz all mine off. Long story."

The girl kept her head down and didn't look at us. "My hair is terrible," she said eventually. "They're right. It's embarrassing." She shook her crow's nest hair around and then turned her face to us with a shy smile, dropped her books to her lap.

"Ah! A bird's in there." We leaned back in mock fright. "Ha ha. Just kidding."

"My name's Jill," she said as she laughed. "Probably are birds in that mess." She patted at her hair down against her head but it bounced back into chaos.

"Hi Jill," we said. "And what if there were birds in there? Maybe that's cool. Anyway, who cares? What do those clowns know? The hockey players have mullets and the toughs still think it's 1975."

"Yeah, they're pretty jerky."

"Hell yeah, they are." Sprout sat up on the edge of the bench and jeered down at the hockey players. Sprout waved them off with a big swooshing gesture. We sat back onto the bleacher seat. "But I know it's no fun to have them make fun of you. But screw them, they don't mean shit." We patted her shoulder a few times.

"It's my own fault," said Jill. "I volunteered. I guess I'm a nerd."

"Hey, nothing wrong with caring about shit. Takes balls to care when others won't."

"Maybe." Jill sat up a bit straighter. Set her notebook and books on the bench.

"Maybe nothing. Obviously I didn't dare volunteer, did I?"

"Doesn't seem worth it if you have to put up with them," said Jill. "The rude comments in the hallways are bad enough. I should have known better. Do you know what that feels like?"

"What? People jeer at you in the hallway? Who? Is it Bully Steve? 'Cause I'll go tell him off right now." Sprout jumped up, ready to go give the third degree to Bully Steve. She decidedly didn't like Bully Steve.

Jill reached up and pulled us down by the sleeve. "No. It's all kinds of kids. Too many to beat them all up."

"Okay. Not today. I don't know what it's like to be picked on in the halls because no one notices me. But I know what other things are like. To be picked on in other ways. It sucks." Jill nodded in agreement. "They're going to be jerks no matter what you do, I guess. I know it doesn't seem worth it right now. But doing hard things is what makes us."

"Makes me what? Make me cry?"

"No, no. That's not what I mean. I mean it makes us tough. We learn to leave our comfort zones. Makes us strong, I guess. Strong enough to tell them all to piss off."

"I don't think I'm going to tell them to piss off." Jill looked at us sheepishly, a little embarrassed by Sprout's language.

"Well, we don't actually have to say it. It's all about attitude. Our inner strength is saying piss off."

"You swear a lot," she said as she looked sideways at us.

"Probably why they don't let us give speeches," we said. I realized we had said *us* too late, but Jill didn't seem to notice. "You gave a nice speech. Those jerks wouldn't dare stand up in front of anyone, even assuming they knew enough to give a speech at all."

"Thanks," she said. She grabbed my hand and squeezed it. "Nice of you to say so."

We squeezed her hand back and leaned into her slightly, bumped her shoulder. "Hang in there, Jill," we said. "And don't do anything with your hair. I mean it." We patted her on the shoulder as we stood up.

She looked up and flashed us a timid smile. "I won't," she said and ran her fingers through her hair.

We smiled back and walked down to our seat. Bully Steve turned and said "Oh, did nerdy girl have a boo boo you needed to kiss. Boo, hoo, hoo!" Bully Steve laughed.

"Don't put up with his shit," said Sprout. "I'll go but you need to confront him, push back." I agreed to that terrible idea but only because having Sprout do it would be worse.

"Shup up, ya dick," I said to Bully Steve. "Rather kiss her boo-boo than your pox-ridden face."

Bully Steve jumped over the seats and stood towering over me. He poked his finger in my chest. "Do you have something to say, pussy boy?"

So much for keeping a low profile. I wanted to run but running wasn't an option. Pinned between the seat rows and the edge of the bleachers, I was going to feel his wrath no matter what so I may as well tell him off. "Yeah, I have something to say. Why do you need to do it? Why do you need to pick on someone weaker than you, different than you?"

"You mean make fun of a nerd like you? Because you're an embarrassment. Because it's funny. Because I can."

"Or maybe it's because you have low self-esteem. You need to lash out because you're ashamed. You feel ashamed for having to hide in your basement closet when you masturbate to pictures of Wonder Woman."

Bam. I crumbled down into the bleacher aisle, my head crammed against the guard rails. Bully Steve lurked over me. For once Bully Steve didn't have anything to say. I should have stayed down and stayed quiet. I did not. I stood, and with my back to the bleacher guard rails, I stared defiantly up at Bully Steve. Other students looked at us now. The audience strangely emboldened me. "Feel better now? Maybe we can find a kindergartner for you to beat up."

Bully Steve shoved me hard in the chest. I felt all my breath leave my lungs and my back jam into the guide rail. I couldn't even fall down without collapsing into him. I waited for the next blow.

"Hey!" One of the teachers yelled as they finally noticed the disturbance. "Sit down."

Bully Steve backed up. "Fuck you, you little pecker." He hid his left hand away from the teacher and flipped me off. He jumped over the bleacher seats back to his friends and grumbled at Rod. Rod looked at me and flipped me off.

I flopped back onto the bleacher seat. I knew this was the price Sprout always said had to be paid. I touched my bruised chest. Tender. But the swelling of pride I felt for having helped Jill was worth the price. I looked back up at Jill. She looked at me with a pained smile. I didn't want her to feel bad for me so I gave her a wink and a thumbs up so she knew I was okay. I could feel the pain later.

CHAPTER 23 – MATURING

UNDERSTANDING. I surely didn't understand anything at fifteen, especially not the real world. Still a child and in no hurry to reach adulthood, growing up was not high on my agenda. In my sophomore year, though, nature and puberty had their own agenda. Society had something to say too. They all had expectations. Expectations that came from without and within.

I began to have an inkling of the world beyond my childish view of it, as well as an awareness that I lacked a basic understanding of the world and my place in it. The increasingly noisy intrusion of life on my awareness seemed to fuel my desire to refuse it. While I wished to reject society's expectations, I knew I needed to understand them in order to navigate in their world. If I for some reason chose to row my canoe over the waterfall, I wanted to do so intentionally and not be at the mercy of the current. However good or bad the decision, I wanted to own it. I could at least hold my breath before I splashed down into the water.

I began to see my tenuous grasp of the world was not my only gap. I needed to understand me. I understood a few of my core qualities like introversion, but puberty had jumbled up the rest of me and I couldn't keep up. I couldn't seem to plug my jumbled sense of self into my jumbled sense of the world.

Walking in the school halls before class one day I stopped to look at one of the bulletin boards plastered with posters. One of the posters announced a writing context. I stopped and looked at it: essays, short fiction, poetry. Winners would read their works at a class assembly and celebration. I didn't have a desire to write anything, not that I knew of. I wrote what my classes required and no more. I certainly didn't want to read at any assembly. What would draw me to a writing contest poster?

"Hi," she said. "We should enter the writing contest."

Here Sprout was in school again, which she knew I hated, but her presence also explained the interest in the writing contest. I'd argued with her about not showing up at school, but she always reminded me my inner needs controlled those decisions. She exhibited a consistent belief we would survive in all situations, that no one would notice, which, to give her credit, had been true so far. I insisted we'd been lucky and eventually sticking our hand in the trap would come back to bite us. She argued I enjoyed her presence despite the risk, so it must be worth it. She liked to redirect the conversation, like she was on a mission and needed to control the narrative.

I stepped closer to the bulletin board to reduce my exposure to the students in the hallway, held my back pack to my chest. A terrible disguise but gave me a slight sense of security.

"What would I write? I'm not a writer."

"You're a writer if you decide to be one."

"I don't think you can just decide to be one."

"Sure you can. We could write a poem. We almost started to write a poem that one time at your sister's house. And we read the poetry we borrowed from the library a while ago."

"That's a bit of a reach, Sprout. We almost wrote a diary but didn't. And reading a few poems by Robert Frost doesn't count toward being a poet."

"Everybody starts somewhere. It all begins with a single word and a belief. Then bam. You're on your way."

"Right. But why do you think I want to write poetry? Nothing about me tells me I should write poetry."

"I'm telling you you should write poetry. I say you should try. And I'm you. The you that you don't understand, remember. So what I want is what you don't know you want."

"Now, that's some convoluted shit. If you have to twist the justification into so many knots, you might be reaching a bit."

"It's not reaching. It's why I'm here. Anyway, it's less about the poetry and more about the trying. Like trying a new food. How do you know if you like it? You try. Sure, sometimes you don't like it. And that's okay. But then you know."

"Okay. I get the point. But I'm boring. What would I write about?"

"Write about yourself. Remember Maya Angelou. She wrote about being human. Well, you're human, so you got that going for you. And other people are humans so they might relate."

"Ugh! I still don't want to."

"I don't care. This isn't about want, this is about need and growth. And you not being a baby."

"You are so annoying."

"I'm not annoying," she said and flashed a quick pout. "It's my job to convince you, which is way harder than it needs to be. You're about as malleable as a brick."

"Okay. Calm down. I'll try to be more open. I still don't know what I would write about."

"Well, it could be a poem about you against the world. All the struggles. Hey, I got it. You could write about me."

"You? Really? No one would believe that."

"So what? Poems don't have to be believed. No one knows whether it's true or not. It's like sci-fi. You make stuff up to make a point, to tell a story. It's not about outside truth. It's about inside truth."

"Where do you dig up this stuff?"

"I just know things. Trailing clouds of glory, remember. Though a poem about me would be true. I'm real. I'm you. I'm certainly a good topic."

"I don't think I want to talk about you in a poem everyone will read."

"It's only a poem. What are they going to say?"

"That I'm nuts. Totally mental."

"Or you're a genius. You tell them you were imagining what it would be like. The whole creative expression thing. You're practicing empathy. Empathy is good. Show people you understand what it's like to be human, to be them."

"Whatever. What's the point? Why would I want to open myself up ridicule? Seems like a bad idea."

"Man, you're a resistant bastard. It's about learning to express yourself. Seeing if you can express how you feel about your inner workings. Don't bottle all that shit up. Whether it's about you or something outside of you. Know yourself. Seriously. This is important for me, for us. For you."

"For you, you mean. I'll think about it."

"Yes, think about it Mr. Resistance." She turned her attention to the students in the hall and dropped the topic.

"Look, here's a poster for the science fair?" I liked science. Physics and chemistry. I could understand those subjects, unlike social norms and poetry. "Why can't I do that?"

"Ugh! Because you're a science geek. You were going to do it anyway. So it doesn't count."

"You have an answer for everything."

"Whatever. Why are you so afraid of writing a poem? Are you afraid of looking inside yourself?"

"Maybe. What if I look inside and nothing's in there?"

"Hmm. Valid fear. I'll give you that. But I'm inside so something's in there, even if it's not especially what you were hoping to find. Looking for love in all the wrong places, as they say."

She had a point. I couldn't be completely empty inside. I felt empty because I didn't know what I was looking at, or for.

I pondered her proposition to write a poem for a few days. I tried to understand the point but it eluded me. One night lying in bed, I thought about what she said. Maybe she was right. Fear of expressing myself clouded my vision inward. Was that the barrier to understanding myself? Maybe writing a poem could help. My family provided zero guidance on this topic. In the family you didn't talk about who you were. You were you and you dealt with it silently. I wanted to move beyond that barrier. I wanted to know who I was dealing with. Who was I? I would have to take it on myself.

Submitting a poem to a contest posed a different question altogether. I could learn to express myself without publicly humiliating myself. What life lesson would come from such self-inflicted pain? Sprout would tell me the reward came with trying. The learning to step into the world. The world I didn't want to step into. But if I didn't step into the world, it would step onto and maybe even trample me. Sprout would tell me to take control or be controlled.

I decided I was open to trying, but I still didn't want to write a poem. The contest had called for essays as well. I could do that. It would be like writing a report.

"Okay, let's write an essay," I said to Sprout one evening. "I'm willing to try that. Let's write about caring about what people think, not about the essay but about people's opinions."

"Ooh, a compromise," she said. "Okay, let's do it."

At least I'd have her energy to keep me going. We had two weeks to work it out. I didn't know much about writing essays so we made a trip back to the library and asked the librarian for some examples of famous essays. We could at least mimic what others had done before.

I struggled with thinking about the psychology of caring about others' opinions, so the essay slowly became about my frustration with caring about other people's opinions, the anger in my inability to not care, about the annoyance of letting those opinions sting me so sharply. The essay slowly morphed into the desire to learn how to truly not care. I wanted it to be true when I said I didn't care.

A dozen drafts, maybe more. The first few drafts involved figuring out what to say. The next few moved on to how to say it and worrying about what the critics would say. Two pages of frustration sprinkled with a few rhetorical devices stolen from famous essayists. The last drafts focused on making sure I said what I thought I was saying.

"Am I done yet? It could be done." I said. "How do you know?"

"Maybe it's never done. Take a break and make one last pass. You'll know when you're done if not when it's done."

I sat down to pound out the last draft. I stared at the words on the paper, tired of them. I didn't have the energy to care anymore. I made more changes than I thought I would. I became so weary of trying I gave up the ghost. I didn't have the energy to take any more effort to say the right thing. I said what I wanted to say.

And bam. The epiphany slapped me in the face. I laughed. That is what she wanted me to learn. To find the way to let go. You didn't let go because you wanted to. You had to go through it. That was the lesson.

"Done," I said.

"Good job. How do you feel?"

"I feel good." I did feel good. For a little while I had stopped dwelling on what others would think. I didn't even care what I was thinking. I sat on a cloud and floated above it all, like the euphoria Sprout often released into my blood. Maybe she wasn't the drug, maybe liberation was. Maybe not blocking your own happiness was the key to the drug.

"Do you like that feeling?"

"Yes." I did like the feeling. The feeling of creating. The feeling of accomplishment. But best of all the feeling of letting go, releasing my own anchors.

"Do you like your essay?"

"Hell, I suppose. How would I know if it's any good?"

"Doesn't matter. Being good or bad isn't the point. Working at it until you moved past caring was the point."

"You could have pointed that out sooner."

"Would you have understood sooner?"

"No." She was right. I needed to go outside my comfort zone to find experiences I liked. Was learning to learn the key? The key to surviving in the world. It wasn't the knowing, it was the learning.

"I'm not sure I'm ready to bare my soul to the world. It's a contest after all. The whole point of the contest is for someone to judge it. I don't need to be judged."

"Fair enough. But did we write this to win? I don't think we did. Did we even think about winning while we were writing it? No."

"I suppose not."

"So we're all set."

"I know. But I can't do it. I can't submit it. I'm not ready for people to see it, even if they think it's good. Especially if they think it's good. I don't want people to notice me. Not for anything. I can't do it." We sat in my bedroom with the printed essay in my hands. The thought of reading it in front of the whole school still terrified me. I shivered at the thought. I was afraid. The fear of the spotlight, the stinging of social awkwardness, sent me into a state of panic. Not caring about the quality of my essay was a good lesson in private, but I wasn't ready to learn that lesson in public. One lesson at a time.

"I'm sorry," she said as she noticed my watery eyes. "I didn't mean to pressure you so much. It's okay. You did the important part. You wrote it.

You tried. The contest isn't important. No one knows you were going to enter it anyway." She wiped away an escaping tear. She sat up straighter. "But we have to do something with it. We did good. We should feel good about it. We should celebrate it."

"How would we celebrate it? It's a piece of paper with a little ink on it."

"It's not just a piece of paper. It's a piece of you. It's a creation." She thought about it for a while. "Okay. So maybe not so much a celebration as a ritual. The ritual will give the piece of paper, your creation, importance. Seal it inside us. Remind us of letting go. Remind us of how we felt." She jumped off the bed, clapped her hands together as she paced around the room. "I have an idea. I know what we'll do. Let's find an old bottle, one with a cap still on it. We're going to the river."

I didn't argue. We found a used Coke bottle in the recycling, grabbed the essay, put on a coat and walked to the river. I walked alone in the cool darkness of the night, no one about. A few cars driving by. We walked up on the pedestrian bridge crossing the river. The bridge didn't have any lights but you could see nearby street lamps reflected off the middle of the river that had opened up during a warm spell.

"Roll the paper up and put it in the bottle. Put the cap back on. Our message in a bottle. Now throw it into the river. Set your thoughts free. Send them out to sea. Out into the universe. Now we're free and can move on."

We threw the bottle. We could hear it plop. Enough light from the streetlamps allowed us to see it as it bobbed along with the flow of the river, slowly moving into the darkness, slowly fading into the universe.

"To the sea," she said.

"To the sea."

She smiled. "How do you feel now?"

"Good." I watched the last few bobs of the bottle before the river and the darkness swallowed it. I felt full of satisfaction, filled with lightness. Accomplished. Proud.

"Yes. Yes it does feel good."

"Now what?"

"Ice cream? You can't have a proper ritual without ice cream."

CHAPTER 24 – RIPENING

SCHOOL SPORTING EVENTS. The emphasis on competing against others. The desire to prove oneself better than another. The need to establish supremacy. Mating rituals where the strongest won the best mate. I did understand the hormone induced tribalism.

What I didn't understand was why was I asked to watch this ritual where I stood to gain nothing? Supply adulation for the victors? Live vicariously through them? Experience the winning I would never have in real life? And what about the losers? Was I providing solidarity for my kind? To say, it's okay, we're all mostly losers anyway.

A labyrinth of social awkwardness lay over it all. The barriers. The noise. The crowds. The overwhelming nature of it all. The competing tribes. The communal need to belong. The rituals performed to gain access. The fear of rejection.

Yet I loved to watch people. Alone in a crowd, allowed to observe humanity on my own terms. To soak it in without interacting. I required a strong and vigilant defense system to ward off the pressure to participate in the adulation and commiseration. To join the tribal rituals. To speak. I rarely had enough energy to venture out, let alone, actively engage.

Every other Friday the boys' basketball team played a game in the high school gym. One Friday Jimmy asked me if I was going. I said I thought I might. When I got home after school, I regretted having shown interest. The weight of the commitment sucked the energy out of me. After a warm spell the weather had turned frigid again. I didn't like the cold much. The biting wind would viciously hunt down and torture my hands into blocks of ice, mocking my knitted mittens for their false hope of warmth. Once back inside, the painful tingle as my hands warmed up cemented my hatred of the cold. I had subzero desire to go anywhere.

I sat in my room after dinner contemplating going upstairs to watch TV, which meant sitting with the family since the house only had one TV, and still that seemed better than going out into the cold. I laid back on my bed to ponder my decision.

"Hi," she said.

"Hi," I said. "What's going on?" I could be more casual about her appearance alone in my bedroom now. I had gotten used to her showing up unexpectedly, except when we were in school. I never liked that.

"So, we're not going to the basketball game, I guess?" She rearranged the pillows and leaned up against the headboard. She folded her arms around our chest, which almost always portended some pouting.

"No, it's too cold."

"It's always cold. You need to learn to adapt, ya big baby. If we used the cold as an excuse, we wouldn't go anywhere for months."

"I'd be okay with the isolation."

"Isolation loses its charm after a while too. Cabin fever."

"I suppose. But not tonight."

"You told Jimmy you were going to go."

"I didn't really commit. And he doesn't care anyway."

"We should go. Don't you feel a tiny bit of tingling curiosity inside you?"

I shook my head no.

"Are you sure you're not smothering it in fear?"

She poked a tender spot. She knew I struggled with trepidation. Fear of interaction. Fear of commitment to action. It wasn't simply fear either. Even when I conquered my fear, the social discomfort caused actual physical pain, which justified the fear. A vicious loop.

"We need to find a way to break through your resistance. Don't focus on all the reasons why not to or on all the barriers to doing it, but on the reasons why you should."

"I think you're making this more complicated than it is."

"I'm not. You don't want to hear it. That's what's going on. I should go then. I'll show you how it's done."

"Why do you want to go to a basketball game? They're mostly stupid. Who wants to watch a bunch of manly jocks?"

"I don't know. I've never been to one. I suppose I want to see how the other half lives. See what people do? I'm curious. What's wrong with being curious? Curiosity is the reason we should go."

"Not exactly anywhere to hide you. A bunch of bare bleachers in a well-lit gym."

"We don't have to hide me. We'll go as me. No one will know it's you. I'll be another pretty girl. We can act normal, no sneaking around. We were just me when we messed with Jerry. He didn't have a clue. Kevin didn't either."

"Yeah, but they only saw you for a few seconds. And they talked about that for weeks. They were all worked up. No one knew who the hell you were. This is way riskier."

"Why? There's no reason they would tie me back to you. And who the hell cares what they talked about. And this won't be so scary. We'll be by ourselves and watch people, right? You like watching people. That's cool. I can tell you what I think of everyone. Maybe we'll talk to Tammy again."

"Shut up."

"Just teasing. Come on. No one will be the wiser. It'll be good for us. I'll be good. I won't slap anyone." She wiggled around on the bed. Pouted. Sat up. "Come on, please. Better than watching TV with Mom."

She was right. Mom had to editorialize on everything, the TV shows, the commercials, pointing out how scandalous and unChristian everything was. To be fair she saw everything as scandalous and unChristian, unless it was actually Christian, however she defined that. Mom made watching TV almost unbearable. You only put up with it if you desperately wanted to watch a particular show.

"You're not going to let me be, are you?"

"No. Don't make me go scorched earth and walk upstairs right now."

"Very funny, Sprout."

"I know. I won't. I'm not a total jerk. I'll find a more ingenious way to torture you with if I don't get my way."

"Okay, you can go." We had talked about the need for confidence over and over again, how I needed to work for it. I knew I hadn't tried hard enough, avoided opportunities knowing they would be painful. I avoided thinking about it at all, except when I failed at it and became frustrated at how it debilitated me. I was tired of being afraid. What I needed was determination. If she could be confident, so could I.

Sprout insisted we wear the blouse and skirt I had bought her. I argued it was too cold for them. She argued this was exactly why we had bought them. Where else were we going to wear the outfit? I agreed to wear the blouse and skirt, but we'd have to exercise extreme caution in getting out of the house. We also needed to cover my close-cut hair. People would notice that, so we found one of my sister's winter hats we could wear inside without overheating.

I wanted to wear a heavy winter coat. I'd go but I didn't want to be cold. She didn't care about being cold. She found one of my sisters' fall coats she liked instead. We could keep it on inside was her argument and we couldn't wear one of my coats anyway. I gave in because it afforded another layer of disguise, but being cold was going to make me crabby.

"We don't need to disguise me," she said. "Except for your hair no one is going to see you at all. And why can't I have hair when I show up anyway? I have breasts. Why can't I have hair?"

'I don't know. You're in charge of my subconscious world. Show up however you want."

"It's not that simple."

"Of course, it isn't."

When we arrived at the school, the only people wearing real winter coats were the adults. So we fit in. The hallways hopped with people loitering or filtering into the gym.

She stared at the crowd as we walked along, fascinated by buzzing social activity. You'd think we'd never been in public before. Her wide-open eyes scanned the crowd as if she were a secret agent looking for a contact.

"Quit staring at everything," I said. "You look like you're from outer space or on drugs."

"Whatever. Freedom is like being on a natural drug." She rattled her head and eyes around to look spacey. She was always saucy when she got her way.

She was right. No one recognized us, though I still thought we probably looked like we'd never been on Earth before. We saw Jimmy in the crowd. She looked right at him. She had to walk past him to prove not even Jimmy had any idea. She was right again.

We stepped slowly into the gym. Bright and loud. Stark and sterile. Two sets of bleachers on either side of the basketball court, folded out of the way most of the time. They set up chairs on one side for the home team and the other for the visiting team. People streamed into the home side, filling most of the seats. The visiting side had a couple dozen people in the front rows.

The raucous noise and bright gym lights immediately overwhelmed me, a sensory blast to my brain that temporarily stopped me in my tracks. If I had come as myself, I might have turned around and left.

Sprout took a deep breath, stood a little straighter, unphased. "Confidence," she said. "Fake it until you make it." She stepped boldly into the gym.

"Okay, you're in charge."

"Up there." She pointed to the top of the bleachers behind the visiting team where no one sat. "People will think I'm a groupie for the visiting team. Nice and isolated. No one will bother us."

We made our way through the gym and split from the crowd headed to the home side bleachers. We sat in the top row, right in the middle. We observed the different groupings of students, cliqued up even at the basketball game. Mostly adults and parents in the front rows. The cheerleaders mulling in front of them. Folding chairs on the gym floor for the basketball players and coaches.

"Look," she said. "There's Jerry. He might remember me. Should I wave?" She laughed. I shook my head vigorously. "Don't worry. I won't."

We had a good view to watch people. The game started. For the first few minutes she paid attention to the boys as they ran up and down the court but soon lost interest. She instead watched the people across from us, watched people coming in and out of the gym, people heading to the concessions stand. Noticed their clothes, the way they held themselves, their body language.

"Most of these people aren't even watching the game," she said.

"Neither are you."

"But I don't care about basketball."

"Neither do they. This is a big social experiment. Packs of animals watching and sniffing each other."

"Hey, that's what we're doing. Don't call me a dog."

"But they are. They're pack animals. We're not. We're outsiders looking in."

"Oh sure, everyone wants to be the lone wolf. Or maybe we're not so different."

"I'm different."

"Maybe. You think being a loner is cool."

"I do."

At half time we stood up to stretch. We looked around the gym. Watching everyone stream out into the hall to the restrooms, the concessions, to the hallways to cluster in their clans.

"I haven't seen Tammy," she said. "We should go find her."

"Shut up. Man, you're pushing all my buttons today."

"Yeah, it's kind of fun. Who else is going to prod you to action?"

"Let's go get a soda."

We walked down into the crowded gym floor and out into the hallways. She smiled at everyone we walked by. She liked to smile. "Costs nothing to smile," she said.

We plodded through the concessions line and bought our soda. We turned around and walked past all the people waiting in line, observing them. We saw a boy near the end of the line looking at us. She returned his gaze and he turned his eyes away. I didn't recognize him. Maybe from the visiting team.

"He's cute," she said.

"Sure."

He looked back at her. She made eye contact and smiled even more. Raised her eyes brows in recognition. Winked ever so slightly. He smiled and turned away again. Embarrassed to have been caught.

She chuckled as we passed by him in the line. "That was fun," she said. "See, you can have confident exchanges with people."

"You can. And he was a boy so that made it easier."

"But I'm a girl. If I can interact with a boy, you can interact with a girl. You see the connection, right?"

"Sort of."

"Oh, come on," she said. "Work with me. We're being confident today."

I did understand her but making eye contact still tightened my stomach. And even though she kept making me practice, and even whenever she was around, she had to try and make eye contact with everyone, I still cringed when I tried. I always felt I crossed a personal boundary when I did it. She said it was a natural connection and not a violation. Not unless I was being a creep, which I wouldn't be.

"Oh relax. It's all fun. And you need to come out of your shell anyway. You're still terrible at it."

We walked back to our seat. The last of the school band marched off the court. They swept off the court, they blew their whistles, and they started the game again. We kept watching the crowd.

"Look at Kevin," she said. "He acts like a little puppy around Jerry. How sad. Remember when I taught you about Jerry?"

"Oh yeah, haven't forgot." I remembered how she felt. Violated. And Jerry had no idea. No clue how his behavior made other people feel. I'd kept my distance from Jerry during cross country practice after the incident, which also meant keeping my distance from Kevin. And since the season had ended, I hadn't seen much of either. I was fine with that. I didn't need their kind of friendship or protection.

"Look," she said. She nodded towards the bottom right of the bleachers. The boy from the concession stand line, hanging at the bottom of the stairs, looking around.

"I think he's watching me," she said.

"Of course, he is."

"I probably shouldn't have winked at him." She laughed.

"No kidding."

"Who is he?"

"I've never seen him before. Probably with the visiting team."

"I wonder if he'll come talk to me?"

"If you keep looking at him, he will."

"Look, he's easing his way up." She sat up a little straighter. "I wonder if I should make out with him?"

"What? No! Where did that come from? You're totally off the rails today."

"Why not? You need the practice. It would be fun."

"Shut up. No way."

"Maybe a little kiss then. You need practice kissing. No one will know. I'll be in charge. It won't be about you at all. It'll be about me. You'll be safe inside."

"Okay," I said, mostly to placate her. I had agreed to let her be in charge after all. If I wanted to learn about confidence, I needed to jump in the deep end with her. She was my mask, my armor. If she could march into the breach, then so could I.

"Hi. I'm Daniel," he said. He had short, blond hair. Taller than we were. A leather coat on, unzipped. He was cautious. "May I have a seat?"

"Absolutely," she said. "I'm Zoey."

"You go to school here?" he asked.

"Kind of," she said. Well, at least he didn't go to school here. We wouldn't have to explain who we were. I wasn't even there, so he wouldn't be confused by that. All he saw was her.

"I'm with the visiting team," he said. "Came to see my friends play."

"I kind of figured that. I came to watch people. Haven't watched the game at all. Is someone winning?"

He laughed. "Someone is, for sure."

She nodded in mock seriousness. She took a sip of her soda, made a loud slurp as she emptied the cup. "Oops," she laughed. He laughed too and imitated her slurping sound.

"Hey, do you want another one? It's on me."

"Oh, a gentleman." She laughed. "I would gladly accept."

We stood up and walked down to the concession stand. we stood quietly quiet while we waited to order, unsure where to start the conversation. Finally, he said. "So you don't like basketball?"

She shook her head, took a drink of her soda. "Look. No slurping."

"No slurping is good. What do you like? I like movies."

"Movies are good. I like music. I like to dance." She pirouetted and spun around. "Like that."

"Excellent dancing," he said and smiled.

We walked down the hall towards the gym. We walked by one of the dark hallways where all the lockers were. She grabbed his arm and pulled him down into the dark deserted hall. He followed her without objection.

"The school's kind of weird at night with all the lights off," she said. Halfway down the hall she stopped and leaned back against a locker. He stood across from her, looking at her a bit awkward. She put her soda on the ground and stepped towards him.

"Do you want to dance?"

"There's no music," he said.

"The music will be in our heads." She grabbed his hand and twirled him in a circle. She spun him away. Pulled him back towards her. Placed her arm around his waist and raised his arm as if to waltz. She led him through a few clumsy steps and stumbled into the lockers. The awkward physical contact felt good. Nature took control. It wanted more contact.

"You need practice," she said and laughed. She guided him back into a dancing position, pulled him a little closer and stole a quick kiss. He hesitated briefly and gave her a quick kiss back. Warmth spread inside us, tingled at our belly.

"Another kiss might be nice," she thought, and she twirled him around again.

"This is too much," is what I thought.

"Hey, none of that," someone yelled down the hall.

"Shut up," she yelled back. She looked at Daniel. "Just one more," she said and stole another kiss, a little longer this time. She leaned back and held a finger to her lips. She released him and skipped down the hall.

"Hey," he called out.

She looked back and waved. "Bye."

We skipped down the hall and back to the gym where ethe game lumbered on. We stood at the bottom of the bleachers, deciding whether we should go back to the top of the bleachers.

"What were you doing?" I said. "I thought no making out?"

"We weren't making out." She rolled her eyes. "You're an idiot. That was barely a kiss. A little bitty one."

"Two."

"Okay, two. Don't be a baby. You liked how we felt, didn't you?"

"Yes." I did like that. The tingle. The little drip, drip of intoxication into the blood. Different than the drip of liberation. Though not exactly how I had imagined a first kiss. "What was that feeling?"

"That was the other side of innocence." She twirled in place. "A little taste of why people step over that line."

"Makes me uncomfortable."

"Good. It should. But now you know how to start. Easy peasy." She smiled and smiled. She beamed out her happiness. Her happiness infected me. We floated. Walking through fear and discomfort led to joy. Who knew?

"But we need more practice kissing for sure. We did good though."

"They're going to talk about that."

"Who cares? They can talk about a non-existent girl all they want because we kissed a boy."

CHAPTER 25 – ABUNDANCE

SOMETIMES SHE SHOWED UP inside my head and didn't manifest herself physically. Voices in your head is what you're thinking, which sounds mentally ill, I know. She would still announce herself. She wanted me to know she had arrived, my secret friend and guide. Maybe to let me know I was talking to her and not myself. But I had learned to feel her arrive, that slight shift in mood, so her announcements were usually just formalities.

We knew each other well by now, though she knew me far better than I knew her, and she often knew me better than I knew me. She certainly knew more about the world than I did, the trailing clouds of glory she liked to talk about. I thought of her as my spirit guide, the wise elder disguised as a young girl, the old soul in me, though I didn't understand the gift it was at the time.

She provided me the guidance my family didn't, though I suspect the family wouldn't have approved of most of her advice. She was a free spirit and wanted me to become one too. In those moments when I followed her advice, the family often rewarded me with disapproval. My family saw my free spirit as irreverent, disrespectful, asocial, offensive, and often incomprehensible. As if my fear of being myself wasn't a heavy enough weight on my shoulders, my family's intolerance and often belittling of my free spirit hung like a stifling albatross around my neck. I was a lost soul to them.

I responded by exercising my free spirit out of sight and out of mind. I kept my family in the dark about anything I did or achieved. If I won an award at school, I wouldn't tell them. Maybe they would applaud or maybe they would wonder why I had even tried. Why put myself in harm's way? In my junior year of high school as a joke among my friends, I ran for class president. The weird kid bucking the system. I didn't tell my family. What but bewilderment would I have gotten from them? I think my dad found out talking to a friend's dad. He mentioned it in passing, but I dismissed it as nothing and walked away. I cherished my free spirit however fragile it was. I took a few lumps before I realized the family wasn't allowed near my spirit.

One day walking down the hall at school, we saw a poster for a school dance. She constantly noticed posters and other communications from the world I didn't bother with.

"We should go," she said. "Look, it's a theme dance. Back to the '50s."

"Those are lame."

"How do you know?

"I just know."

"I don't think you know. I think you think anything you don't understand is lame. With your attitude, most of the world is lame."

"Whatever."

"Don't whatever me. That's my line. But seriously. Because you think stuff is lame doesn't make it so. People like different things. Maybe understand it from their perspective before shitting all over it. Doesn't mean you have to like it. Show some empathy."

"I have empathy."

"Sure, on your terms."

"Whatever."

"Yes, I know. Whatever. Look, there's going be a DJ and a live band. Jimmy will probably go. You could go with him."

"Yes, he'll go. He likes social events."

"See. Jimmy knows."

"I'll think about it."

"It's like a party. You like those, don't you?"

"Sort of. But it's not a party."

"You should go. You can build your confidence. We're getting better. We talked to Tammy at the mall. We kissed a boy. Come on, going to a dance will be easy."

"Are you going?" I asked. Sometimes when she said I should go, she meant I should go. And sometimes she meant she should go. I always made sure to clarify which she meant.

"Totally. But I can stay hidden if you want. No one will know. I can help you navigate the scary dance."

"I'm not scared. And help me with what?"

"With dancing. With girls."

"And kissing, I suppose."

"Only if you want." She puckered her lips and laughed.

"Great."

She was nothing if not persistent, and persuasive. She knew what buttons to push. And she was right. I needed to work on my confidence. Even though she egged me on often enough to let my free spirit out in the world, I resisted often and found it easier to retreat into myself where I could fence off the fear. But I did want to be free, which meant facing the fear. No retreating.

I called Jimmy to gauge his interest in the dance. If he was in, I would go. Otherwise, I wouldn't. The thought of going by myself still made me uneasy. My level of self-consciousness would tear through the roof. If I dressed up like the '50s, people would stare. If I didn't dress up, I might feel excluded. But Jimmy wanted to go so I committed. If we both dressed up, we had strength in numbers.

The night of the dance I met Jimmy in front of the school. We had dressed alike. We apparently both understood the '50s as depicted on the TV show *Happy Days*. I wore a white t-shirt underneath an old leather coat I found in the basement storeroom, jeans rolled up above the ankles, white socks and black shoes. I didn't have any hair to slick back so my buzz cut had to suffice, which fit the period just as well. Jimmy dressed in almost the same outfit. We extended a unified front, except for the hair.

We paid the $5 admission. The dance took place in the school gym. The band and the DJ had set up at the far end of the gym. The bleachers had been pushed back against the walls, the gym had a semi-circle of high and low-top tables surrounding a wooden dance floor set up in front of the band. A handful of colored streamers and other decorations hung from the rafters to provide an inkling of ambiance, but it was hard to hide the fact you were in a gym.

We arrived an hour after the official start. The DJ was spinning music when we walked in. A handful of students danced. Most students clustered in groups around the high-top tables, and more were standing behind the tables and chairs, apparently concerned the dancers might deviously suck them in.

A concession stand had been set up in back of the gym, selling candy and soda and such. We bought sodas and looked for an empty table. We saw a group of our cross-country friends at a table at the top of the semicircle. Most of them hadn't dressed up, but Jimmy and I still held a united front.

"Nice outfits, losers," they mocked us.

"Sit on it," we said together, the one insult we knew from *Happy Days*. "We look fab," Jimmy said.

We joined the semi-circle of friends. I looked around the gym to see if I noticed anyone, curious about who showed up to these events.

"Look, there's Tammy," Sprout said, pointing across the dance floor to our right.

"Don't point." I looked down quickly. Thank god she wasn't physically with me. I never knew when she would do that, though she had promised she wouldn't show up physically tonight. Right now would have been a bad time.

"Don't panic," she said. "She looks good, doesn't she? See, she's wearing a themed skirt. See, I told you skirts were cool. And she does look good in it."

"Yes, she does. Don't stare at her."

"She's not going to notice you looking at her."

"Maybe not. But just in case."

"Okay, I won't. But we're all here to be looked at or to be looking, so we may as well look. No other reason to be here, though I suppose someone might actually want to dance."

"Apparently not many people." A handful of students danced randomly around the dance floor.

"They will. Takes time to warm up. Takes the right song. Once the band starts playing, they start moving. The poster said it was cover band. Once they play a cool tune, they'll jump out." I wondered why she would know anything about high school dance etiquette, but I guess she did know people.

Jimmy and I chatted with the cross-country boys. Jerry and Kevin weren't there, clearly beyond school dances and way too cool for this, which was fine by me. And Sprout despised Jerry. She might have made us leave. Or worse she would have confronted him, given him the business for being an asshole.

Eventually the band kicked back up with a popular song we all recognized. Kids started to jump out on to the dance floor. The ice had broken.

"This song is awesome," said Jimmy. "Let's go." He motioned everyone at the table to follow him. I trotted after him onto the dance floor. We jumped around and spun and hopped in a big jumble. You could call it dancing. The dance crowd swelled. We thrashed in the thick of it. We saw Tammy across the crowd. She swirled around and around, her skirt billowing up, her hair tossing around. She smiled and laughed. She looked pretty. I knew I was attracted to her and knew what that feeling was. I had no idea what to do with the knowledge so there was nothing to do. After a while I lost track of her in the crowd.

We stayed out on the dance floor for another song and then it was time for a break. Back to the table. Time for another soda. The band played a few more upbeat songs before turning to the ballad and slow song portion of their set. Time for couples to dance. The dance floor emptied, leaving a half dozen couples swaying slowly.

"Let's dance," said Sprout. "You should go ask Tammy."

"Are you kidding? She's not going to dance with me."

"Why not? She's nice. You're nice. She's pretty. You're sort of pretty."

"No one else is asking anyone to dance."

She pointed to the dance floor full of dancers. "Someone must have asked."

"Whatever. They' probably all couples. Seems like a bad idea."

"It's not a bad idea. You're afraid."

"I'm not." I was. Sure, I had said a few words to Tammy at the mall but that had been a chance meeting without intention, without risk. And the dancing in Jimmy's basement was just an accident. Asking her to dance was intentional. Asking her to dance would put me out on the ledge.

"You're afraid. But that's okay. It would be weird if you weren't."

"It's not my style."

"That's why I'm here. Obviously, you need to expand your style. Stretch your boundaries. Just do it. Confidence, remember."

"Easy for you to say."

"I know. That's why I said it."

I stared across the dance floor at Tammy. She sat at a table with her friends. They chatted and laughed. Tammy laughed with them. She looked happy. Wouldn't it be nice to share in that?

The thought of going over churned up my stomach. I started to sweat, felting myself blushing already. She was right. I was afraid. All my past fears seemed small compared to this.

"Now's the time," she said. "It's a dance. People are supposed to ask others to dance. Practice your social skills. Not like you're going to walk over all naked."

"I can't." Cement encased my feet. I didn't know if I could take a step even if I wanted. The larger the desire the larger the fear.

"If you don't, I will. You know I will. And I know you won't like what I do. She'll think you're you and then she'll see my breasts and be freaked out. Things are going to get ugly."

"Don't you even think about it. You promised."

"I did. But I also said I'd help you dance. So let's do it. I'll go with you. We'll do it together."

"This is a bad idea."

"Probably. Only one way to find out."

"Okay." I was in. The only excuse I had was fear. I was tired of fear ruining everything. I took a big drink of my soda as if it were a stiff drink that might give me a jolt of liquid courage. I set my soda down and walked to the outside of the semi-circle of tables. Jimmy asked where I was going. I said, "You'll see." I walked around the edge of the crowd and cut back into the table where Tammy sat. I recognized her three friends but didn't know them. I didn't actually know Tammy either except from history class and the brief encounter in Jimmy's basement. I approached her from the side until I encroached on her line of sight. She noticed me as I walked up and smiled. "Hi," she said.

"Hi," I said, my voice weak and wavering. "Keep eye contact," said Sprout, "Don't panic." I smiled but what I wanted to do was run away. I blushed and sweated even more. I felt myself trembling. "Ask her about her shoes," she said. "The hard part is over."

"Hi," said Tammy timidly again.

"Did you ever find any good shoes?"

Tammy looked confused then a look of remembrance flashed across her face. She nodded and smiled. "Oh, no. I didn't find anything I liked."

"That's too bad. Some saddle shoes would have been good for this dance." Tammy nodded. I didn't know where to go with that. Tammy looked across at her friend's a little puzzled. I noticed them watching me. A wave of paralysis ran through me. I felt stuck in time. I looked down at the table.

"Ask her to dance." Sprout prodded me. "Look her in the eyes. Remember."

I looked back at Tammy and met her eyes. "You want to dance?" Time did stop this time. The music faded from my awareness. Her friends faded into the background. An eternity passed while I waited.

Time moved again. Her friends giggled. Sprout gave them a quick icy glance. They were lucky Sprout wasn't physically there. She would have told them off. I looked at her giggling friends and back at Tammy.

Tammy pulled back a little before she answered. She shook her head but didn't actually say no. "Thanks for asking though." She looked down and away, perhaps a little embarrassed.

"Cool," I said. What more could I say? I wasn't going to plead. I made the mistake of looking back across the table at her friends. They snickered as I turned and walked away. I felt terrible. I felt heavy. Humiliated. I could hear outright laughter from her friends.

"You want me to go tell them off?" said Sprout. "Bitches. They don't know shit."

"Oh gawd. Please don't. You'll make it all worse."

The walk back to the table took forever. I imagined everyone stared at me in my failure. Jimmy looked at me as I walked up to him. He smiled. "Rejected," he said.

"Shut up." He had noticed. He had probably watched the whole thing. Watched me fail.

He punched me in the shoulder. "Hey, everyone gets rejected. Don't sweat it, loser."

Everything moved on as if my rejection had never happened. Lost in the muddled group of people in a dark gym. I lost all enthusiasm to stay but made myself hang with the guys until the dance petered out. Jimmy tried to pull me onto the dance floor for more dancing, but I resisted.

"That sucked," I said, lying in bed after the dance. "It still sucks. How embarrassing. I'm never asking anyone to dance again. You knew how it was going to feel, the rejection, didn't you?"

"Well yes, I knew how it could end up feeling. But the possibility she might have said yes. Think of that. How good would you have felt? It was so worth it."

"How would I know it's worth it? I don't know the feeling."

"But you had an inkling of it, you felt it when we kissed Daniel. Otherwise, you wouldn't have done it. One day you'll know it's worth it. Like the liberation of flying but better."

"It still sucked."

"It did. I was sure she would say yes. Maybe she was embarrassed too. I think she was."

"They laughed."

"Tammy didn't laugh."

"Maybe not. But her friends certainly did."

"Oh, I know. Teenagers are mean. They excel at cruelty. Don't take it personally."

"How else can I take it?"

"Take it as learning. You actually did it. You didn't think you could do it. You took a risk. You knew she might say no, but you still did it. Be proud of that. The good thing is it gets easier, or maybe you learn to care less. One of those two, maybe both."

"I'll have to put up with the shame on Monday."

"You'll be fine. There's no shame here. No one will remember. Not like you bloodied your pants with a period."

"Not funny. They'll whisper about me."

"They'll whisper about stuff no matter what you do. No avoiding gossip and no controlling it. It's learning shit doesn't matter even if it feels right now like it does. Or maybe have empathy for them. They do it because they're insecure. They hide it behind their cruelty."

"I'm not ready to have empathy for them and their cruelty."

"Maybe later."

"Maybe."

CHAPTER 26 – THE HARVEST

WINTER DRAGGED ON and cabin fever set in even for me, who often cherished the solitude winter brought. I didn't like the cold, so I stayed home even more than others. My friends would go to the mall for escape. Despite my brief shopping spree with Sprout, I still immensely disliked the mall. Except for an occasional movie, I turned to running as an escape, but I could only do so much of that. I poorly balanced restlessness and lethargy, like a hibernating bear who had drank too much caffeine before crawling into the cave.

March came and the promise of spring came with it. Hope popped it's head out into the world like a ground hog. My mood changed. I had more energy, ready to go out into the world again. I ventured out more but not enough to break free of my winter malaise. Sprout was right. Even I needed to consciously and intentionally break out of cabin fever.

One day at school we saw a poster for another school dance. The last dance had been a month ago, my last real attempt to fight winter. Though I didn't think of it often, Tammy's rejection at the dance made me wince in pain. I had a deep-rooted belief she would snicker at me if we ever ran into each other. I could envision her thinking, "there's the stupid boy who dared to ask me to dance." The reality was more likely she never thought of me at all.

I ignored the poster. I felt like a child who had touched a hot stove. Don't do that again. I turned to move on, but Sprout had shown up and she stopped to look at the poster. She showed up frequently now. Though often for only a few minutes. Bolder and bolder, Sprout forced us to interact with the world more often. When we would go shopping, she made small talk with the cashiers. She knew I hated the social interaction. She would initiate contact herself if I hesitated, but she preferred to coax me into doing it. We needed the practice, she said. She was right, however much I didn't want to agree. I found myself able to break my social paralysis and more frequently initiate the small talk on my own. I felt a little bit of pride when I pulled it off. I liked that.

"The 'Spring is Here' dance" She read the poster out loud. "Friday, March 16th at 7."

I turned away from the bulletin board. I hoped if I ignored it, she would move on. I liked to think I had some say. If she could persist so could I.

"Let's go." She let us walk away from the poster, but she hadn't let go of the idea. She insisted this is exactly what we needed after our winter induced solitary confinement.

"No way. I don't even like to dance." I liked to dance around by myself. Dancing in front of others was the real problem. I lied because I didn't want to talk about the pain of Tammy's rejection still lingering.

"Oh shut up. That's not why you won't go. You danced with Jimmy at the last dance. Anyway, the point of the dance isn't really the dancing. Are you still embarrassed by your rejection? Come on, you shouldn't be. You should be over it. Water under the bridge."

"I was embarrassed. I didn't like feeling like crap, okay. That's normal."

"Totally normal. But it's also normal to move past it. Time has healed you, I'm sure. I'm sure Tammy isn't hung up on it. That's old news to her."

"Good for her," I said sharply. "She's not the one who got rejected."

Sprout wisely let the topic die. We walked away from the posters and headed to my locker. I thought about the history test I had today. Of course, it was the history class Tammy was in. Fortunately, the class consisted of boring lecture after boring lecture where we never left our seats, so I never had to interact with her.

"Okay," she said as we walked to our first class. "What if," she started and then stopped. I assumed she stopped to ponder how to convince me. "What if I went to the dance?" She started to say more but stopped again and kept silent, waiting for my reaction before making her case.

"I don't know how that's better." I knew running into Tammy at the dance even as Sprout would open the wound. Letting her be in charge wouldn't stop me from feeling awkward and stupid. And she might go ask Tammy to dance anyway.

"Of course, it's better. You'd be like anonymous, like at the basketball game. No one would know who you were. You wouldn't be in disguise, you'd be me. Remember how that works? We could do whatever we wanted."

"I'm not convinced this isn't a terrible idea."

"Oh, come on," she said. "We have to get out of the house. You need to get out. You know you do."

"I think better ways might exist."

"They do. But you won't do them." She pouted as we sat through first period. She pouted and fidgeted so much I could barely concentrate on class.

On the way back to my locker after class, she started up again. "Okay, listen. What if it's not about cabin fever? And obviously it's not about dancing." We opened my locker and exchanged books, then she continued. "So, what if it's about getting back on the horse, the horse who bucked you off. Going back to where you were embarrassed and showing how you're stronger now."

"I'm not going to ask Tammy to dance again. I've moved on or it's not worth it. Or whatever excuse you'll buy."

"Ha! I'm not buying any excuses. Anyway, first, we're going to go as me. And second, we don't need to ask Tammy to dance to conquer the fear. We only need to show we're not afraid to go back. You need to show yourself you can do it. We don't need to show it to anyone else." She was persistent. I told her I would think about it. I had a week and a half to think about it. I had time to come up with a better excuse.

So I thought about it. She'd wouldn't relent so I'd have to come up with good reasoning on why not to go. I couldn't pretend I was sick since she would know I wasn't. How did I counter her argument about going back to the scene to conquer fear? Yes, we needed to conquer fear as a whole, but maybe not as a specific. Couldn't I conquer a different fear? Or was this particular fear like a regret, like a pebble in your shoe that would eventually give you a blister because you were too afraid to remove it? You had to get used to blisters, didn't you?

The night before the dance I decided I needed to choose. As I lay on my bed, all I saw in my mind was Tammy blankly staring at my foolishness. I felt the roiling of my stomach as I recalled her look. Did I have to experience a pang of pain every time I thought about the dance or every time I saw Tammy? What a terrible life to lead. I couldn't respond like this to every unpleasant experience. I had to stop the pattern. We should go to the dance. She was right. I would not let fear dictate what I did and how I felt. I would let go of the pain and embarrassment.

We decided we would go as her. She wanted to experience the dance. We would wear her one outfit. She looked good in it. We'd still have to wear a hat or a scarf to cover my hair. She said if the hat fell off we could say we shaved our head for swimming. She wanted us to put on makeup, but I told her I had to draw the line somewhere. She didn't persist on the makeup, but only because she had already won the battle.

"I'm so excited," she said. "Let's do this."

We needed to sneak up into the porch and grab a coat, open the door quietly and slip away. We could hear people watching TV upstairs, hoping the voices would cover any noise we made. I made sure I had a little money and my school ID. I listened at the flimsy accordion door for any signs of activity. All quiet.

We slid open the door and stepped quietly into the dark hall. We didn't turn the light on so we wouldn't attract attention, easily able to navigate the hallway with my eyes shut. Still no one. We stepped all the way out into the hallway and turned toward the stairs when the door to my brother's room slid open. The brightness from his room filled the hallway with light. My brother's shadowy body filled the doorway.

I tried to keep moving but he grabbed me by the shoulder and spun me around. He stared at us in our blouse and skirt. Maybe he thought I was one of his sisters. He looked us up and down.

"Sprout?" he eyes opened wide. "Sprout?" His big hands grabbed me by the cheeks.

"I don't have time for the punching game." I squirmed but couldn't pull out of his grasp. "Leave me alone."

"Fuck you. What the hell? Are you dressed up like a girl, Sprout?"

"There's a costume party at the school. I'm a schoolgirl." I blurted out the quickest lie I had ever told and no better time for it.

"There's no costume party, loser." He let go of my face. Looked me up and down again. "That's one hell of a costume. You look like a real girl." He tugged at the front of the blouse. Let it go. "You're a real girl. You have boobs and everything. What the hell?" He gave us a shove in the chest and we staggered back. "What the fuck are you?"

"Oh, none of that," she said with her teenage girl's voice. She said it forcefully. She took over. "I'm not taking this shit anymore."

"Fuck you, Sprout." He said and pushed us again.

We stumbled back but she quickly regained her balance. She stepped back towards my brother. "Okay, you are a fucking idiot, aren't you? See. I am a girl. A real girl. Anybody can see that. Are you fucking blind? Look at these cheeks. Do boys have cheeks like these?" She patted her cheeks and grinned hard at him.

"Holy shit," whispered my brother. And then louder, "Holy shit!" He looked us up and down again. "Are those real too?" He thrust left hand at our chest and grabbed one of our boobs. His eyes popped wide as if he had seen a ghost. Then with both hands he grabbed the front of her blouse and yanked the front open. I could hear the fabric tearing and the buttons flying. Our breasts stared back at him. No bra. I didn't own a bra. She didn't need a bra. So there they were in all their glory. Her breasts.

"Holy shit," he said again.

Undeterred, she cupped her breasts. "See, girl. Is this what you want to see?" She edged a little closer to him. In a cold hard voice, she continued. "Is this what you think I am? Is this what you want me to be? You think I am so girlie and weak all you see is a girl. Well, here I am. All girl. Are you mad? Do you need to see my pussy too? Are you fucking sick in the head? You pathetic boy."

He didn't say anything. He stared hard at her breasts. He stepped back into his room. When he came back to the door he had a dirty steak knife in his hand. "Shut the fuck up, Sprout. You fucking freak. You fucking fag."

We stared at the steak knife in his hand and before we could react, he had stabbed us in the left breast. The sharp knife cut right through our fleshy breast. Thank god the knife ran into a rib and stopped with a thud. We looked down at our breast. Blood ran from the wound, down our breast and over our belly and onto our skirt.

Time stopped. We watched the blood ooze out of the cut. We knew pain would come but we didn't feel it yet. We looked up to see the rage on his face, his mouth contorted and his eyes wide, filled with hate. Why did he hate us? We stared into his eyes and buried behind the hate we saw fear. Unlike us, he didn't know fear. Fear wasn't manly. Fear was physical weakness. Fear of something he didn't understand generated a new emotion in him. This new emotion made him angry.

He pulled the knife back seemingly in slow motion. Our wound began to bleed even more. She instinctively put her hand to the wound. "Holy crap, you stabbed my boob. What the hell is wrong with you?" She looked up at him and gave him the coldest stare she had ever mustered.

He didn't respond. He hesitated briefly as he stared at the blood then struck at our other breast. Time sped back up. Taking the hand from her bleeding breast, she flung it at his incoming arm and knocked it off target, like we had learned in self-defense class. The knife arced near her breast but didn't connect and his arm swung violently past and across his own chest.

She didn't hesitate. She kneed him in the groin. Again. So in shock and unprepared for retaliation, he didn't defend himself. He buckled forward. She grabbed his hair and pulled his head down. His body followed. As he lurched forward she kicked his knee out from under him and he crumpled to the floor.

The knife fell from his hand when his arm crashed to the floor. He screamed. Sprout jumped on his back and pulled his right arm behind him. She wrenched on his wrist. He groaned again. She slammed his head into the cement floor.

Blood flowed down her breast. Dripping onto his back and neck. Covering her belly, her hands, her arms. Her chest heaved up and down. She pulled his head back and slammed his face into the floor again.

"Yes, I'm a girl. Sprout has sprouted breasts. Are you seeing these? Is that what scares you? That I'm a pussy and a little girl you need to terrorize all the time. Either you're a boy or a girl, right? Manly or a pussy. You see me as a girl cause I'm not a manly jerk. Sorry, life doesn't work that way. It's not masculine or feminine. It's both. It's supposed to be both."

She started to sob. She wrenched his wrist again. "You can be tough and kind. You can be confident and compassionate. You can be open and closed. You can be strong and soft. Do you understand? We can be both. You're just not. You're just a manly asshole. And fuck you, because I'm not."

"I'm going to kick your ass," my brother groaned. He started to regain his composure. We weren't heavy enough to keep him down once he regained his composure. We needed to escape soon.

"Yes, kick my ass," she yelled. "Solve everything with violence. But I'm not going to stop being thoughtful, and empathetic, and compassionate, and creative. You stabbed me, you asshole. You stabbed my fucking boob. And I'm bleeding all over myself and I'm bleeding all over you. You could have killed me." She looked at all the blood. "Fuck." She wrenched his wrist again. He grunted. She pushed his head hard into the floor once more and jumped up.

We ran to the bathroom. We grabbed a hand towel off the floor and wiped at our bloody chest. We ripped off the remains of the blouse. Threw it in the corner of the bathroom. We walked into the laundry room and grabbed a dirty shirt and pants out of a laundry basket. We raced up the stairs into the porch. We could hear BJ groaning in the hallway. He hadn't moved yet but he would. Hastily we pulled on the shirt and stuffed the hand towel underneath to soak up the blood. We could bandage it later.

I pulled my pants on under the skirt. Took the skirt off and pulled on my winter coat. We ran out the door. I didn't know where to go. I looked into the back yard and ran that way. I stumbled through the little snow left on the ground, leaving a bright red trail on my way to the garage.

We slammed the garage door shut and locked it. We sat in the cold dark of the garage, pressed up against a cabinet in the corner. Chest rising and falling. Shaking. We held the towel against the wound. The cold air in the garage gave us some comfort. We sat quietly. What was there to say? She started to cry. I cried with her.

CHAPTER 27 – CORNUCOPIA

THE COLD SLOWLY SPREAD UP from the frozen garage floor and began to chill our bones. The adrenaline had worn off. The shaking muscles no longer staved off the cold. We stood. The wound on our breast reminded us of its existence with a sharp jab of pain. We pulled the towel out, avoided looking at the blood, unfolded it and rolled it back up. We stuffed it back up under the shirt to make sure it would stay in place. Reminded me of movies where the hero is injured, wraps his wound with an old shirt, grunts a bit and carries on. I was obviously not a movie hero because I couldn't ignore the searing sting from the slice in our boob.

We were still cold. We looked around the garage and found an old jacket of my dad's. The jacket dwarfed me, sleeves hanging long, zipper so low I could hardly reach it. It would keep us warm. We peeked out the garage door. The empty backyard stared back at us. Silently we walked out of the yard, past our trail of blood-stained snow and down toward the river. We walked briskly and warmed up quickly. We stumbled and slid down the riverbank to the frozen water's edge and headed for my favorite bridge.

We stood under the bridge and flung a few rocks onto the river, but the throwing motion tugged at the wound, so we stopped. We sat down on a large flat rock and withdrew our hands up into the lengthy sleeves of the jacket. We stared at the frozen ripples, the nearby streetlights illuminating the caps of a few finger drifts here and there.

"I'm sorry," she said after a long time staring at the ice. "I snapped. I shouldn't have snapped. This is my fault." She touched the towel over the wound.

"Don't be sorry. I'm glad you stood up to that asshole. He deserved everything we did to him. I could never have stood up on my own."

"He stabbed us. Holy crap. Really stabbed us. Has that sunk in yet?"

"What the hell is wrong with him? He's messed up."

"I have no idea. We should have run away. But the cat had jumped out of the bag. I couldn't put it back in. I guess we didn't have a choice but to stand up and fight."

"I would have regretted running away. You were so strong though. You didn't flinch. Not at all."

"We didn't flinch. That was us. You did good. I mean, despite the gaping hole in my breast." She started to laugh but that only made the wound hurt more. She touched the towel again. I could still feel the wet blood though it seems to have stopped running down my belly.

"I should go. You warned me about getting caught. You said there would be repercussions. You were right." She cupped our face in her hands, shook her head slowly. "I was naïve. I put you in danger. My arrogance almost got us killed." She stifled a sob. A tear welled but didn't fall. "Dammit." She lowered her hands and sat up straighter.

I felt the tear though and cradled her cheeks with my hands. "It's okay. We made it. I can handle the danger."

"Can you? You do feel the blood oozing from my fucking boob, don't you? We could be dead. The blade was a few centimeters from plunging through our ribs into our heart." She was right, but I couldn't process a near death experience that quickly. It was just a blur.

"You can't go." I stopped. I couldn't wrap my head around her leaving. However weird all this was she had become a normal part of my life. She had become essential, my coping mechanism of choice, my drug of choice. The addict in me didn't want to let go of her. I could already feel the pain of withdrawal starting. "Why would you go? We're learning to be good at this. You make me confident. And strong. You're part of me now. I can feel it."

"I was always part of you. I was always open about that. I was here to help you see inside. We're one now."

"I understand. But why should this," I pointed at the wound, "change your mission. It's one more learning. I'm sure we can learn more things together. We're just getting started."

"You'll always have more things to learn. But maybe my job is done here. Maybe you're on the right path and you can learn these things on your own."

"There are still so many things I don't understand."

She laughed. "Welcome to life. Always something to not understand. You'll figure it out, one lesson at a time."

"Easy for you to say. You're the trailing clouds of glory."

"I know. But I'll still be here inside you." She rested her hand on our chest. "You can channel me when you need me. I'll be part of your gut instinct. I worked hard to showed you your intuition for a reason."

"What do I do about my brother? We beat his face into the floor. That

159

was some violent shit."

"Yeah. Because he stabbed us in the fucking boob. He's lucky we didn't do worse."

The image of his head pounding into the floor. Bam, bam, bam. We did that. The sound of him groaning. The sound of him swearing and yelling my name. All too vivid and shocking. "He's going to kill me."

"Maybe not."

"What? Are you kidding? He's not going to forget I pummeled his face."

"Absolutely not. That was a life-changing event. For all of us. We fought back and we won." She reached inside the jacket and touched the now bloody shirt. "I think we won, anyway. He certainly had never lost before. How does it feel to win?"

"Besides the blood and the pain and the shock, you mean? I feel good. Proud. Maybe liberated. Sounds weird, I know."

"No, it's not weird. It's exactly right. Remember, liberation isn't free. At the end of the day, we didn't even have to win to feel it. We had to stand up."

"And get stabbed."

"People don't always stab you when you stand up to them. At least, I hope not. So probably not. Think about it. In the future when you stand up to someone, you probably won't get stabbed, so that's good." She laughed and then winced. "Everything else will be easy. You're a pro now."

"Not sure about that. You might be stretching the deeper meaning here."

"Hey, I'm bleeding from my boob here. I'm taking anything I can to make that worth it."

We laughed. The wound hurt and felt better at the same time. The emotional wound enjoyed the laughter as well, though I suspected the emotional wound would take much longer to heal.

"Okay, so you're telling me that I'm oddly the winner in this fight. I'm a better, stronger person. But what about my brother? How is he different? How does this stop him from pounding me?"

"Well, we can speculate he'll have to come to grips with the fact he stabbed you. His own brother. Lots of blood and a gaping wound. Even he won't be able to ignore that. He'll have to come to grips with the idea he could have killed you. Even now he has no idea whether you might be bleeding to death somewhere. The idea might even cross his stunted mind. I don't know if he'll feel bad, but he'll feel something."

I couldn't imagine him feeling bad. I'd never seen him show remorse for anything. He was such a jerk. If he ever had remorse, he hid it well.

"And add the shame he'll feel for his beaten face. A face that looks like it lost terribly to someone. Don't know if he'll be able to come to grips with his humiliation, but he'll have to explain his pulped-up face or lie about it. My bet is he won't talk about it and certainly lie about it if anyone asks. He can't bring it up to your parents because he won't be able to lie about it. He can't threaten you because all you have to do is pull your shirt up and he's screwed. You own the trump card."

"Gawd, I hope so. But it's going to be weird for a long time."

"Yeah. Going to be a lot of awkward silences. I don't know if he'll learn anything. His pride will take a blow for sure. Maybe he gets better, maybe he gets worse."

"So did we go through all of this for nothing? The bleeding, the fight, the everything."

"On no. It was all worth it. You have to understand you can't control him. He'll change or he won't."

"That's a tough lesson to learn."

She laughed. "Hell yeah, it is."

"But this moment and everything up to this moment has been good. Every time you let me stay. Every time you let me have my way. Every time you didn't run away. You were accepting me. You were taking a risk. That's openness. That's growth."

"You did all that. That was all you."

"No. It wasn't. We did all these things together. You and me. You had to navigate the waters. You had to feel it. That was you. You and me. You still think I'm a strange ghost haunting you or a mentally ill hallucination. I'm not. I'm you. I need you to accept me." She put her hands to our face and held our cheeks. She wanted to cry but didn't. She clasped our hands in front of us. "I'm your trailing clouds of glory. The glory is a little less cloudy and a little less trailing than before, I hope. And it's here." She touched our chest. "The clouds of glory are in here. I'm in here. Accept me. Let me stay in here."

"You can stay in there. But don't go yet. I'm afraid when you go, everything I've learned will flee with it. I won't be able to find you. I'll lose everything about you. I know I resisted you a lot but, now that you want to leave, I realize how important you are to me. I don't want to go back to the way I was."

"Trust me, you won't. How could you? I'm part of you now. Now you're aware of me. Your awareness makes all the difference. You can't get rid of me now even if you wanted to. Why would you? You think I'm seriously cool."

"Well, you're seriously confident, that's for sure."

"Ha! Well, then you're confident too. We're integrated now. You have to remember you're confident now."

"I think I'm still learning."

"You are a slow learner, for sure. Just kidding. Remember, nothing is free. Not liberation, not confidence. It's all about knowing what price you're willing to pay. You've tasted liberation so you know it's worth it. You'll find the same thing with confidence."

"I still don't want you to go."

"It's the right thing. You know it deep down."

I nodded. She was right. The danger was right in front of us, running down our chest. I desperately didn't want her to be right, but I knew. My gut knew. She had taught me to understand that.

She stood and unzipped the bulky jacket. I'd forgotten about the cold. It had lost importance.

"Well, you better take one last look at my breasts before I go, blood and all." She pulled up our shirt and stripped away the bloody towel. "Ouch, that does not look good." She dabbed at the skin around the wound and winced. "But they still look good."

"Yes, they do."

"See, you won't forget me. This will be one bad ass scar. You'll think of me every time you look in the mirror."

"Always something there to remind me."

"Exactly. Let's go home. Better bandage this up before it gets infected."

"We can go in a minute. I need to sit here a little longer."

She nodded. We sat back on the big rock. Stared into the murkiness beneath the bridge. I wondered what Tammy would think of me sitting under a cold bridge with a stab wound in my boob. Indeed, what would anyone think? I think they would find it interesting. I chuckled. The most interesting thing about me now would be an experience no one would ever know about or understand. Perhaps that was fitting. Now I had a secret. Now I was mysterious. I know something you don't know.

A cold gust of wind swept under the bridge and raked across our face. We startled back into the reality that we were shivering under a bridge with a knife wound that needed attention. After a while we stood up and headed home.

"I guess we missed the dance," I said as we climbed up the river bank. "Though he ruined your cute outfit, so we wouldn't have had anything to wear anyway. Maybe we could buy you another one?"

She didn't respond. She was gone. I touched my chest. The wound still bled there but the breasts had gone. Was she gone for good? Was she serious about leaving for good? I'd have to wait and see, though deep down I knew the answer.

I felt suddenly alone. I felt wobbly. I leaned against a tree to keep steady. I wanted to cry. She would've said that was okay. I smiled. I would cry later. She would like that.

ABOUT THE AUTHOR

Sometimes author, sometimes painter, sometimes not. Minneapolis-based human.
@joegergen

Made in USA - North Chelmsford, MA
1312604_9781734736625
04.27.2022 0956